D0445466

G

A
MAMMOTH
MURDER

▼

A
MAMMOTH
MURDER

▼

BILL CRIDER

THOMAS DUNNE BOOKS
ST. MARTIN'S MINOTAUR
NEW YORK

THOMAS DUNNE BOOKS.
An imprint of St. Martin's Press.

www.minotaurbooks.com

Library of Congress Cataloging-in-Publication Data

Crider, Bill, 1941–
    A mammoth murder / Bill Crider.—1st ed.
       p. cm.
    ISBN 13: 978-0-312-32387-5
    ISBN 10: 0-312-32387-5
    1. Rhodes, Dan (Fictitious character)—Fiction. 2. Sheriffs—Fiction.
3. Texas—Fiction. I. Title.

    PS3553.R497M36 2006
    813'.54—dc22

                                                    2005054755

First Edition: April 2006

10 9 8 7 6 5 4 3 2 1

To Bob Crider,

Mammoth Hunter

A
MAMMOTH
MURDER

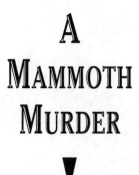

1

▼

BUD TURLEY, CALLED BUD SQUIRRELLY BY THOSE WHO THOUGHT he had a lot of peculiar ideas, put the gigantic tooth down on Sheriff Dan Rhodes's desk and said, "I want you to take custody of this tooth, Sheriff."

Rhodes looked down at the tooth. He was sure he'd never seen a bigger one. It was six or seven inches tall and two or three inches wide. It wasn't exactly in prime shape. It was more of a fossil than an actual tooth. Rhodes looked up at Turley.

"The county doesn't generally take custody of teeth, Bud. Not unless they're evidence."

"This one's evidence," Turley said. "Evidence that I've been right all along. We'll see who's crazy now."

"I meant evidence in a crime," Rhodes told him.

"There might be a crime involved. I just haven't uncovered the body yet."

Turley was a big, red-faced man, at least six-two. He was completely bald, and he had on a long-billed welder's cap, black with white polka dots. His arms looked as if he'd just come from pumping iron at the gym. Or in a prison yard, considering the tattoos. A devil with forked tail and pitchfork dancing in flames on the left bicep, and a cow skull on the right. Under the skull was the word "Moo."

Turley wore a "concealed carry" vest with more pockets than Rhodes could count. They were stuffed with things like binoculars, a cell phone, an opened package of jerky, a ballpoint pen, a water bottle, a flashlight, and other paraphernalia that Rhodes couldn't see. The lawman knew that there were at least two pockets inside the vest for holding sidearms. He figured that some of the outside pockets held extra magazines for the pistol that Turley was surely carrying, considering the sag of the vest.

Underneath the vest Turley wore a T-shirt with the arms ripped out. The vest hung open, and Rhodes could see that the T-shirt was emblazoned with an eagle's head in front of an American flag. Turley's blue jeans were faded almost white, and the bottoms were crusted with drying mud, as were the leather hiking boots he wore.

"You know it's against the law to carry a firearm in a correctional facility," Rhodes said.

Turley's head lifted, and something flared in his eyes as if they were reflecting a match flame. Rhodes wondered if he might pull out the pistol and start shooting, but Turley got a grip on himself, and the little flame disappeared. Turley took off his cap and ran his hand across the top of his perfectly smooth head. He settled the cap back and smoothed it down, using both hands on the sides to get it just right.

"Sorry, Sheriff. I forgot. I guess I was in too big a hurry to get that tooth in here. I'll go and lock my gun in the Jeep if you're not going to arrest me."

The implication was that if Rhodes intended to arrest Turley, he'd have to pry the pistol from Turley's cold, dead fingers.

"I'm not going to arrest you," Rhodes said. "This time."

"Thanks. You watch that tooth while I'm gone."

Turley went out, and Rhodes's hand went to the crown of his head. He thought he might be getting a little bald spot back there. He couldn't see it in the mirror, but his father'd had a bald spot, and Rhodes could be getting one now. He was about the right age.

"I always wonder if I'm goin' bald when I see that fella," Hack Jensen said.

Hack was the dispatcher, and although he was much older than Rhodes, his hair was still thick. Totally gray, but thick and carefully combed. He would never go bald, and he knew it.

"How did you know what I was thinking?" Rhodes said. "Have I got a bald spot in back?"

"Nah," said Lawton, who'd been sweeping the floor. "You got plenty of hair."

Lawton was the jailer, and while his hair was thin, he still had plenty of it. It was black, too, which puzzled Rhodes since Lawton was as old as Hack. His hair should have been gray, too, but it wasn't, and Rhodes was sure he didn't dye it. Most likely he didn't even know that there was such a thing as hair dye for men.

Lawton looked over at Hack, and the two grinned at each other. Rhodes was sure they were grinning because he was going bald, though of course they'd never admit it.

The door opened, and Turley came back inside the jail. "You still got the tooth?" he said.

"It's right there," Rhodes said, looking down at it again. "Now, where'd the tooth come from, and what's this about a body?"

"It came from the bank of Pittman Creek, up around Big Woods. I've been saying for years that I'd find Bigfoot there, and now I have."

"I thought you said it was a tooth," Hack said.

Turley turned to look at him. "It is a tooth. A Bigfoot tooth."

"Could be somethin' else, couldn't it?"

"No. It's a Bigfoot tooth. And I think there's part of a jawbone there, too. So the rest of the body must be somewhere around."

"What if that was the last of 'em?" Lawton said, clasping both hands around the broom handle and leaning on it. "All dead, and that tooth there's part of the last of the Bigfoots. Or Bigfeet. Which is it?"

"I didn't come here for some ignorant old fart to make fun of me," Turley said, glaring at Lawton.

Lawton's hands tightened on the broom handle.

Rhodes stood up behind his desk. He wasn't as tall as Turley, but he was tall enough. Besides, he was the sheriff. That counted for something.

"You'll have to watch the way you talk in here, Bud," he said.

Turley turned back to him, took off his cap, ran his hand across the top of his head, and put the cap back on. "Sorry. I didn't mean to get ugly. I guess I've just been made fun of for too long. I don't much like it."

"I wasn't makin' fun," Lawton said. "Just askin' a question."

"Yeah," Turley said.

Rhodes sat back down and looked at the tooth. He didn't know what a Bigfoot tooth looked like, or even if there was such a thing, but whatever that tooth belonged to would have been huge, far larger than any Bigfoot could be.

"You should have it looked at by an expert," he said.

"I've already called the expert. He's coming here to look at it. I don't want anybody to steal it. That's why I think you should take custody of it. This is going to be the biggest thing that's ever happened in Blacklin County."

Rhodes would have mentioned something bigger, but he couldn't think of anything. A Sasquatch would be big news indeed.

"You say you found it up by Pittman Creek?"

"That's right. Close to Big Woods."

Pittman Creek had been named for George Pittman, one of the county's early settlers. Just after the Civil War, he'd come to Texas from Mississippi and built a house near the creek that now bore his name. Not much else was known about him except that he liked to read Shakespeare and that he'd started the first rumor about something large and strange that lived in Big Woods.

"Do you want to be more specific about where you found it?" Rhodes said. "That creek runs all the way across the county, and Big Woods covers quite a stretch, too."

"I'll save the exact location until somebody looks at that tooth," Turley said. "Will you keep it for me?"

Rhodes had an idea Turley was being cagey because he didn't know who owned the land where he'd found the tooth. Or maybe he just didn't want anybody else horning in on his big discovery.

"I'll hang on to it." Rhodes picked up the tooth, which was heavier than he'd thought it would be. "I'll put it in the evidence locker."

"I appreciate it," Turley said.

"What's the name of this expert you're calling in?"

"Name's Vance. Tom Vance. He teaches at the community college. He has a couple of classes here tomorrow, so he'll be in town then."

A community college from another county had recently opened an extension campus in Clearview, the county seat of Blacklin County, and the only town in the county of any real size. None of the college instructors, except for a couple of adjunct instructors, lived in Clearview. They all drove to class from their homes near the main campus, which was a couple of counties away.

"This Vance know anything about Bigfoot?" Rhodes asked, resisting the urge to say "Bigfoots."

"He knows about all kinds of things. About dinosaurs and all that. He teaches biology, but he's a paleontologist, too." Turley looked at Lawton. "That's somebody who studies prehistoric animals."

"I knew that," Lawton said.

Turley ignored him and said to Rhodes, "He's interested in Bigfoot, too, because it could be some kind of survivor from prehistory. Some kind of giant primate." He looked at Lawton. "That means a big monkey."

Lawton didn't bother to respond.

"Don't think monkeys are native to North America," Hack said. "Don't think they ever lived here."

"They could have," Turley said. "Big ones. And I might have one's tooth right here."

"Don't get your hopes up," Hack said. "Better wait for that expert."

"He'll be here tomorrow," Turley said. "Eleven o'clock, he said. And this tooth better be here, too."

"It will be," Rhodes said.

2
▼

When Turley had gone and Rhodes had stowed the tooth, Hack said, "I wonder where Squirrelly's runnin' buddy was? Usually those tinfoil hat boys stick together."

"You mean Larry Colley?" Rhodes said.

"That's the one. Those two been huntin' Bigfoot together since they were teenagers. That is, when they weren't gettin' abducted by flyin' saucers or pickin' up radio signals from the CIA through the fillin's in their teeth."

"It's only Larry who got abducted," Lawton said. "Bud's never got over it, if you ask me. Larry kinda holds it over him."

"Well, his Bigfoot tooth oughta put him back in the race," Hack said.

"Yeah," Lawton said. "Larry'll be mighty put out if Bud's found Bigfoot without him."

"Bigfoot," Hack said. "How much danger do you think there is of him really havin' found one? Or even a part of one?"

"Not a whole lot. That's sure a big tooth, though."

"Too big, if you ask me. Even Bigfoot wouldn't have a tooth like that. You think it's real, Sheriff?"

Rhodes said it looked real enough to him.

"We oughta analyze it ourselves," Lawton said. "Send it to our crime lab."

"Right," Hack said. "It could be the first episode of *CSI: Blacklin County*. Now there's a hit TV show if I ever heard of one."

Rhodes laughed. Their crime lab wasn't exactly state of the art. In fact, he wasn't sure there was a crime lab in the state that matched the kind of thing people saw on TV. Houston had certainly had its problems because of its lab, and a lot of people were getting out of prison because the evidence against them didn't hold up under independent examination. Hundreds of cases were being reopened. Maybe thousands.

"I don't think any answer our lab came up with would satisfy Bud," Rhodes said. "He's picked his own man, so we'll wait for his expert."

"Well," Hack said, "maybe that Vance fella can tell us whether that tooth came from a Bigfoot or not. And maybe he can't. No matter where it came from, though, I'd just as soon not be mixed up with Larry and Bud. The wonder of it is why somebody didn't do away with those two a long time ago."

Rhodes had often thought the same thing. Turley and Colley had few friends in Blacklin County. They earned a bare living as shade-tree mechanics, although they didn't actually do any jobs under a tree. They worked on cars, trucks, tractors, and lawn mowers in an old barn behind Turley's house.

They couldn't do much with recently built engines, since they didn't have a computer or any other modern equipment, but they still managed to find a few customers among people who owned older vehicles and hoped to save a little money. Lawn mowers were a big part of their business. It seemed that mowers were always breaking down.

There had been several complaints against the two men for overcharges, and Colley had been arrested a time or two for his unorthodox collection methods, which included showing up at a person's front door armed with a baseball bat and a threatening manner. A couple of broken windshields figured into things as well.

Both Colley and Turley had been arrested more than once for their involvement in bar fights that had escalated into general brawls. Witnesses had at first claimed that the two friends had instigated the fighting, but all the witnesses had retracted those statements sooner or later, usually, or so it was said, after a visit by Turley or Colley or both. There was no proof of that, though, as it was a matter that none of the witnesses wanted to discuss, either on or off the record.

Neither Colley nor Turley had ever been convicted of anything, not even of littering, which Rhodes thought was too bad. If Turley had a record, he wouldn't be walking around with a concealed handgun.

"You know, Sheriff," Hack said, breaking into Rhodes's train of thought, "we have had a few calls lately about funny things goin' on around Big Woods."

"That's just hogs," Lawton said. "They're takin' the county."

Lawton was right. According to one estimate Rhodes had seen, there were a million and a half feral hogs in Texas, but most people thought that that guess was far too low and that the actual number of feral hogs was at least twice that large. Sometimes it seemed to Rhodes that there were at least a million and a half of them roaming around in Blacklin County, damaging fences, rooting up the bottomlands, destroying wildlife habitat, ruining crops, and even eating small animals like baby goats, calves, and fawns. It was like a bad Hollywood movie from the early seventies, the kind Rhodes loved to watch on late-night TV back in the days when such movies were actually run during the wee hours.

A little like *Frogs,* maybe. Or, even more likely, *Night of the Lepus,* the one in which the National Guard had to be called in to save mankind from the giant mutant bunny rabbits. Except that nobody was calling out the Guard to fight the hogs. Farmers and ranchers were doing most of it on their own, but it was a losing battle. If people thought that rabbits reproduced rapidly, then they should consider the hogs, which ran them a close second.

Rhodes had once had an encounter with feral hogs, up close and personal as they said on TV, and he'd wound up spending some time in the hospital. It had been a few years, but it wasn't an experience he cared to repeat.

"You ever eat any of that feral hog meat?" Hack asked. "They say the young ones taste pretty good."

Rhodes said he wouldn't touch it. He knew too much about the diseases the hogs carried and the kind of things they'd eat, which included everything. The hogs didn't care. They'd eat sewage if it was the only thing available.

"I don't think I'd eat one, either," Hack said. "How about you, Lawton?"

"I'd just as soon eat a possum."

"Possum's not so bad," Hack said.

Lawton made a face. "Man that would eat a possum would eat a raccoon."

"Raccoon's not so bad," Hack said. "Not as good as possum, though."

"What about armadillo?" Lawton said. "Would you eat an armadillo?"

"If it was cooked in chili, I would. Armadillo chili's pretty good."

Rhodes didn't want to get into the culinary discussion, so he just listened while Hack defended several unlikely delicacies and Lawton made occasional gagging noises.

When he'd aggravated Lawton about as much as he could, Hack turned his chair so that he could see Rhodes and said, "So we got wild hogs and Bigfoot, not to mention Bud Squirrelly and Larry Colley. What next?"

Rhodes said that he didn't know but there was always something.

"Who was it used to say that?" Lawton asked.

"Roseanne Roseannadanna," Hack said.

"Well," Lawton said, "she had a point."

Lawton was right, but the rest of the day, while busy, was mostly routine.

A man called up to say that he was on probation but had been out sinning and wanted to be jailed while he repented. Rhodes was glad to accommodate him, as he was wanted for questioning in a daylight burglary that had occurred a couple of days earlier.

An auto repair shop—a legitimate one, not the one run by Colley and Turley—reported that a stack of inspection stickers had been stolen.

A cow had escaped from a pasture and was wandering down a county road.

A tractor had disappeared from a barn on a farm near Thurston, and the owner wanted immediate action.

Someone called to say that there was a dead animal in the middle of the road near the town of Obert.

Then they got the call about the Bigfoot sighting.

3

▼

"YOU WANT TO LET RUTH GRADY TAKE IT?" HACK ASKED
Rhodes.

"What's the location?"

"Louetta Kennedy's store."

"There was a Bigfoot in the store?"

"No," Hack said. "That's just where the call came from. It's
some fella named Johnson. He was plumb out of breath and
mighty excited. Must've been runnin' for a mile or so before he
got to the phone."

Rhodes was surprised. He didn't think there was anyone left
without a cell phone in all of Blacklin County. Except for himself,
of course.

"I'll drive down there and have a talk with him," Rhodes said.

"Ruth's not all that far away. She could handle it."

"I'd rather do it myself. Maybe there's a connection with that
tooth we have in the other room."

"All right, then, but somebody's gonna have to get that dead animal out of the road."

"Have Buddy take care of it."

Buddy was another of the deputies. Rhodes knew he was on patrol in that part of the county.

"Buddy's not fond of dead animals."

"Neither am I," Rhodes said. "What this county needs is an animal control officer."

"If we had one, would he be in charge of the Bigfoot cases?"

"No," Rhodes said. "I get to handle all of those."

When he drove through Thurston, Rhodes passed by Hod Barrett's grocery store. At one time Thurston had been a thriving town, with doctors, drugstores, variety stores, even a movie theater. That had been long ago, when cotton was still being grown on the farms that had surrounded the town. The cotton gin was gone now, and so were all the stores. Only a few buildings were still standing, and one of them was Barrett's.

Barrett was standing out in front, and he waved when Rhodes went by, but Rhodes thought that Barrett probably hadn't recognized him. He'd never been one of the sheriff's biggest fans.

It didn't take long to get into and out of Thurston, maybe a minute, and then Rhodes turned onto one of the county roads that led to Big Woods.

Blacklin County wasn't one of the state's major population areas. There was nothing there to attract tourists except for an old restored fort and a couple of lakes that bass fishermen visited. No major industries had ever shown a desire to move there and provide employment. Most of the farms were now fallow land, and while there were some cattle ranches, they were all small operations.

As a result, there were places in Blacklin County that had remained pretty much as they had always been. Big Woods, located in the southernmost part of the county, was one of those places. It was an area of about six square miles covered with tall trees and almost impenetrable brush. People avoided it, even the people who owned the land it covered.

A number of years ago, a boy named Ronnie Bolton had wandered away from a family reunion at a farm near the woods and never been seen again. Rhodes had headed up the search party, which had included Bud Turley and Larry Colley, but no sign of the child had ever been found. The Bigfoot rumors had run rampant for a long time after that. The family hadn't used the house since the reunion, and it remained vacant even now.

The woods were home to deer and feral hogs, and it was there that Rhodes had experienced his little run-in with the hogs. The woods were home to other things, too, things just as unpleasant as the hogs. Snakes for one. Copperheads for sure, and rattlers almost certainly, though Rhodes had never seen one there. And he never wanted to. He didn't like snakes, not even harmless hognose snakes.

The snakes existed. No question about that. So did the hogs. Rhodes wasn't so sure about Bigfoot. If some kind of primitive creatures really lived in those woods, why hadn't anyone ever found any bones or other traces? Rhodes wasn't counting the tooth that Bud had brought in as a trace. Not yet, anyway.

The county road that Rhodes drove along was covered with white rock, but the passage of the car brought up only a small amount of dust. The summer had been dry for a good while, but when the rains had come, they'd come in force. So although it was the middle of August the weeds in the pastures were green. The trees that grew so close to the road that they hung over it in some places were even greener than the weeds. It was dry again now, and Rhodes figured they wouldn't be having any rain for a while, not until up into the fall.

Rhodes pulled off the road when he came to Louetta Kennedy's store. It might have been prosperous once, back in the days when the farms in this part of the county had been producing tons of cotton every year, but now it was a dilapidated, unpainted shell of its former self. Hardly anyone even passed by there anymore.

The front porch slanted downward at an alarming angle. The tin roof was so rusty that there wasn't a shiny spot on it anywhere. The only concession to modern times was the Handi-Ice freezer that sat precariously on the porch. Beside the freezer there was a plastic chair where Louetta usually sat when there were no customers in the store. Rhodes wasn't sure why she didn't slide out of it, considering the slant of the porch.

On one side and to the back there was another, smaller building that was in even worse shape than the store. It leaned to the left, as if a giant had pushed it out of alignment. It was where Louetta stored cattle and chicken feed. The Sunglo feed sign on one side was so faded that it was hard to make out the original colors.

A forty-year-old black Ford was parked in the shade of a pecan tree near the building. That was Louetta's car, Rhodes knew. It probably didn't have more than a few thousand miles on it. She drove it only from her house, which was less than a quarter of a mile away, to the store. And on Sundays she drove it to church.

The only other vehicle around was a battered green GMC

pickup. Rhodes figured the man who'd called about Bigfoot must be the owner. Hack had been exaggerating when he'd said the man had run all the way from Big Woods.

Rhodes parked near the ramshackle porch and got out of the car. It was hot and humid, and he had to wipe sweat off his face by the time he'd walked the five or six steps to the building. He went up on the porch, made sure he had his balance, and went in through the rusty screen door.

The wooden floor creaked under his feet as he entered. The boards were worn from years of footsteps and broom sweepings, and there were gaps between some of them wide enough to drop a candy bar through.

The old wooden building wasn't air-conditioned, but it wasn't as hot inside as might have been expected. There was a little circulation through the front and back screens, and there were screened windows on both sides. An oscillating fan sat on a wooden box and stirred the air. The only light came from a couple of bare bulbs that hung from twisted electrical cords attached to the central rafter.

On the left was a glass candy case that contained only hard candy, nothing that would melt in the heat. A big red and white Coca-Cola box sat down beside the case. On the right there was a counter that held an old-fashioned cast-iron cash register. Shelves ran along each wall, and they were poorly stocked with canned goods.

Louetta Kennedy stood behind the counter. She was short and wrinkled, and she wore a pair of men's overalls over a blue work shirt. A black baseball cap with CORNELL HURD BAND in white letters on the front covered most of her thin gray hair, though some of it stuck out around the edges.

A man sat at the end of the counter in a wooden chair that must have been a hundred years old. He was thin and wiry, and his hands were twisting together in his lap. He wore faded jeans, a red and blue print shirt, and a black cap that said CLEARVIEW CATA-MOUNTS in red letters on the front. His jaws were working rapidly. Rhodes smelled the distinctive odor of Juicy Fruit gum.

"Hey, Sheriff," Louetta said. "You must think this is important if you come all this way yourself instead of sendin' a deputy."

"I'm always interested in Bigfoot," Rhodes said. "Is that what you saw, Mr. Johnson?"

The man in the chair nodded. His head bobbed on his thin neck like a fishing cork on a windy day.

"He's a little spooked," Louetta said. "It's not every day a man sees a Bigfoot."

Johnson kept right on nodding. Rhodes was afraid his head might come off his neck and bounce across the floor.

"You want to tell me about it?" Rhodes said.

Johnson couldn't seem to stop nodding. But he didn't stop chewing his gum, either.

"You might want to get yourself a Coke, Sheriff," Louetta said. "He's been like that ever since he phoned your office. Hasn't said a word, not since he asked me for some chewing gum."

Rhodes went over to the cooler, which was bound to be an antique. It was, at any rate, a good bit older than anybody in the room except for Louetta. There was one other like it in the county that Rhodes knew of, and that was the one in Hod Barrett's store. It didn't dispense the drinks. They sat inside it in glass bottles, in cold water up almost to the top of their necks. A small pump circulated the water.

Rhodes took hold of a Dr Pepper bottle and pulled it out of the water. Louetta handed him a cheap brown paper towel that was instantly soaked through when he wrapped it around the frigid bottle. He pulled the top off the bottle with the opener on the side of the cooler and took a drink. As far as he was concerned, you couldn't beat the taste of an icy cold Dr Pepper in a glass bottle.

He paid Louetta for the drink and set the bottle on the counter. He looked over at Johnson, who was still as nervous as a cat in a kennel. Whatever he'd seen, it had made quite an impression.

"Would you like something to drink?" Rhodes asked him.

"He looks to me like he needs something stronger than a Coke," Louetta said. "And I don't sell that stuff."

Rhodes had another swallow of his Dr Pepper and walked down to stand in front of Johnson.

"You'd better go ahead and tell me about it," he said. "What's Bigfoot look like?"

"He . . . he . . . he's big," Johnson said between chews.

"How big?"

"W-well, I didn't quite s-see him. J-just his s-shadow."

Rhodes took a swallow of Dr Pepper. The paper towel was so wet that it was coming apart in his hand.

"Must have been a pretty big shadow to upset you so much," he said.

"Yeah. R-real big." Johnson stopped chewing his gum and wiped his mouth with the back of his hand. "B-but that's not what scared me."

"What did, then?"

"The dead man," Johnson said.

4

▼

CHESTER JOHNSON'S STORY WAS THAT HE'D GONE TO BIG WOODS
to hunt feral hogs on some land owned by Gerald Bolton. It was
Bolton's family that had held the reunion from which Ronnie
Bolton had disappeared. He was, or had been, Gerald's son.

"Mr. Bolton lets me kill all the hogs I want," Johnson said.
Rhodes didn't ask how many that might be. "He's glad to get rid
of 'em. You know some people hunt 'em with dogs?"

Rhodes nodded. They were still in Louetta Kennedy's store. It
didn't seem likely that they'd be interrupted by any customers, so
Rhodes figured the store was as good a place to talk as any. If
there was a dead man in the woods, he'd wait there for them.

"Well," Johnson said, "I don't use any dogs. They say it's a
sport, but I don't see any sport in it, not for the dogs or the hogs
either one. I hunt for the food. I eat some myself and sell the rest."

"When did you go to the woods today?" Rhodes asked.

"It must have been around four o'clock when I got there. I like to go in the afternoon. They sleep in the woods in the heat of the day, and sometimes I can scare some of them up while they're still a little groggy."

The call had come in to the jail about four thirty, Rhodes thought, so it had taken Johnson a little while to find the body. Johnson was a little more self-possessed than he'd been earlier. His head was no longer nodding, but he was still chewing the gum, and his hands still twisted in his lap. Rhodes was a bit surprised that a man who'd hunt feral hogs would be bothered by a little thing like a corpse.

"Tell me about the dead man," Rhodes said.

"Not much to tell. I was walking along in the woods, and there he was, just lying there. I thought for a second or two that he might be sleeping. You know, like the hogs."

"But he wasn't sleeping."

"No. And I knew he wasn't, just as soon as I thought it. Who'd go out and fall asleep in those woods, what with the hogs and Bigfoot around?"

When he mentioned Bigfoot, he started chewing the gum violently.

"How long had he been dead?" Rhodes asked. "The man, I mean."

"Not long. The hogs hadn't got at him yet."

"What about Bigfoot?"

Johnson closed his mouth and swallowed. "W-well, I was l-looking at the man who was lying there, and I could tell right off that he was dead. He wasn't moving the least bit, no sign at all that he was even breathing. There was blood on him, and I thought the hogs had got him." He paused. "Damn, Sheriff—" He looked at Louetta. "Sorry about that, Miss Louetta."

"You should be," Louetta said from behind the counter, where she was looking over some account books.

Johnson turned back to Rhodes. "What I was gonna say is that we'd better get down to those woods. The hogs will tear that dead fella apart if they find him."

Rhodes should have thought of that himself. The dead man wasn't going anywhere, but the hogs could do a fine job of destroying any evidence there might be. If there was a dead man at all. Anybody who saw imaginary creatures like Bigfoot might see imaginary dead men, too. Rhodes couldn't take that chance.

"Let's go find him," Rhodes said.

He took another pull at the Dr Pepper bottle and put it down on the counter.

"I guess I meant *you'd* better get down there," Johnson said. "I don't think I can go back, Sheriff. I j-just can't."

Rhodes looked at him. "Sure you can. I won't be able to find the dead man without you."

"If the hogs are at him, you'll know about it."

"We'll hope they aren't," Rhodes said. "Come on."

Johnson got up. For just a second Rhodes thought he might bolt, but after a little chewing and head bobbing he got control of himself and said, "All right. I'm ready."

In the county car, Rhodes turned the air conditioner on high and let the cold air blow against his face as he followed the pickup along the graveled road. It turned in at an open gate in the barbed-wire fence that ran along the ditch beside the road. Rhodes didn't see any cattle grazing nearby, so he didn't bother to close the gate. It had been open for quite a while already, and any cattle that were going to get out would already have escaped. Rhodes hadn't seen any along the road, but that didn't mean much. They could be anywhere. Everybody who owned land had cattle. They had to keep cattle on the land to get the agricultural tax exemption.

The pickup followed a two-rutted path through the pasture, and Rhodes trailed along behind. The weeds were as high as the windows on the county car, and they brushed the sides of it as Rhodes passed them.

At the end of the road was Big Woods. There was no real transition from the pasture to the trees. It was as if they'd sprung up right there in a solid line.

Rhodes had no idea why the land in that part of the county had never been cleared. Certainly most of the large wooded areas had disappeared long ago, back when most of the land had been covered with cotton farms, but this one large patch of woods had been left alone.

Colley and Turley would have said it was because the early settlers were afraid of destroying Bigfoot's habitat, afraid of the revenge that the monster would take on them. If they wanted to believe that, it was fine with Rhodes, but he thought there must be another reason.

Johnson stopped his pickup near the tree line, and Rhodes parked beside him. Johnson sat in his truck for a second or two, then got out and looked into the woods, as if he was hoping to see something. Or hoping *not* to see something.

The trees were so thick that it wasn't likely Johnson would see much of anything, Rhodes thought. Then he noticed that not far from where Johnson stood there was an opening into the woods.

"Hogs made themselves a trail," Johnson said when he noticed where Rhodes was looking.

Rhodes went over and looked at the ground. It was churned up by the cloven hooves of the feral hogs, and the ground, which had been soft the last time it rained, had hardened to a thick crust that wasn't likely to take any new impressions.

"Is this where you went into the woods?" Rhodes asked.

"Yeah. If we're going in there, I'd better get my gun."

Rhodes told him to go ahead, and Johnson went to his pickup. He opened the door, folded down the seat, and pulled out a .30-30 rifle.

"You got a gun?" Johnson said, slamming the pickup door.

There was a shotgun in the county car, and Rhodes could load it with single-ought buckshot. Each individual pellet was about the size of a .32 caliber bullet, and a charge from the shotgun would cut down a small tree. Rhodes thought that Johnson had enough firepower for both of them, though.

Johnson wasn't so sure.

"I'd feel better about it if you were armed," he said. He touched his hand to the rifle he was holding in the crook of his arm. "This'll stop a hog. I'm not sure about anything else that might be in there."

Rhodes nodded and walked back to the county car. He got the cartridges out of the ammo locker and loaded the shotgun. Then he pumped a cartridge into the chamber.

"All right," Johnson said. He sounded reassured. "I guess we're ready."

They followed the hog track into the woods, and Rhodes asked if Johnson had followed that same path earlier. He said that he had.

"'Bout the only way to get in here," Johnson added.

Rhodes had to agree. The trees on both sides of the path were so thick that it would have been hard to blaze a new trail, and once you got a little way into the woods, you might as well have gone a hundred miles, or a hundred years back into the past. It was quiet and still and hot, and no breeze stirred the leaves. Hazy light filtered in, but it was almost as if twilight had come on a little early. Rhodes felt the sweat trickling down his sides under his shirt.

Off to one side of the trail, about ten feet into the trees, there was an old deer stand that had been made of plywood and spray-painted green and black in a semblance of camouflage. It had stood up about ten feet off the ground, but now one of the legs of the stand had broken and the whole thing had collapsed. The plywood sides were rotted and falling apart. Vines grew around it, and a small tree was growing right up though the middle of it.

"I didn't know anybody hunted deer in here," Rhodes said.

"They don't," Johnson said. "Not anymore. There's not as many of 'em as there used to be. Hogs eat a lot of the young ones."

Johnson acted jittery. He worked his jaws on the chewing gum, and Rhodes thought that it must have lost all its flavor by now.

"The dead man's not far now," Johnson said.

"What about Bigfoot?" Rhodes said.

Johnson stopped so abruptly that Rhodes almost ran into him.

"I kinda wish you hadn't mentioned that," Johnson said.

"Sorry. But I'd like to know."

Johnson cocked his head and stood still.

"You hear anything?" he said.

Rhodes could hear nothing except the distant chattering of a squirrel and the call of a rain crow. There were no hogs on the loose nearby as far as he could tell. No Bigfeet, either, unless they were very quiet.

"Not a thing," Rhodes said.

"Me, neither," Johnson said. "Didn't hear anything when that Bigfoot snuck up on me, either. But there it was."

"What did it look like?"

Johnson looked thoughtful. "I can't really say."

"Didn't you see it?"

Johnson's thoughtful look turned defensive. "Sort of," he said. "It wasn't like I was gonna take a picture of it."

Rhodes wanted to sigh but didn't. He asked Johnson to describe exactly what he'd seen.

"Well, I guess you could say it was more of a shadow than an actual thing. Rose up behind me and raised holy hell. I didn't hang around for any conversation. I got out of here quick." Johnson's jaws worked on his gum for a few seconds. "And to tell you the truth, I'm not all that happy to be back."

That was the way of most Bigfoot stories Rhodes had heard. When it came right down to it, nobody had seen anything. Not really. A shadow, maybe. Something that moved in the trees. Or they'd heard a noise. If someone was in an agitated state, as Johnson had been, a shadow, a movement, or a noise would be enough to persuade you that you'd seen something. Bigfoot, say, or the Creature from the Black Lagoon.

There was no use in discussing any of that with Johnson, though. He was convinced of what he'd seen, and nothing Rhodes could say would change his mind. Rhodes was having doubts about the dead man again.

"Let's find that body," he said.

Johnson wiped his mouth with the back of his hand and started walking. Rhodes stayed right behind, trying to avoid the feeling that the trees were closing in on him. He remembered the time he had been in the woods chasing after one of his own deputies and what had happened when the feral hogs had caught him.

He pushed the memory aside, but it was replaced by one of the time he'd led the search for the lost boy, Ronnie Bolton. The official search had gone on for a week, and Rhodes had searched on his own for days afterward. But Ronnie Bolton had completely and utterly disappeared.

Johnson stopped and pointed. "There he is."

Rhodes looked. Sure enough, there was a body lying not far away, just off the side of the path in a little clearing.

Johnson's head bobbed and swiveled. "If you don't need me anymore," he said, "I'm gonna get out of here."

"You'd better stick around," Rhodes told him. "Just in case."

He stepped off the path and into the clearing. The dead man lay facedown, and Rhodes could see that the back of his head had been smashed in.

"Take something real strong to do that," Johnson said. "Something real big."

"There's nothing around here now," Rhodes said.

Johnson didn't appear convinced. His head swiveled as he looked around for signs that Bigfoot was in the vicinity.

Rhodes scanned the clearing for any signs of evidence: footprints, a piece of torn cloth hanging from a sticker vine, something that the killer might have dropped. His Social Security card would have been nice.

There was nothing, though, not that Rhodes could see.

"You gonna turn him over?" Johnson asked.

Rhodes didn't answer. He was staring down at the body. It was wearing a T-shirt, grease-streaked overalls, and work shoes. There was something missing, but Rhodes couldn't quite figure out what it was. It would come to him eventually, he was sure.

He handed the shotgun to Johnson, who took it with his free hand, and went to the body. He knelt down beside it and looked at the wound. The dead man had been hit on the right side of the back of his head by something hard and heavy, something that had left a depression several inches long. Rhodes lifted the head up and looked at the face.

"You know him, Sheriff?" Johnson said.

"I know him," Rhodes said.

The dead man was Larry Colley.

5

▼

RHODES AND DEPUTY RUTH GRADY WORKED THE CRIME SCENE until almost dark, which at that time of the year came around eight thirty. Mosquitoes buzzed around them, and Rhodes was glad that he always carried insect repellent in the county car. Even the repellent didn't keep all the pests away, though, and he had been bitten a couple of times.

After three hours, he and Ruth hadn't found a single clue.

"We know someone else was here," Ruth said. She was short and stout and probably the best deputy in the department. "That's about all."

"By someone," Rhodes said, "do you mean *something*?"

Ruth grinned. "You don't really think Bigfoot bashed in Larry Colley's head, do you?"

Rhodes wasn't sure what he believed. Right at the moment, it seemed that either Bigfoot had killed Colley or that Colley had just dropped out of the sky into the woods. The area where Colley had been killed had been so little disturbed that it was as if he'd been alone all the time.

Johnson's pickup had driven into the pasture and out of it, and then Rhodes had followed it back in with the county car. So any tracks from another vehicle, assuming that there had been any, were obliterated. Johnson claimed that he hadn't seen a car or pickup anywhere around, but there were plenty of places where one could be hidden.

The hog path was too hard to take footprints, and the floor of the woods, even in the clearing, was thick with leaves and sticks and vines. There was not much chance that a heavy man, even one carrying a body, would have left any impression.

Rhodes didn't think Colley had been carried in, anyway. The path was too narrow for anyone to walk along while carrying a body without snagging something, and Rhodes had looked along every inch of the path all the way out to the edge of the trees to see if there was anything caught on a tree branch. He'd found nothing.

The path, of course, went on past the clearing and farther into the woods, where it eventually petered out near another little clearing where the ground was concave and had held water from the rain. The hogs used it for a wallow when it was wet like that.

Rhodes had gone down the path to the wallow. He'd found nothing. Nothing at all.

Colley might have been dragged into the clearing, Rhodes thought. It was possible, but there was nothing to indicate it. If someone had dragged him, the signs had been obliterated. So it was possible that he'd walked there under his own power.

"I wish we had a murder weapon," Ruth said. "If Bigfoot did it, he was at least smart enough to carry his blunt instrument away."

"We'll know more after the autopsy," Rhodes said.

The justice of the peace had been there and declared Larry Colley dead, and the body had been taken away in an ambulance. Dr. White would work on it later that evening.

"Do you really think we'll know any more?" Ruth asked.

Rhodes didn't, but he didn't want to admit it. He looked around the clearing and wiped sweat off his face while trying to look thoughtful and confident. He wished he had a Dr Pepper.

"We'll at least get some idea of the time of death," he said.

"The heat and humidity in here might make that hard to determine."

Ruth wasn't making Rhodes feel any better.

"At least the hogs didn't get him," she continued.

"Where are those hogs?" Rhodes said. "I haven't heard a sound out of them."

"It's almost as if something's keeping them away from here," Ruth said, and started humming something that approximated the theme from *The Twilight Zone*.

"Bigfoot again," Rhodes said. "You'd think a shaggy fella like him would leave some hair stuck on a twig now and then."

"There you go, being logical again."

Rhodes didn't recall having been logical before.

"Do you have any suspects?" Ruth asked.

"Sure. Everybody Colley ever knew."

"That must be a pretty long list. What will you do about it?"

"Start narrowing it down," Rhodes said.

Bud Turley's house was a few miles outside the Clearview city limits, about halfway to Obert, a small town that had long ago been home to a small college. The campus was now used for retreats and a workshop for aspiring writers. Rhodes had been more involved with the last workshop there than he'd wanted to be, mainly because of a murder that had occurred.

Rhodes pulled his car into the graveled driveway behind Turley's Jeep. The house was old, and the paint was flaking off the sides. It was nearly ten o'clock. There were no lights on inside the house, but Rhodes could hear loud music, and there was light coming from somewhere in back.

Rhodes got out of the car and walked around the house. A big sheet-metal barn squatted there. Several cars and an old pickup were parked in the darkness, either repaired or waiting for someone to tinker with them. Rhodes walked past them without paying them much attention.

Turley's Jeep was parked near the wide doors in one end of the building. The doors were open, and the place was lit by fluorescent bulbs. The floor of the barn was hard-packed dirt, darkened in most places by stains made by oil and other automotive fluids.

Bud Turley was working on something under the hood of a rusty-fendered Oldsmobile. Rhodes didn't know how old the car was, but he didn't think Oldsmobiles were even being built anymore.

A country song from around 1975, something by Don Williams, played on a black plastic radio that sat on a workbench. The radio was almost lost in the litter of tools and oily rags that covered the top of the bench.

Because the music was turned up loud and because Turley had his head well up under the hood of the ancient Oldsmobile, he didn't see Rhodes come in. Rhodes waited until the song stopped playing and said, "Hey, Bud."

Turley slipped out from under the hood. He held a spark-plug wrench in his right hand, and there was a dark line of grease on his cheek.

"Hey, Sheriff," he said. He gestured with the wrench. "You got some car trouble you need fixed?"

"Not that kind of trouble," Rhodes said. "This kind can't be fixed. Not with a wrench or anything else."

"Sounds bad," Turley said.

He put the wrench down on the top of a red rolling tool cabinet that was nearby. Rhodes thought it must have come from a flea market, because it looked as if it had fallen down a flight of concrete stairs. Turley wiped his hands on a greasy rag he pulled from his back pocket. He wasn't wearing a cap, and the lights reflected from his shiny head.

"You haven't lost that Bigfoot tooth I gave you, I hope," he said.

"No, it's not that." Rhodes had never found a good way to tell someone that a friend or family member was dead. "Somebody's killed Larry Colley."

Turley didn't change expression. He kept right on wiping his hands. It was almost as if he hadn't heard. Finally he said, "That's not very funny, Sheriff."

"It's not a joke," Rhodes told him. "Someone found his body out in Big Woods late this afternoon."

Turley stuck the rag back in his pocket and walked over to the workbench. On the radio Conway Twitty was singing now, something about a woman who wore tight-fitting jeans. Turley turned off the radio, and in the sudden silence Rhodes could hear the humming of the fluorescent light tubes. A wooden folding chair stood at one end of the workbench. Turley sat down in it and looked up at Rhodes.

"You sure it was Larry?" he said.

"I saw the body. I'm sure."

"Larry was supposed to be here tonight, help me work on that Olds." Turley shook his head. "I wondered why he didn't show up."

"You'd been friends for a long time," Rhodes said.

"Since junior high. We hunted arrowheads together all over this county before we started to look for Bigfoot. Larry was the only one who never laughed at me about that." Turley shook his head. "He always claimed he was abducted by a UFO, but I never believed it."

He pronounced UFO as a word: "you-fo."

"Some people think you were a little jealous about that."

"Then I'm going to be a lot more jealous now. First he gets abducted and then he gets killed by Bigfoot."

"I don't think he was killed by Bigfoot," Rhodes said. "I think it was somebody like you or me."

"You don't know what's in those woods, Sheriff. Nobody knows. Larry should never have gone in there by himself."

"Somebody was with him," Rhodes said. "The person who killed him."

"If you say so."

"You weren't with him, were you?"

Turley tried a grin. It didn't work. He said, "You think I killed Larry? Why would I do that? Because he got a ride in a UFO and I didn't?"

"I didn't say you killed him. I was wondering if you might have any idea what he was doing in Big Woods."

"He was supposed to come over here and help me this afternoon. I didn't know where he was." Turley ran a hand across the top of his head. The rag hadn't removed all the grease, and he left a black mark just above his forehead. "The son of a bitch."

"Hard words for a friend."

"I'm thinking of why he was out at the Woods. He must've been looking for where I found that tooth. He was mad when I called and told him about it. He said I shouldn't have gone off without him. But he had something else to do, so I went. He must've decided to look for the place instead of helping me with this car."

"You mentioned that he had something else to do this morning," Rhodes said. "What was it?"

"He wouldn't tell me. Said it was none of my business."

"He wasn't doing any bill collection, was he?"

"Is that supposed to mean something?"

"There'd been some complaints about his methods."

"None of 'em ever stuck, though, did they?" Turley rubbed his chin. A black mark appeared on one side. "Larry could be a little rough sometimes, I guess. You think somebody killed him because of that?"

"I don't know. I'm just asking questions to see if I can find out something that will help me. Can you think of anybody who might want to kill Larry?"

"He has a couple of ex-wives. You talk to them?"

"I will," Rhodes said.

Rhodes knew about the wives. He'd given Ruth Grady the job of notifying them of Colley's death. He wasn't sure that either of them would be grief-stricken, not from what he'd heard about Colley's domestic affairs.

"What about enemies?" Rhodes said. "People he'd been in fights with, people he'd threatened."

"Sheriff, you know as well as I do that Larry liked to fight. Hell, I've been in a few fights with him myself. You know that, too. You've put a stop to one or two of them. He might have been in some I didn't know about. I don't have him on a leash."

"What about other friends, people I should talk to?"

"Larry wasn't a friendly sort. People thought he was a little crazy." Turley tried another grin. This one stayed on his face. "They think the same thing about me, but that tooth will prove they're wrong."

"Has he been doing any work lately?" Rhodes looked around the shop. "I don't mean here with you. He did some odd jobs now and then, didn't he? Fence building, house painting, that kind of thing."

"Yeah, he picked up a little money like that when things were slow around here, but not lately. Damn. I just can't believe he's dead."

"He was your friend," Rhodes said. "You must have some idea about what he was doing."

"I can't think of anything," Turley said. "I'd tell you if I could. I want you to get whoever did it. And then I want you to let me share a cell with him for about half an hour."

Rhodes didn't bother to comment on that idea. He said, "If you think of anything that might help me, give me a call."

"I will," Turley said, and Rhodes started out of the barn.

He hadn't gotten far when Turley called him back. Turley was standing in the wide doorway, silhouetted by the lights. He looked a little like Bigfoot himself. Rhodes returned to the barn to see what he had to say. He could hear music from inside. Turley had turned on the radio again.

"I just remembered," Turley said when Rhodes got close

enough to hear clearly. "Larry *had* been doing a little work on the side. You know Gerald Bolton?"

"He owns the land where Colley was found," Rhodes said.

"Yeah. I thought he might. Anyway, Larry was doing something for him."

"What?"

"There's an old camp house down near Big Woods. The Bolton family used it for reunions and things once upon a time. They stopped after that kid, Ronnie, wandered off and Bigfoot got him."

"Nobody knows what got him," Rhodes said. "Maybe nothing did."

Turley shook his head as if to say *That's what you think.* He said, "OK. Anyway, Bolton was thinking about having the house fixed up. Larry was doing a little work on it. That might be why he was down there."

"I'll check it out," Rhodes said.

"I don't see why Bolton would want to fix up that old house," Turley said. "It's too dangerous to be near those woods, and bad things happen there."

"I can't argue with that," Rhodes said.

6

▼

When Rhodes got home, his wife, Ivy, was watching the ten o'clock news. The weatherperson was saying that the next day would be hot and humid.

"Now that's what I call news," Rhodes said.

Yancey, the inside dog, was circling Rhodes's feet and yapping. Yancey was a Pomeranian and did a lot of yapping. Rhodes ignored him.

"The crack Channel Eleven news team is always on top of things," Ivy said. "Scoops are their life. How was your day?"

Rhodes had called to tell her about Colley and to explain that he'd be late getting home. It seemed he told her that a lot.

"About what you'd expect, not counting the Bigfoot tooth."

Ivy used the remote to turn off the TV set. "You didn't mention a Bigfoot tooth on the phone. You want to tell me about it while you eat?"

"Sure," Rhodes said.

He picked up Yancey to pet him. Yancey squirmed, either in pleasure or because he wanted to be put down. Rhodes set him on the floor, and he ran toward the kitchen.

"Yancey's excited to see me," Rhodes said.

Ivy laughed. "I don't want to hurt your feelings, but Yancey's excited all the time, whether he sees anybody or not."

"I think he likes me, though."

"I'm sure he does. You can count on his vote in the next election. Come on to the kitchen."

Rhodes himself wasn't much of a cook. In fact, his own special version of beanie-weenie was about the only dish he could whip up. He was also good with bologna sandwiches, but he wasn't sure that sandwiches counted as cooking.

Ivy was much better in the kitchen than he was, but she was currently in a low-fat phase that seemed to Rhodes a bit restrictive. He'd argued for a change to the Atkins regimen. He thought he could get along just fine on a diet that allowed him to eat bacon and eggs and cheese, although he knew he'd want a piece of toast from time to time to go along with it.

When they got to the kitchen, Rhodes set his place at the table while Ivy got out the food: grilled chicken and steamed vegetables. Broccoli, carrots, and cauliflower. She put it in the microwave to heat.

Rhodes was glad he'd cheated at lunch and gone by the Dairy Queen. He didn't think he'd mention the Blizzard he'd had to Ivy, however.

While Rhodes ate, he told Ivy as much as he knew about the Bigfoot tooth and Colley's death. It wasn't much in either case.

Yancey yapped until he got tired and lay down in a corner where he could watch in case anything fell from the table.

Rhodes didn't think the dog would want anything that he might let drop.

"Do you know anything about Colley's life insurance?" Rhodes asked Ivy, who worked in an insurance office in downtown Clearview.

"What did you have in mind?" she said.

"He has a couple of ex-wives. I wondered if either one of them was going to cash in big now that he's dead."

"I don't know," Ivy said. "If he has insurance, I don't think it's with us. People who don't have a regular job don't usually have big policies. Maybe something to cover burial, but that's about all. And the ones with insurance usually remember to change their policies when they get divorced. I wouldn't be looking there for a motive if I were you."

Rhodes hadn't really thought it was a possibility, but ex-wives might have other motives. He'd have to find out what he could from them tomorrow.

"Do you remember Ronnie Bolton?" Rhodes asked.

"The boy who disappeared from that family reunion? That was a long time ago. Before we met. Why do you ask?"

"No reason. It just seems that a lot of things happen in that part of the county." Rhodes thought about what Turley had said. "Bad things."

"Those woods are where the feral hogs got you. I hope you're being careful."

Rhodes knew that Ivy hadn't quite gotten used to the idea that she was married to someone who occasionally got into dangerous situations. She'd thought that the sheriff sat around the jail and delegated everything to the deputies, and it worked that way in some of the bigger counties in the state. In those places, a sheriff was a politician and an administrator first and a lawman second. Rhodes didn't think he'd like a job situation like that.

"I'm being careful," he said.

And he was. So far there was no way to be anything else.

He finished his meal and went outside to see Speedo, the outside dog. Speedo was a border collie, and he was much bigger than Yancey, though Yancey had never acknowledged the fact. In spite of his size, Yancey was louder than Speedo ever was. He went along into the yard with Rhodes, and the two dogs sniffed each other and ran around the yard for a while.

It was hot and muggy, and when Rhodes looked up at the sky there was so much moisture in the air that the stars appeared almost fuzzy. Rhodes thought about going back inside to the air-conditioning, but Speedo found his ball and brought it over to Rhodes, who threw it for him to fetch.

Yancey got to it first, by virtue of being much closer to where it landed, and tried to grab it, but Speedo skidded into him and snatched it away. He took it to Rhodes and dropped it, but when Rhodes reached for it, Speedo grabbed it again.

Rhodes tried to take it away, which was exactly what Speedo wanted. He shook his head and growled and wouldn't let go until Rhodes pretended to lose interest. Then Speedo dropped the ball again.

That went on for a while, and then Rhodes went back inside, with Yancey yapping at his heels.

The next morning Rhodes was at the jail early. Hack and Lawton were there, waiting to hear if he had any more to tell them about Larry Colley than they'd already learned from Ruth Grady.

Rhodes knew they'd have pumped her for all the information she had, so he couldn't give them much satisfaction.

When he was finished, Hack said, "I was just sayin' yesterday that it was a wonder nobody'd killed them two. You remember me sayin' that?"

Rhodes admitted that he remembered.

"Nostradamus," Hack said. "Me and him have a lot in common."

"Is that anything like the Cosa Nostra?" Lawton said.

Rhodes interrupted them before they could get an argument started. If he let them go on, they'd jaw back and forth all morning.

"Do either of you remember Ronnie Bolton?" he said.

Hack, who had been about to light into Lawton, turned to Rhodes. He said, "You think this has anything to do with Ronnie Bolton?"

Rhodes said that he didn't know but that it didn't seem likely. Larry Colley hadn't been at the Bolton family reunion. "That was a long time ago," he said.

"Still bothers you, I bet."

"You'd win."

Rhodes didn't like leaving things undone, and he'd never found out what happened to Ronnie Bolton. As far as he knew, no one else had, either. At the time, there had been no suspicions of foul play. Everyone at the reunion alibied everyone else. Rhodes had still never been satisfied with the idea that Ronnie had simply wandered off and disappeared.

Some people thought that the most likely explanation was that he'd been picked up by someone driving along the county road. Or that he'd been killed by feral hogs. Rhodes supposed that was possible. A lot of things were possible. Bigfoot? Even that had been suggested.

Gerald and Edith Bolton, the boy's parents, had been distraught, and Rhodes could understand why. They'd called him daily for weeks, and regularly after that for a year or more before they'd finally stopped. Rhodes doubted that even now they'd given up hope. As long as no trace of the boy had been found, they'd think there was a chance he'd come home. Rhodes thought it was unlikely, and he'd told them so, but he knew that wouldn't change their thinking.

"You gonna talk to the Boltons?" Hack said.

"I might," Rhodes told him. "I have some other people to see first."

"Don't forget that professor from the college is coming to see that tooth."

Rhodes said he wouldn't forget, and Hack and Lawton got back to work, or pretended to. Rhodes looked through the things on his desk and found the inventory of Larry Colley's personal property that Ruth Grady had written out. Colley's billfold still held his driver's license and credit cards, as well as forty-six dollars. He'd had thirty-seven cents in change, a Timex Ironman wristwatch. No rings or other jewelry.

No cell phone, either. That was interesting. Either Chester Johnson wasn't the only man in Blacklin County besides the sheriff without a cell phone, or Colley's was missing.

Around nine thirty, Rhodes decided that he'd done all he could at the jail, so he told Hack he was going to have a talk with Larry Colley's ex-wives.

"You think you have time?" Hack said. "Before the professor gets here, I mean."

"I have time to see at least one of them, if not both. I'll be back. Don't worry."

"I'm not worried. I'm just lookin' out for you."

Rhodes told him that he appreciated it and left.

The first thing Karen Sandstrom told Rhodes was that she didn't care one way or the other about Larry Colley.

"He was a lifetime ago, as far as I'm concerned," she said. "I haven't heard anything from him in ten years, and that's just the way I wanted it."

Sandstrom was a slim blonde who worked at the circulation desk of the Clearview Public Library. She and Rhodes were at a round table in one of the meeting rooms so as not to disturb the library's patrons, who were looking through the new books, working at the computers, reading the magazines, or just browsing the used paperbacks that were being sold off a cart for a quarter a pop.

"You haven't had any contact with him lately?" Rhodes said.

"No, I haven't. I made a big mistake when I married him, Sheriff. The day my divorce was final was the happiest day of my life. I've remarried now, and I'm very happy. I never even think about Larry Colley."

While she spoke, she toyed with the wedding band on the ring finger of her left hand.

"No calls, no cards, no nothing," Rhodes said.

Sandstrom laughed. "Cards? You don't think Larry was a sentimentalist, do you, Sheriff? The kind who remembers birthdays and anniversaries? He didn't even do that when we were married, much less afterward. When he walked out the door, it was as if our marriage had never taken place." Her face clouded. "It was that way for most of the time we were married, in fact. Larry spent more time with that friend of his than he ever did with me."

"You mean Bud Turley?"

"That's the one. Those two were closer than Larry and I ever were."

"What about that UFO?" Rhodes asked.

"That happened before we were married, if you want to believe it happened at all. I always thought he just made it up to make Bud Turley jealous. The story changed every time he told it. It was something to tell in a bar, for a drink."

"What about enemies, people who might have wanted Larry dead? You know anybody like that?"

"Not a one. I've been telling you, Sheriff, I haven't talked to him in ten years. I wish I could help you, but I just can't."

She sounded convincing, and Rhodes supposed that he believed her. He hadn't expected anything, really, but he'd had to try. He thanked her and left the library, being careful not to make any noise. He didn't want anybody to have to shush him.

He looked at his watch when he got outside. He still had forty-five minutes until Tom Vance was supposed to show up at the jail to have a look at the tooth, so he could either talk to Colley's other ex-wife or visit Dr. White and see if he'd completed the autopsy on Larry Colley.

He decided on Dr. White. One ex-wife was enough for one morning.

7

▼

CLYDE BALLINGER WAS IN HIS OFFICE IN BACK OF THE FUNERAL home when Rhodes arrived. He was reading an old paperback, which was not unusual. His desk was covered with them, and he read them at every opportunity. The one he held up for Rhodes to see was called *The Green Wound.*

"They don't write 'em like this anymore," Ballinger said. "And nobody would buy 'em if they did."

"Why not?" Rhodes asked.

"Because people don't have any taste. They want four hundred pages of serial killers, car chases, and explosions."

"You must be thinking about the movies," Rhodes said. "They're all long and loud. Sometimes when I see one of the new ones, I feel like I've been on a carnival ride."

Ballinger put a piece of paper between the pages to mark his place and laid the book on his desk with all the others. "Did you ever consider the fact that it might be you and me who're out of step?" he said.

"You mean that books and movies are actually a lot better now and we're wrong to think the old ones are better?"

Ballinger nodded. "Hard to believe, isn't it. What it means is that we've become old farts."

"It's barely possible that we could be right. There's always a chance of that."

"Two chances," Ballinger said. "Slim and none."

"And we're not that old," Rhodes said. "Middle-aged at most."

"Yeah, if you're planning to live to be a hundred. In my business I see a whole lot of dead people, but I don't see many that age. Come to think of it, I haven't seen one that age in years."

"Speaking of your business," Rhodes said.

"Dr. White finished the autopsy, if that's what you mean. He wrote it all up, and he's probably delivered it to your office by now. It won't tell you anything you didn't already know, though."

Rhodes had been afraid of that. The language would be a little fancier, but what it would add up to was the fact that someone had hit Larry Colley in the back of the head with the traditional blunt instrument and killed him. Well, it wasn't as bleak as that. White would know whether Colley had died in the clearing or been brought there.

"What about the clothes?" Rhodes said.

"We can go get them." Ballinger stood up. "You think they'll be full of clues?"

"Two chances they will be," Rhodes said. "Slim and none."

* * *

Ballinger's funeral home had once been one of the grander mansions in Clearview, with a big front lawn and oak trees for shade, tennis courts in the back, and even a little building that was used for servants' quarters. That building was where Ballinger now had his office. He and Rhodes had to walk across a small parking area to the main structure. Rhodes supposed it was ironic that this place that had been home to a large and prominent family was now used for a mortuary, but it wasn't something that bothered him.

They went in through a back door, and Ballinger led Rhodes to a small storeroom. He opened the door and took out a plastic bag.

"Shoes, shirt, pants, underwear," he said. "Your deputy took the other things."

Rhodes took the bag. He didn't open it. He'd have a look later, after he'd talked to the professor about the Bigfoot tooth.

"When's the funeral?" he asked.

Ballinger didn't know. "Nobody wants to make the arrangements."

"You've talked to his ex-wives?"

"Both of them. Maybe the county will have to bury him."

"Try Bud Turley," Rhodes said.

"I should have thought of him first," Ballinger said.

Tom Vance looked like Rhodes's idea of a college professor. He had gray hair, parted neatly on the left, and he wore a light blue dress shirt with a dark blue tie.

"I just had my last class of the summer session," he told Rhodes, "not counting the final exam. I'm ready for a break."

"How long do you get?" Rhodes asked.

They were in the jail. Vance sat in a wooden chair by Rhodes's desk, while Hack and Lawton pretended to be busy. Rhodes knew, however, that they were listening to every word.

"Less than a week," Vance said. "When I started teaching, I thought I'd have great summer vacations, but every summer I wind up teaching classes."

"You must enjoy your work."

"That." Vance paused. "And I need the money."

"Don't we all. Bud Turley tells me you're a paleontologist."

"That's right. I like to dig up prehistoric animals."

"What about Bigfoot?"

Vance laughed. "I've never seen one, and I've never seen the bones of one. But when Turley called, he sounded pretty excited about this tooth he found."

"It's a big tooth," Rhodes said. "That's all I know about it. I'll get it and let you have a look."

Just as Rhodes got to his feet, Bud Turley came through the front door. Right behind him was Jennifer Loam, a young, intense-looking woman who was a reporter for the *Clearview Herald.* Or, Rhodes thought, *the* reporter for the *Herald.* The local newspaper didn't have a lot of employees.

"I hope you weren't going to start without me," Turley said. "I had to stop by the newspaper office first."

"Had to alert the media, huh?" Hack said.

Rhodes gave him a look. So did Turley.

"Sorry," Hack said, but Rhodes could tell he didn't mean it.

Jennifer Loam had something new, a tiny digital recorder. Rhodes knew it would already be turned on.

"Sheriff," she said, "would you like to comment on the Bigfoot tooth that Mr. Turley has found?"

"We don't know what kind of tooth it is," Rhodes said. "We're just about to get an expert opinion."

He introduced Vance to both Loam and Turley and went to the evidence locker. He got out the tooth and took it back to his desk.

"Well," Vance said after giving it a cursory glance, "it's a tooth, all right, and it came from an animal with big feet."

"Bigfoot," Turley said. His face broke out in a wide grin. "I knew it."

"I said the animal had big feet," Vance told him. "Not that it was Bigfoot."

Turley's grin disappeared. "It's not?"

"No. That's a tooth from a Columbian mammoth."

Rhodes knew next to nothing about mammoths. In fact, as far as he could remember, he knew only one thing: that they were woolly.

"A woolly mammoth?" he said.

Vance disappointed him.

"No. There were never any woolly mammoths in Texas. The Columbian mammoth was an even bigger animal. Bigger than any Bigfoot, I promise you. They could stand as high as twelve to thirteen feet at the shoulder. A woolly mammoth would have been about three feet shorter."

So Rhodes had known even less about mammoths than he'd thought. He said, "All right. We know it's not Bigfoot. I didn't ever think it was."

He didn't look at Turley, who said, "Is this a valuable find?"

Vance did look at Turley. "I'm sorry to have to tell you that it's not very valuable. Mammoths are a dime a dozen in Texas. People find their remains all the time when they're building highways or digging foundations. Where was this one found?"

"Down on Pittman Creek," Turley said.

He didn't sound happy about the fact that his Bigfoot dream had been shattered, but then he had other things to be unhappy about, including the death of his best friend.

"And that's in Blacklin County?" Vance said.

"Yeah, the southern part."

"That at least makes it interesting, because as far as I know, there's never been a mammoth find in this county." Vance reached out and touched the tooth. "Besides that, this one seems to be in a very good state of preservation, which would make it worth more."

"How old is it?" Turley said.

"I don't really know. I'd say at least ten or twelve thousand years old. Maybe much older. But if it's from more recent times, say ten thousand years ago, there's a bare chance that we'll find that it was in some way associated with humans. The Clovis people, to be specific."

Rhodes didn't think ten thousand years ago was exactly recent times, but then he wasn't thinking in terms of geologic eras.

"Larry Colley and I found some Clovis points in that area a few years ago," Turley said.

"If we could find Clovis points associated with the bones, that would add to the historical value," Vance said.

"How much money are we talking about?"

"Hard to say. If the tusks are there, they're valuable for their ivory. People love to make pistol grips from them. If the skull is intact and well preserved, then you're talking about something worth still more, and it's more interesting besides. But even at that, you're not talking about huge amounts of money. The main interest would be purely scientific, but I wouldn't mind doing the dig."

Turley didn't look too pleased with that idea. "A dig?" he said.

"A proper one. In some ways, this is even better than Bigfoot. It's from something real, something that can tell us about the history of this county."

"It won't tell us anything about Bigfoot, though," Turley said. "That's what I was hoping for."

"I don't think you should hope too hard," Vance said. "As a scientist, I can tell you that there's not much likelihood of a Bigfoot ever turning up here. Or anywhere else."

Turley opened his mouth to say something, then closed it and shook his head.

"I think a dig for the mammoth bones would be a good idea," Vance continued. "We'd have to find out who owns the land first, and then get permission. Do you know, Mr. Turley?"

Turley hemmed and hawed and finally said he believed that the land was owned by Gerald Bolton. Rhodes had suspected as much. The bones had been found not far from Big Woods.

"I'll try to get in touch with him if he's in the phone book," Vance said. "A dig would be interesting for my students, and maybe some of the local science teachers would like to get involved. It would even bring the county some good publicity."

At the word "publicity," Rhodes looked at Jennifer Loam, who was jotting some notes on a notepad rather than relying on her little recorder. Maybe she didn't trust technology. That seemed to Rhodes to be a sensible attitude. He didn't trust technology himself.

She must have noticed Rhodes looking at her, because she stopped writing and said, "Speaking of publicity, do you think there's any connection between the mammoth bones and the murder?"

* * *

If Jennifer had been trying to get everyone's attention, she'd certainly succeeded.

Tom Vance turned to her and said, "Murder?"

"A man named Larry Colley was killed in the vicinity of Gerald Bolton's property yesterday," Jennifer said. "I believe murder is suspected. Isn't that right, Sheriff?"

Rhodes said that it was but that as far as he knew, there was no connection between the mammoth and the murder. He didn't see how there could be.

"It seems like a strange coincidence, then," Jennifer said. "A mammoth's bones are found, and a man is killed not far away on the same day."

Rhodes wasn't fond of coincidences, but as far as he could tell that's what they were dealing with.

"Have you made any progress in your investigation?" Jennifer asked.

"Some," Rhodes said. He noticed Hack looking at him from across the room. "Not much, though," he added.

For Vance's benefit, he went on to explain about what had happened to Larry Colley.

"It shouldn't interfere with whatever you want to do," Rhodes said. "In fact, I have to see Gerald Bolton, so I'll ask him about the dig."

Vance didn't appear to be very happy with the turn of events. Murder was bad enough, but Rhodes had also happened to mention the feral hogs that roamed the area.

"Maybe we should just forget about the dig," Vance said. "It sounds as if you might be inconvenienced. And I don't like the idea that feral hogs are running around out there. They could destroy the dig without half trying, and they might hurt someone. There might be liability questions."

"You don't have to worry about interfering," Rhodes said. "Probably not about the hogs, either. They don't come out of the woods much in the daylight, and maybe you could put a fence up around the dig. That might keep them away. Why don't we ride out and have a look at the place where the bones are. I'm sure Bud would be willing to show it to us. Isn't that right, Bud?"

Turley hemmed and hawed some more and appeared more reluctant than ever to give up his secret, but eventually he agreed. He must have known that sooner or later he'd have to tell someone where the bones were.

"I'm going, too," Jennifer said. "I want some pictures for the paper."

Rhodes had a feeling she wanted more than that. She wanted to pump him about Colley's death.

"Can you not print the location for a while?" Vance asked her. "People have a way of trampling all over the place and spoiling things, and they like to take souvenirs. They could really mess things up. Not as bad as feral hogs would, but bad enough."

Jennifer thought it over before saying, "All right. I won't print the location."

"No pictures, either," Vance said. "People could figure out the location from them."

"Fine. But people will find out the location soon enough without any help from the paper. And pictures or no pictures, I'm still coming along."

"You can ride in the Jeep with Bud, then," Rhodes said. He didn't plan to be trapped in the car with her.

Even that didn't discourage her. "That's fine," she said.

8

TOM VANCE WAS QUIET AS THEY DROVE SOUTH. RHODES FIGURED
that the teacher was thinking about the possibility of digging for
the mammoth, or maybe he was more concerned with the possibility of being attacked by feral hogs while looking for old bones.

Rhodes didn't mind the silence. He was trying to remember a
little about the autopsy report that he'd hardly had time to look at
before Vance arrived at the jail.

In the report Dr. White made it clear that Colley had died at the
place where he'd been found. The postmortem lividity indicated
that quite clearly.

Dr. White had also concluded that Colley had been killed by
the traditional blunt instrument. Not a tree branch or something
handy in the woods, because there was no sign of anything like
that in the wound. More likely it had been something metal, like a
jack handle. Dr. White had made a cast of the wound, in case
Rhodes turned up a weapon that he'd like to try to match to it.

Rhodes wasn't sure he'd ever find a weapon, certainly not before he found a lot of other things. He'd looked all over the area where the body had been found, but there was no sign of a heavy piece of metal. So what Rhodes was wondering about was how Colley had gotten to Big Woods, and why he'd gone there. There had been no sign of a vehicle, and since there was nobody living in the area, there was no chance that anybody had seen one.

The county car was passing through Thurston about that time. Someone in the little town might have seen the killer's car, but because the road through town was a fairly busy highway, no one would have paid any special attention to a car driving through.

There was one person who might have noticed a car, though. Louetta Kennedy. Rhodes told himself that he'd have to stop by her store on his way back to Clearview and have a little talk with her.

As it happened, the route Turley was driving took them right by Louetta's store, which meant that Turley and Colley had been near the woods at the same time. Louetta's old Ford was parked in its usual place. Rhodes looked for Louetta on the porch, but the plastic lawn chair was empty. Maybe it was cooler inside, or maybe Louetta had some shelves that needed stocking.

Rhodes followed Turley's Jeep past the road he'd taken the previous day through Bolton's land to Big Woods, but not far past it. Turley pulled off to the side of the road just before he came to an old wooden bridge over Pittman Creek. He parked the Jeep with two wheels on the road and two off in the ditch beside it, leaving the Jeep leaning to the right at a sharp angle. It didn't seem to bother Jennifer Loam, who climbed out without any trouble. Turley, who was going uphill, had a harder time of it, but not much.

Rhodes parked the county car behind the Jeep. He and Vance had to contend with heavy doors, so it was harder for them to get out than it had been for the passengers in the open Jeep. Rhodes let the door on his side slam shut behind him. Vance left his open while he took off his tie and tossed it inside the car. Then he shoved hard on the door and closed it.

Rhodes and Vance walked to the bridge where Turley was standing with Jennifer. Turley was telling the reporter how he'd found the mammoth.

"All that rain we had this summer really washed along this creek," he said. "And naturally it washed away a lot of soil."

Rhodes looked down at the trickle of water that ran along the creek bed. It was hard to believe, now, that earlier in the summer water had been rushing along it at a depth of eight or nine feet.

"Indians camped all along this creek," Turley said. "Larry and I found arrowheads here a long time ago, like I said."

The creek had likely looked pretty much the same when the Comanches had lived there a hundred and fifty years ago or more, but Rhodes was sure it had been different when the Clovis people had been there.

Rhodes wondered what Vance thought about Turley's arrow-head hunting. The few archaeologists Rhodes had talked to over the years didn't like to have amateurs picking up arrowheads or pieces of clay pots. They thought things should be left in place for the professionals to find them, even if there were no professionals in the area at the time.

"I figured that maybe the rain had washed up some more ar-rowheads," Turley continued. "Clovis points, and some that are a lot newer than that. When it's rained a lot, you never know what you might run across. And I thought maybe if a Bigfoot had walked along the creek, it might have left some footprints."

Rhodes looked at Vance, who smiled at the Bigfoot reference.

Jennifer kept a straight face. Rhodes didn't know if that was because she was a believer or because she didn't want to upset Turley.

"I asked Larry to come looking with me," Turley said, "but he didn't want to. Said he had something else to do."

Jennifer Loam had probably questioned him about Colley during their ride, Rhodes thought, assuming she could be heard over the roar of the wind in the Jeep.

Turley looked off into the distance, as if he might be thinking about Colley and how things would have been different if his friend had come along with him to look for footprints and arrowheads.

"Do you think this creek was here ten thousand years ago?" Rhodes asked Vance, who was already beginning to sweat through his blue dress shirt.

"Not likely," Vance said. "A lot of this area was under water. We might be standing on the edge of what was once a huge lake. Or there might have been a creek here, just not this one. We can tell more about what was here when we see where the bones are."

Rhodes glanced down at Vance's feet. The professor was wearing black dress shoes.

Vance noticed where Rhodes was looking and said, "Don't worry about me. I've ruined more than one pair of shoes in my day."

There was still some mud along the sides of the creek down near the water, but the upper sides of the bank had dried out on both sides. Tall weeds grew along them, and Rhodes thought about mosquitoes and chiggers. He could see the trees of Big Woods about a quarter of a mile away.

"How far from here did you find the tooth?" he asked Turley.

Turley took off his welding cap and wiped the top of his head. "Maybe a little more than fifty yards," he said as he put the cap back on. "You know, I didn't really notice the other day, but this land's not even fenced on the other side of the creek."

Rhodes hadn't noticed, either, but now that Turley mentioned it, he saw that the fence ended at the creek.

"Maybe Bolton thinks the creek is enough of a fence," he said, and maybe it was.

The banks were steep and the creek was plenty wide, at least fifteen yards wide, maybe twenty. Bolton's cattle wouldn't want to go to the trouble of crossing it, not when there was plenty of grass on their side.

"If the place isn't fenced, Bolton's not gonna have much to say about anybody digging for a mammoth's bones," Turley said. "I found that tooth on the unfenced side."

Jennifer Loam swiped her hand at a bug that flew in front of her face. "Why don't we look at where you found it, if we're going to," she said.

"Sounds like a good idea to me," Rhodes said. "You lead the way, Bud."

Turley went down into the ditch beside the road. The weeds reached up to his armpits, and he shoved through them to the creek bank. Jennifer was right behind him, followed by Vance and then by Rhodes.

The ground along the creek was rough, and the weeds didn't make the walking any easier. Bugs swarmed in their faces. Rhodes wasn't sure if he wanted to look for mammoth bones, but he did want to see the location where Turley had found the tooth, so he pushed on.

When they came to the spot they were looking for, Turley stopped and pointed to a chinaberry tree on the other side of the creek. "We'll have to cross over here," he said.

Rhodes wondered why they hadn't crossed on the bridge and walked along the other side. He didn't ask, however. He just tried to keep his balance as he followed the others down to the trickle of water at the bottom of the creek bed. When they reached it, Turley, Jennifer, and Vance stepped across with no trouble, not seeming to mind that their feet sank into the mud on the other side.

Rhodes minded, but he didn't say so. He stepped over the water and into the mud on the other side. There was a sucking sound when he pulled his foot free. He looked down at the mud on his shoes and thought about the way Turley's shoes had looked when he brought the tooth into the jail.

About halfway up the bank, Turley stopped and peered closely at the ground. He took a couple of steps to his right and said, "This is it. I found that tooth right here."

"If you don't mind," Vance said, "I'll have a look around."

Rhodes understood that what he meant was *If you three amateurs will keep out of my way, I'll see what a professional can find.*

"Why don't we go up in the shade," Rhodes said, and he walked up the bank to stand under the chinaberry tree.

Turley and Jennifer came up and stood beside him while Vance probed in the earth of the bank with his hands.

"Do you think he'll find anything?" Jennifer said.

Her face was red, and a rivulet of sweat ran out of her hair and down her temple.

"If it's on top of the ground, he'll find it," Rhodes told her.

"There's stuff there," Turley said. "If there was a tooth, there's bound to be more."

He was right, and it didn't take long for Vance to prove it. He came up to join them under the tree with a satisfied look on his face, and in his hand he held another tooth, just as well preserved as the one Turley had found.

"From just my quick look around," Vance said, "I'd guess the bones are here in a layer of sediment and gravel. Maybe this was the edge of a lake, or a slowdown in some ancient creek like the one that's here now. The rainwater rushing down the creek has washed away a lot of the topsoil, so the bones might not be too hard to find."

Vance handed the tooth to Rhodes and told him to let the others see it. While Rhodes was examining the fossil, Vance looked at both sides of the bank and said, "I think I could rig up a canopy to shade a dig here, and I can get some of my students to help. And, as I said, maybe there's someone at the high school who'd be interested, too."

"How soon would you want to get started?" Rhodes asked, handing the tooth to Jennifer.

"As soon as I can. This weekend would be best. Once the fall semester starts, I won't have much time other than on Saturdays. When did you say you were going to talk to Mr. Bolton?"

"I'll do it this afternoon," Rhodes said.

"Good. Give me a call when you find out something."

Vance reached into a back pocket and brought out his billfold. He took out a business card and handed it to Rhodes, who put it in his shirt pocket.

"I need to get back to town and write this up for the paper," Jennifer said, wiping away the sweat on the side of her face.

"I'd like to stay for a while and check things out, if you don't mind," Vance said.

"I can take you back when you're finished," Turley said. "I'll help you look."

"You'll have to be very careful," Vance told him.

"I will."

Jennifer looked at Rhodes.

"Well?" she said.

Rhodes managed not to sigh. He knew what was coming as soon as they got in the car.

"You can ride with me," he said. "Let's take the easy way and cross the creek on the bridge."

"Good idea," Jennifer said. "No wonder they keep electing you."

"I knew there must be a reason," Rhodes said, and he shoved off through the weeds.

He didn't look back, but he knew that Jennifer was right behind him.

By the time they arrived at Louetta Kennedy's store, Jennifer Loam had learned almost everything Rhodes knew about Larry Colley's death.

Although she'd gotten all the facts, he'd managed to withhold a couple of his guesses, but that was only because she hadn't had more time with him. She was smart and persistent, and Rhodes had a feeling she wouldn't be staying in Blacklin County for long. As soon as she had a little more experience, she'd be off to Dallas or Houston for a bigger and better-paying job.

"This place looks as if a good strong norther would blow it right over," Jennifer said when Rhodes parked beside the store in about the same spot he'd used the day before.

"It's probably sturdier than it seems," Rhodes said.

Jennifer looked skeptical. "I suppose it would have to be if it's still in use."

"It's been here a long time and withstood a lot of northers. I expect it'll hold up for a little while longer."

"Why are we stopping here, anyway?" Jennifer asked. "It's not just because you want a Dr Pepper, is it?"

"No," Rhodes admitted, getting out of the car. "The Dr Pepper was just an excuse. I want to ask Louetta a couple of questions."

Jennifer got out on her side. "Then I'm coming in. It's always enlightening to hear an experienced sleuth do an interrogation."

"Sleuth?" Rhodes said.

Jennifer laughed. "It's a word we professional reporters like to use."

"Louetta must be busy inside today," Rhodes said when he stepped up on the porch.

Jennifer stayed back, as if wondering whether the ice machine was going to slide off and crush her.

"She's usually sitting out here in her chair," Rhodes said, opening the screen door.

As soon as he looked inside the store, however, he knew that Louetta wasn't busy. She wasn't ever going to be busy again.

She lay on the floor in front of the counter, her gray hair falling over her face. Her head was twisted at an odd angle, leaving no doubt in Rhodes's mind that she was dead.

9

▼

Seeing a dead body always made Rhodes feel a little empty, as if his stomach had suddenly been hollowed out. Sometimes the feeling was stronger than at others. He hadn't felt it so much when he'd seen Larry Colley lying in the woods. He felt it more this time.

He turned away from the door and told Jennifer to stay outside because the store was now a crime scene. She wanted to know what was going on, but he didn't tell her until after he'd radioed Hack. Then he filled her in on what he knew and told her to stay out of the way.

"Don't worry," she said. She had the professional's calm demeanor in the face of unexpected events. "I know how to behave at a crime scene. But I would like to have a look, if you don't mind."

"Louetta's dead," Rhodes reminded her.

"And I'm a reporter," Jennifer said. "I have a job to do."

Rhodes nodded. "Go ahead, then. You can look through the door, but don't go inside."

Jennifer went up on the porch and peered in through the screen. Rhodes knew she was taking in every detail and would provide her readers with an accurate description even though she didn't have her camera.

"Why would anyone want to kill her?" Jennifer said after they'd gone back to stand beside the county car. Her eyes were a little damp, which didn't really surprise Rhodes. "She was an old woman. She couldn't hurt anybody. It doesn't make sense."

Rhodes thought that killing never did. It was a way of avoiding something, or a way of getting something, but it was never fair and it never made sense, except maybe to the person who'd done it. He wasn't good at saying things like that, however, so he offered a motive.

"Robbery?" he said.

Jennifer gave him a look. "There couldn't have been much money in the cash register, not in a place like this."

"Probably not," he said.

"Why, then?"

"I don't know. I'll try to find out, though."

"I hope you do," Jennifer said.

Rhodes waited with her beside the car until the justice of the peace got there, and then he had to go back into the store.

The JP agreed with what Rhodes had already decided: that Louetta Kennedy had been killed by person or persons unknown. She had been a small woman, and it seemed to Rhodes that someone much bigger than she was had argued with her and then hit her. Hard. So hard that her neck had snapped.

The JP left and the ambulance arrived. Rhodes had a good look at the body before he let it be taken away. Aside from the mark on the side of her face where she'd been hit, there was nothing to indicate any kind of a scuffle. The cash register hadn't even been opened.

Rhodes looked at everything in the store. It seemed to him that something was missing, but he didn't quite know what it was. He shifted his feet, and the old wooden floor creaked. If only he could interpret what it was saying, he thought, maybe he'd have his answer.

Or maybe not.

Jennifer rode back to town in the ambulance, which pulled away just as Ruth Grady arrived to go over the crime scene with Rhodes. Not that he expected to find anything.

"Do you think this has something to do with Larry Colley?" Ruth asked as she snapped on her rubber gloves.

Rhodes looked at the items on the sparsely stocked shelves. Dust on some of the cans showed they'd probably been there a while. He wondered much how longer Louetta would have been able to keep the store open if she'd lived.

"I wouldn't be surprised," he said, and he went on to explain why he'd stopped there.

Ruth nodded. "So you think that whoever killed Colley thought he might have been seen yesterday. He came back to make sure she didn't tell, and they got into an argument."

"That's what I think," Rhodes said. "Something like that, anyway. I wish I'd come by a little earlier."

But he knew that it wouldn't have done any good. He knew that Louetta had been dead for a good while. Hours, probably. She had so few customers these days that it wasn't surprising no one had come in and found her.

While they were working the scene, Rhodes asked Ruth if she'd found out anything that morning. He'd asked her to check into Colley's whereabouts on the day he was killed, and he was hoping that she might have learned something.

She hadn't.

"Nobody saw him around," she said. "At least not in any of the usual places he'd go."

"What places are those?"

"The Pool Hall," Ruth said. "And the Dairy Queen. He hung out at both places."

The Pool Hall was an imaginatively named establishment that had set up shop in one of the formerly vacant buildings in downtown Clearview. It had quickly become a favorite spot for people like Colley who lived with hardly any visible means of support but who could somehow afford to pass the time in games of chance and skill. Not that there was any gambling going on there. Rhodes would have been shocked to learn that was the case.

Colley hadn't been there, though, and Rhodes wondered again what business might have kept him from going to hunt for Bigfoot tracks with Bud Turley.

"What about his house?" Rhodes said. "Did you have time to get a look at it?"

"It's not a house," Ruth said. "It's a trailer." She told Rhodes where it was. "And I didn't get by there. There was a little car wreck out on the highway, and I helped clear it."

"I'll go by there later today, then," Rhodes said.

They searched the store diligently for clues, but there were none. The killer had not thoughtfully left a Dr Pepper bottle with his fingerprints on it sitting on the counter, nor had he left any other sign that he'd ever been there.

"I wish I'd thought about talking to Louetta yesterday," Rhodes said. "She might still be alive if I had."

"Or she might not," Ruth said. "She might not have remembered a thing, but the killer would have paid her a visit anyway. Besides, this might not even be connected to Colley's murder."

"You don't really believe that, do you?"

"No," she said. "I don't think I do."

Rhodes had missed lunch again, so he stopped by the Dairy Queen when he got back to town. He figured that a Blizzard wouldn't hurt him, not as long as nobody, and by nobody he meant Ivy, found out about it. He had one with crushed Heath Bar mixed in. If that wasn't nutrition, he didn't know what was.

He talked to the counter workers about Larry Colley, but they didn't know much about him other than that he was a regular customer and preferred his burgers without onions and his Blizzards with crumbled Butterfinger. None of the patrons in the place knew Colley at all. Or so they all said.

After he finished his Blizzard, Rhodes went by the jail. It was getting close to four o'clock, and he still wanted to see Bolton and Colley's other ex-wife. He also wanted to go and have a look at Colley's place of residence, that trailer on a lot just outside of town.

When Rhodes went inside the jail, Hack and Lawton were waiting for him. He knew they wanted all the details about Louetta Kennedy's death, and he also knew that he didn't have time to make them drag the details out of him the way they would have done if they'd known something he didn't know.

So he just told them everything as quickly as he could and then asked if anything had happened in his absence, hoping that they'd do him the favor of responding as concisely as he had.

He should have known better.

"We got a couple of calls," Hack said, looking over at Lawton, who looked down at the floor.

Rhodes waited, but of course Hack didn't say what the calls were about. Rhodes knew that if he waited forever, Hack wouldn't tell him outright. He'd have to ask. So he did.

"Important calls?" he said.

"You could say that."

"Do you want to tell me about them?"

"One of them was from somebody callin' about Vernell's goats."

Vernell Lindsey wrote romance novels and was doing fairly well for herself by all accounts. Her sales had soared after she'd held a writers' workshop on the old college campus near Obert. The sales hadn't been a result of her improved writing abilities, however. They'd come about because a famous cover model had been murdered in the course of the event. It was the kind of publicity that money couldn't buy. Vernell got an interview in *Romantic Times,* and sales skyrocketed.

Vernell was considered by nearly everyone in Clearview to be a little eccentric, though not excessively so for a writer, and she owned three goats named Shirley, Goodness, and Mercy. They didn't stay penned and were always getting off her property to bother the neighbors.

"Tell Buddy to take care of them," Rhodes said, naming the other deputy on duty.

"I already did," Hack said.

"Good. Now tell me about the other call."

Rhodes knew the other call would be the important one. Hack always liked to hold the good stuff back as long as he could.

"It was from a couple of friends of yours," Hack said.

Rhodes waited.

So did Hack.

After several seconds had passed, Rhodes said, "What friends?"

"It's nice to know you have so many that you can't figure it out," Lawton said, speaking up at last. "It's not ever' sheriff that can say that about himself."

"Especially if it's women friends," Hack said. "I wonder if Ivy knows about this."

"About what?" Rhodes said.

He was pretty sure Hack wasn't referring to the Blizzard, but with Hack you never knew. He had sources everywhere.

It wasn't about the Blizzard. Hack said, "About your women friends."

"What women friends?"

"See?" Lawton said. "What did I tell you? He's got so many of 'em, he can't even figure out which ones you're talkin' about."

"They're writers," Hack said. "Or at least that's what they told me. Like Vernell."

"Nobody's like Vernell," Lawton said. "I bet they don't have goats, for one thing."

"I don't know about goats," Hack said, glaring at Lawton. He didn't like to be one-upped when he was dragging out a story. "All I know is what they told me."

"And what was that?" Rhodes said, hoping to get things back on track.

"That they were coming down here from Dallas to write about the murder."

"What murder?"

"The only one they knew about. I didn't tell 'em about Louetta. Did you want me to?"

"Probably not," Rhodes said. "But then I don't even know who you're talking about."

"Those two women friends of yours," Hack said. "I thought I told you that."

Rhodes was dangerously close to losing his temper, but he controlled himself because Hack and Lawton would have enjoyed seeing him lose it entirely too much. He counted to ten silently and slowly and said, "Tell me their names."

"Claudia and Jan. 'Course, they didn't both talk at the same time. First one of them did, and then the other one."

"And they're coming here to write about the murder."

"I *know* I told you that."

"You sure did," Lawton said. "I heard you."

Rhodes counted to ten again. "I thought they had jobs," he said when the counting was done. "Claudia is a social worker, and Jan's a college dean."

"It's summer," Hack said. "The dean is about to have a week or so off from the college, and Claudia's taking vacation. Claudia's the one I talked to, mostly. She says they have a contract with some Sunday supplement to write an article about small-town murders. They got it because they were at that writers' deal in Obert where Terry Don Coslin got killed."

Rhodes remembered Claudia and Jan well. Claudia was a blonde with startlingly blue eyes. Jan had dark hair and dimples that Shirley Temple would have envied. The last Rhodes had heard, the two women had planned to collaborate on a mystery novel. Now all of a sudden it seemed that they were true-crime writers.

"She mentioned how much help they were to you in Obert," Hack said. "She said they'd be glad to help out again."

"Great," Rhodes said. He remembered, all right. "How did they find out about Larry Colley in the first place?"

"Heard about it on a Dallas radio station and called up the editor of that magazine right then."

Rhodes had hoped the news wouldn't get out so fast, but he should have known better.

"When are they coming?"

"In the morning," Hack said. "They'll be staying out at the Western Inn. And they want to interview you as soon as you can see them."

"I don't know when that will be," Rhodes said.

"I'll tell 'em to come early in the morning," Hack said. "You always come by here before you do anything else."

"I might not."

"They sound mighty determined. I have a feelin' you're not gonna get out of talkin' to them."

"I can try, though."

"Good luck," Hack said.

10

▼

GERALD BOLTON LIVED IN A BIG HOUSE WITH A BIG YARD AND tall pecan trees. Rhodes thought he might like the house, but he knew he wouldn't like the yard, not if he had to mow it. Not even if he had a riding mower, which he didn't. He suspected that Bolton hired someone to do the job.

There was a Hummer parked in the driveway, a yellow one. Rhodes didn't like the color, and he was sure he wouldn't want to pay for the gasoline a Hummer required. Maybe if he were going to hunt wild game in Africa, like John Wayne in *Hatari!,* a Hummer would be practical. Otherwise, he couldn't see a use for it, not in Blacklin County.

Rhodes parked at the curb and walked up the neatly trimmed sidewalk and admired the gardenia bushes in front of the house. The bushes were blooming, as they often did in August. The blooms weren't as big as the ones that came in the spring, but they were just as fragrant.

Edith Bolton answered the door. The first time Rhodes had seen her, she'd been a plump woman with a ready smile. Now she looked almost anorectic. There were dark circles under her eyes, and she wasn't smiling. Rhodes tried not to show his surprise.

"Hello, Sheriff," she said. Her voice was light and whispery, as if it had faded away with the rest of her. "Come in. Gerald's in the den."

Rhodes had called ahead and explained why he wanted to talk to Gerald. He hadn't wanted to take them by surprise. That was a useful technique in some cases, but Rhodes thought it would be cruel in this instance. If he just showed up, they might think he had something to tell them about Ronnie.

He followed Edith into the den, which was paneled in dark wood in the fashion of years earlier. There were bookshelves on one wall, but they held only a few books. Most of the rest of the space was taken up by knickknacks. Glass skunks in one area, glass boots and shoes in another.

On another wall there was a fifty-two-inch plasma TV screen. Rhodes stood and admired it for a second.

Gerald Bolton got up from a La-Z-Boy chair and came over to shake Rhodes's hand. He was big, as big as Bud Turley, and if his wife had lost weight, he'd put it on. And if some of it was fat, it was hard fat. He looked like a man who worked out at a gym, but since there wasn't a gym in Clearview, he must have had some home equipment. He could afford it.

He didn't try to crush Rhodes's hand, which Rhodes considered kind of him. He could have done it easily. He said, "Glad to see you, Sheriff. I was sorry to hear about Larry Colley. Have a seat and tell me what I can do to help you."

Rhodes sat in a platform rocker, and Bolton sat back down in the

La-Z-Boy. Edith floated away like a ghost. After a second or two, Rhodes heard the sound of music from another room. Songs from a generation or two earlier. Rhodes didn't really recognize any of them.

"She hasn't been the same since we lost Ronnie," Bolton said, looking toward the wall that separated them from his wife. "I haven't, either, I guess, but she's taken it harder. There's not a minute that goes by that she doesn't think about Ronnie. They say time heals, but it hasn't helped Edith."

Rhodes didn't know what to say to that, so he didn't say anything.

"But you didn't come here to talk about Ronnie," Bolton said. "When you called, you mentioned that Larry Colley had the misfortune to get killed on my property."

"That's right. On that land you own near Big Woods," Rhodes said.

"I own quite a few acres in that area. Where exactly did it happen?"

Rhodes told him.

"That's my place, all right. Colley was doing some work for me not far from there. I was having our old camp house fixed up. You might remember it."

Rhodes said that he did, but he didn't mention Ronnie again. Neither did Bolton.

"I thought I might use the house again," Bolton went on. "As sort of a weekend place. I never go down there now except to feed the cattle and check on them now and then. But having the house fixed up was probably a bad idea. Edith would never go there. I realize that now."

"Do you know if Colley was working there yesterday?" Rhodes asked.

"Well, he might have been. He and I had one of those deals where there was no real schedule. He'd go down there and do what he could whenever he got a chance or felt like it. I didn't supervise him or anything like that."

That was the kind of job Colley would have liked, Rhodes thought. He didn't have to be anywhere at any specific time, so he could shoot pool or have a DQ Blizzard with Butterfinger crumbles mixed in whenever he pleased and then go off to work. Or not go, if that was his preference.

"How far from that clearing is the house?" Rhodes asked.

"You can't see it from the road you took to the woods. It's around a little bend from there. You remember."

Thinking back to the Bolton boy's disappearance, Rhodes did remember. He thought it might be a good idea for him to have a look at the house, so he asked Bolton's permission.

"Sure, go ahead. I haven't been down there in two or three weeks, so I don't know how much Larry managed to get done. I really hated to hear he was dead. He seemed like a good worker, never complained about anything, never pressed me for money."

"Did he have any helpers?"

"Not that I know about. If he did, he was paying them out of his own pocket."

"What about friends? Did you ever see anybody with him?"

"I hardly ever saw him at all. I'd talk to him on the phone now and then, and he'd send me a bill for supplies through the mail. Then I'd send him a check."

"So you wouldn't have any idea why someone would want to kill him."

"No idea at all. I didn't know anything about him except that he was doing a job for me. That's it."

Rhodes asked a few more questions, but he didn't learn anything that he didn't already know. He had some news for Bolton, though.

"There's something else on your property," he said. "A mammoth."

"A what?"

"A mammoth. Well, not really. Just its remains. Bud Turley found it on the bank of Pittman Creek, where your land joins it. There's no fence on the other side, so I guess that's your land, too."

"It is. I never knew there was a mammoth on it, though."

"The rain washed it up this summer. There's a professor at the community college, Tom Vance, who wants to dig for the bones. He asked me to see if you'd give permission."

Bolton leaned back in his chair and thought it over for a while. Rhodes looked at the skunks while he did. Rhodes had never understood the urge that some people had to gather odd things like glass skunks into a collection.

"Where did you say that mammoth find was located?" Bolton said.

"About fifty yards from that wooden bridge that crosses the county road," Rhodes said. "On the unfenced side."

Bolton thought some more. Rhodes looked at the skunks. He still didn't see any point to owning them.

"I don't really need a fence there," Bolton said after a while. "My cattle never cross the creek."

"Might be a good idea to put one in," Rhodes said. "There could be some ownership issues if you don't."

"You're right. I'll get it done. Is there any money in this mammoth deal?"

Rhodes knew that Bolton didn't need money. He already had as much as anyone in town, and a lot more than most. His great-grandfather had owned land in Clearview during the oil-boom days nearly a century ago, and the family had enjoyed their wealth ever since. Bolton had a little office on the second floor of one of the banks in town, but he didn't work there. He might have been there for four or five hours a week, going over paperwork connected with his holdings, but that was all.

"No money," Rhodes said. "Mammoths are a dime a dozen in Texas." He didn't explain that he'd just learned that fact. "It's all for science and maybe some good publicity for the county."

"All right," Bolton said. "I guess it would be okay. But if there are any damages, somebody will have to pay for fixing things up."

Rhodes supposed that wealthy people were always more concerned with who would pay for things than ordinary mortals.

"There won't be any damages," he said. "The professor told me that he'd have his students help and that maybe some of the high school students would be interested. They'll just be digging in the creek bank, very carefully. It's not like they're going to bring a backhoe in there."

"You can tell that professor that I said it's okay, then. But he should come by and talk to me about it before he gets started. Have him call me."

"I'll do that," Rhodes said. He stood up to leave and then, feeling a little like Columbo, he said, "There's one thing I forgot to mention."

Bolton was standing, too. "What's that?"

"Somebody killed Louetta Kennedy today."

Bolton sat back down. "Jesus Christ. That's terrible. She was just a harmless little old woman. Who'd do a thing like that?"

"I don't know," Rhodes said. "Yet."

"Did they rob the store?"

"No. It wasn't about money."

"What was it about?"

"I don't know that yet, either."

Bolton leaned back in his chair. "But you're going to find out, aren't you?"

He didn't say *It won't be like it was with Ronnie, will it?* but Rhodes could hear it in his tone.

"I'm going to find out," Rhodes said, and he meant it. Meaning it and doing it were, however, two different things. Rhodes hoped he wasn't lying.

Bolton stood up again. "There are too many people getting killed and disappearing down by those woods. I'm not so sure Bud Turley's not right about Bigfoot being there."

"It's not Bigfoot that's killing people," Rhodes said.

"Maybe not. But somebody is, so that mammoth dig might not be such a good idea. I can't be liable if anything happens to those people."

"I'm sure Dr. Vance would be glad to sign a waiver and get everybody else to sign one, too."

"That's a good idea," Bolton said. "I guess it would be all right for them to dig if they signed something like that. I'll have to get one drawn up. But even at that, I still don't want anything to happen to those people."

Rhodes wished he could assure Bolton that everything would be all right, but he knew better than to try.

Bolton walked him to the door. On the way there, Rhodes could hear the music from the other room.

"She listens to music all the time," Bolton said with a nod toward the room the sound was coming from. "It's about all she does."

Some people listened to music, some people worked out, Rhodes thought. He didn't say it. He just thanked Bolton for his time and got out of there.

11

▼

MARY JO COLLEY HADN'T REMARRIED OR TAKEN BACK HER surname, but that didn't mean she was any more fond of her ex-husband than Karen Sandstrom was. At least to hear her tell it.

"Larry Colley is a horse's ass," she said. She lit a Marlboro with a paper match from a little book. "Or he was. Now he's just a dead horse's ass." She took a drag off the Marlboro and stuck the matchbook back in her hatband.

Mary Jo was a server at the Round-Up Restaurant. Once upon a time, Rhodes would have referred to her as a waitress, but he knew that wasn't the proper term any more.

The Round-Up was owned by a man named Sam Blevins, who believed in the virtues of Texas beef. The restaurant's credo was simple and was printed on the outside of every menu as well as being displayed on a sign out front: ABSOLUTELY NO CHICKEN, FISH, OR VEGETARIAN DISHES CAN BE FOUND ON OUR MENU!

In keeping with the cowboy-ish name of the place, Mary Jo was dressed in blue jeans so tight that it would have been difficult, if not impossible, for her to put the matchbook in one of the pockets, which Rhodes supposed was why she kept it in her hatband. She also wore a pair of cowboy boots and a white western shirt with gray pearlized buttons. Her hat was a gray felt Stetson. Or maybe it was only a knock-off of a Stetson. Rhodes never wore a hat and had never owned a genuine Stetson, so he couldn't tell.

It was still too early for people in Clearview to come out for the evening meal, and things were slow in the Round-Up. Rhodes had talked to Sam Blevins and asked him if it would be all right to have a little chat with Mary Jo, and Blevins had said it was fine with him.

"Why don't you bring Ivy out here tonight and have yourselves a couple of my steaks?" Blevins said. "I'll see to it that they're cooked the way you like them."

Blevins was tall, wiry, and thin as a broom handle. Rhodes asked him if he ate steak all the time.

"Steak and potatoes. Healthiest diet there is. Well, you can have barbecue, too, and beans. Cobbler and ice cream for dessert. That's how I stay in shape."

"If I ate like that, you'd have to wheel me into this place on a cart," Rhodes said, conscious that he wasn't exactly the picture of physical fitness. "You're sure you don't mind if I borrow Mary Jo for a while?"

"Hell, no," Blevins said. "She'll be glad of the break, especially if you'll go outside where she can smoke."

So Rhodes and Mary Jo were standing in back of the Round-Up, where Mary Jo was puffing away at a Marlboro and talking about her ex-husband in terms that couldn't be construed in any way as flattering.

"I take it he wasn't the light of your life," Rhodes said.

Mary Jo snorted smoke out her nostrils and nearly choked. When she recovered, she said, "You missed your calling, Sheriff. You should've been a comedian."

"I couldn't stand the heckling," Rhodes said.

Mary Jo snorted again. "I'll bet. Well, I already told you what I thought of Larry. I'm lucky to be rid of him, but I didn't kill him." She took a puff on her Marlboro and blew out a cloud of smoke. "Can't say I'm sorry that someone else did, though. He was a lowlife if there ever was one. Spent all his time off with that Bud Turley looking for arrowheads and Bigfoot and whatnot, and if he wasn't doing that, he was shooting pool or chasing some woman at a honky-tonk. I guess I shouldn't complain. At least that kept him out of the house." Another puff, another cloud of smoke. "He met me in a honky-tonk, come to think of it, and I took him away from Karen. He was cute, and he could be funny. I have to say that for him. We had a lot of fun together at first. But cute and funny don't go very far, and when I got to know him better, it turned out that he was just a horse's ass."

Rhodes asked her about Colley's friends, but she couldn't come up with any names other than Turley's.

"Larry liked to have a good time in the evenings, but he didn't run with anybody special. Just any woman he could pick up. And Bud."

"Have you seen him lately?"

"Bud?"

"No. Larry."

"Why would I see him? I work at this place six days a week, and he doesn't ever come in. His idea of eating out is to get a Beltbuster and fries at the Dairy Queen."

"I was hoping you might be able to tell me what he'd been doing lately. Any jobs he might have had, anything like that."

Mary Jo tossed what was left of her Marlboro on the ground and squashed it under the toe of her boot. Rhodes thought about writing her up for littering, but he didn't think about it very long or very seriously.

"As far as I know," she said, "Larry hadn't worked a day in years. Odd jobs now and then, and he'd help Bud out with his mechanic work, such as it was. It's funny."

"What's funny?" Rhodes asked.

"He always seemed to have money. We never had to stall the electric company on the bill or anything."

"You were working and bringing in a salary," Rhodes pointed out.

"Yeah, there's that. And he made a little from those jobs." Mary Jo tucked a loose strand of hair back up under her hat. "You know something?"

"What?" Rhodes asked.

"I've always been glad we didn't have any kids. We weren't married that long, just over a year, but we could've had a kid. I'll bet if we had, it would have turned out just like Larry."

"Maybe it would have turned out like you."

Mary Jo lit up another Marlboro and breathed out smoke.

"I'll tell you a little secret, Sheriff," she said.

"What's that?"

"I'm no bargain, either."

Larry Colley might have had money to pay his bills, but he didn't spend much on his living quarters.

His trailer was located less than a quarter of a mile outside the

Clearview city limits, but it might as well have been on Mars. It was on a little-used county road on an overgrown lot that was thick with trees and bushes that had never been trimmed. The area surrounding it wasn't kept up any better.

Near the trailer was a magnolia tree at least thirty feet high, with limbs that grew right down to the ground, which was covered with a thick carpet of dead brown leaves beneath the limbs. Some tall pecan trees and even a walnut tree grew a little farther from the trailer and, with the help of some thick hedge bushes, concealed it from the road. If Rhodes hadn't known the trailer was there, he would have driven right on by without seeing it.

He parked the county car and got out. He walked up the rutted drive that led through the bushes and trees to the clearing where the trailer sat.

Rhodes stopped and had a look around. On down the path, there was an old Chevrolet sedan up on blocks. The car was covered with rust, and the windshield and headlights had been broken. The windows on the side facing Rhodes were shattered but still clinging to the frame of the old car.

There was no other car, and Rhodes wondered what Colley drove when he went to work on Bolton's camp house. He had to have some way to get around.

Like the Chevy, Colley's trailer was up on blocks. It didn't have a skirt around it, which would make the dark area underneath a haven for all kinds of critters, including skunks. Some concrete steps sat in front of the door, but there was a gap of several inches between them and the trailer.

A rusty oil drum stood by the steps. It was filled to the top with trash. Rhodes could see a couple of tin cans and several empty frozen-dinner boxes sticking out the top.

The windows of the trailer were all covered with aluminum foil. The air-conditioning must have been unable to keep the metal trailer cool, so Colley had tried to reduce the heat by blocking the sunlight that came into the clearing. It would have been intense during the middle of the afternoon, and Rhodes doubted that the trailer had any insulation to speak of.

Rhodes mounted the steps and knocked on the door. "Anybody home?" he said, not that he expected an answer.

He didn't get one, so he tried the door. It wasn't locked. Colley probably didn't have anything worth locking up.

Rhodes opened the door, and a wave of hot, musty air washed over him. He went into the trailer and felt along the wall for the light switch. When he found it, he flipped it up.

A lamp came on, but the light lasted only for a second. There was a *pop,* and the bulb burned out.

Rhodes stood and waited. A little light from the outside came through the open door, and after a few seconds Rhodes could see a little bit of the trailer. It was a mess.

Magazines were scattered everywhere, and so was some of Larry's clothing. The tattered couch looked as if mice might be nesting in it. For all Rhodes knew, they were. Foam rubber stuffing poked out of the cushions. There was an odor of cooking grease and garbage.

Rhodes's first thought was that Larry had been a miserable housekeeper. He probably had been, but as Rhodes looked around the room more carefully, it seemed to him that even a miserable housekeeper couldn't make that much of a mess. Someone had searched the trailer.

Rhodes went back out onto the concrete steps and looked

around. He couldn't see much other than the trees and the old rusted-out Chevy, so he went out to the county car.

No other cars were parked anywhere in sight. Rhodes got a flashlight out of the car, then walked back to the trailer and went inside again.

He turned the flashlight on and shined the light around the room. It didn't look any better. It didn't smell any better, either.

Rhodes put the flashlight down on the coffee table and peeled the aluminum foil off the windows. With more light, the room looked even worse.

Rhodes couldn't say much for Colley's taste in reading matter. *Hustler* and *Juggs,* mostly. Maybe they were looking matter rather than reading matter, but even at that Larry didn't have a lot going for him.

The couch cushions had been ripped with a knife, and the stained shag carpet had been pulled up at the edges. Rhodes wondered how old the carpet was. He hadn't seen shag in years.

He went into the small kitchen and pulled the foil off the window above the sink.

There were a couple of dirty dishes in the sink. Colley must have eaten most of his frozen dinners in their own little plates.

A black iron skillet with half an inch of grease in the bottom sat on one of the stove burners. Colley apparently cooked his own bacon, which was a little surprising. Rhodes would have expected him to use precooked microwave bacon instead.

All the cabinets in the kitchen had been opened, both high and low, but there wasn't much in them. A few dishes and some glasses. Salt and pepper. An opened box of Wheaties. Most of the cereal had been poured out in the sink with the dishes.

Rhodes wondered what Larry Colley could have owned that someone would be searching for. Maybe it was money, but no matter what Mary Jo had said, there couldn't have been much of that.

The door from the kitchen to the next room was closed. Rhodes thought that there would be a bathroom there, and the bedroom would be right on past it. He opened the door, thinking of the shower scene in *Psycho,* but Colley's bathroom had a small shower stall with a glass door. No curtain, and no place to hide. There was no foil over the bathroom window, but the glass was frosted to give a semblance of privacy.

The bathroom had been searched, too. Aspirin, cold pills, and cough drops lay on the counter by the sink beside a razor that hadn't been cleaned in a while. If ever.

Rhodes slid back the flimsy door between the bathroom and the bedroom. It was so dark in there that he thought he'd better go back for the flashlight, but then he saw the thin line of light where the foil didn't quite cover the windows and decided he'd just turn on the light, cross the room, and pull off the foil.

He stepped into the room, fumbling for the light switch. He heard a rushing noise and tried to turn, but he was too late. Before he got halfway around, he was enveloped in darkness and stink. Something struck his legs, and then he was falling.

12

▼

For the first few seconds Rhodes had no idea what was going on. All he knew was that he'd hit the floor too hard with his head, and he felt as if he were suffocating.

Now someone was trying to beat him to death.

Rhodes tried to fight back, but he was wrapped up in cloth like a mummy and could hardly move his arms. He had a bit more freedom with his legs, and he kicked them as if he were trying to swim. He made contact with something, and the pounding stopped for just a moment, long enough for Rhodes to roll over on his side, but not long enough for him to get free.

He was barely able to loosen his arms before the pounding started again, and he realized that someone was standing over him and kicking him in the ribs and chest and arms and legs. He didn't have long to think about the damage that was being done, because something hit him in the face, just on the point of the chin. His teeth clicked together, his head snapped back as far as it could in the confined space, and he blacked out.

When he came to, he was still enfolded in cloth and darkness.

At least nobody was kicking him.

Rhodes didn't know how long he'd been unconscious, but he thought it must have been only seconds—no more than a minute, surely. He fought his way out of the wrapping. It was still so dark in the room that he couldn't see what had enfolded him, so he tried to stand up and get to the window.

He got about halfway to his feet before he started to fall again. He put out a hand and caught himself on the end of the bed. Somehow he managed to sit on the bed instead of sinking back to the floor.

He sat there for a while, watching what seemed to be fireflies flit about the room, until the dizzy spell passed. When it did, the fireflies disappeared along with it.

Rhodes gripped his chin with his thumb and forefinger and wiggled it. It was sore, but he decided that it wasn't broken. That was nice to know.

The mummy wrapping was still tangled around his feet, and he kicked it off. He tried standing up again, and this time he was able to stay on his feet. He walked slowly and carefully over to the window and tore off the foil. He blinked in the late-afternoon light, and then he opened the window and breathed in the fresh air.

While he was standing there, he thought he heard the sound of an ATV four-wheeler in the distance, but the sound faded away before he was sure.

After a minute Rhodes turned from the window and looked around the bedroom. It was a mess, as he'd expected. A filthy chenille bedspread lay tangled on the floor next to a pair of old running shoes. Not so long ago, Rhodes had been wrapped in it.

Whoever had searched the trailer had waited for him in the bedroom, probably not wanting to leave by the front door even while Rhodes was getting the flashlight because of a fear of being seen. There certainly hadn't been much chance of Rhodes seeing anybody while he was wrapped up in the bedspread like a caterpillar in a cocoon and getting kicked around like the ball at a kids' soccer game.

He was bruised all over, and when he rubbed his chin, he thought of Louetta Kennedy. He wondered if she'd been kicked or hit with a fist. Maybe Dr. White could tell him. Rhodes thought that in a way he'd been lucky to be covered with the bedspread. It helped to soften the blows he'd taken.

He didn't think there was much use in having a closer look at the bedroom, but he did it anyway. If he didn't move around a little, he'd stiffen up, and he didn't want that.

Rhodes started with the closet. Pretty much everything except some wire hangers had been tossed out onto the floor, which was covered with dirty socks and another old pair of shoes. He looked in the dresser and the nightstand, but he found nothing of interest. After a while he gave it up and left the room. He'd send Ruth Grady back to do a more thorough job. He'd ask her to check on the whereabouts of Colley's car, too.

Before he left the trailer, Rhodes picked up his flashlight from the coffee table. Lying not far from it was a portable telephone. Rhodes picked it up and called the jail.

Hack answered, and Rhodes told him to have Buddy or Ruth call the telephone company and get Colley's phone records.

"You think he's been talkin' to his killer?" Hack said.

"Maybe," Rhodes told him. "Any lead is better than what we have now, which is none."

"You sound funny," Hack said. "Are you okay?"

"I'm fine," Rhodes said.

"Well, you don't sound fine."

"Trust me."

"Uh-oh. Now I know somethin's wrong. Where are you?"

"I'm at Larry Colley's trailer. Get Ruth on the radio and tell her to come out here."

"I will. Are you all right?"

"You're repeating yourself," Rhodes said. "And I'm still fine."

"You don't sound fine," Hack said, but Rhodes had hung up the phone before he finished.

Rhodes sat at the table enjoying another low-fat meal, a cold tuna-and-pasta salad. It had black olives in it, and pimientos, along with celery and other things that Rhodes couldn't identify. Yancey kept him entertained by barking around the kitchen while Rhodes tried to downplay his little fracas at Colley's trailer to Ivy.

"I'm sure I'll be a little bruised," he said, glad that he was being allowed to have a few crackers with the salad. "But it won't be so bad."

"I'll be the judge of that," Ivy said. "Do you want some more water?"

There was something pretty spicy in the salad, and the olives were salty. Rhodes said that more water would be nice.

What would have been even nicer was one of Sam Blevins's

steaks, one that was marbled with fat and sizzling from the grill. Rhodes tried not to think about it.

"I just wish you'd be more careful," Ivy said, taking his glass and putting some more ice in it before she refilled it. "I worry about you all the time."

"You don't have to worry," Rhodes said. "I'm fine."

She looked at him the way Hack had no doubt looked when Rhodes had said the same thing to him. "It might even be different if you were making any progress," Ivy said. "But you aren't, are you."

It wasn't a question, but Rhodes answered it anyway.

"Not a lot."

"You will, though. You always do."

"I appreciate your confidence. I wish I felt the same way. A lot of things are going on, and they're all connected some way or other, but I can't make the connections that I know are there."

Rhodes thought about the crime scenes. He knew he'd overlooked something at both of them, but he couldn't figure out what it was.

"You'll feel better about things tomorrow," Ivy said.

"Stiffer," Rhodes said. "I'll feel stiffer tomorrow."

He finished his pasta salad and got up from the table.

"I think I'll go see how Speedo's doing," he said as he put his plate in the sink. "Come on, Yancey."

He went to the door and opened it. Yancey bounced out into the yard, charged over to Speedo, and started running in circles around him, yipping with joy. Speedo ignored him and looked at Rhodes as if to say *You're the one who brought this mutt here.*

"I know it," Rhodes said, sitting down on the porch. It didn't hurt as much as he'd thought it might. "Where's your ball?"

Speedo ran off to get it.

* * *

The next day didn't bring anything new on the murders, but it brought a lot of other things, none of them good ones.

Ruth Grady searched the trailer and found no more than Rhodes had. She checked the phone records, but the only calls Colley made or got were to or from Gerald Bolton and Bud Turley. Nothing suspicious there.

"And he didn't have a cell phone on him," Rhodes said. "Hard to believe."

"Not everybody carries one," Ruth said. "You don't."

"I don't count. Check with the local provider and see what you can find out."

Ruth said that she would.

None of Louetta's regular customers, the few of them that were left and that Rhodes could track down by phone, remembered that she'd ever said anything about threats or that she'd ever had arguments with anyone at all. She was quick to let people have groceries on credit, and she never pressed them to pay up if they couldn't afford it. The general consensus was that everyone liked Louetta. No one would have wanted to hurt her.

Someone *had* hurt her, however, but Rhodes didn't bother to point that out.

He looked over Dr. White's autopsy report and found nothing he didn't know already. Louetta's neck had been broken when she was struck by whatever it was that struck her. Dr. White didn't say what that might have been, nor did he say that it could have been a kick.

Just as Rhodes finished going over the report, Claudia and Jan arrived at the jail. They were excited to be back in Blacklin

County and excited that they had an actual writing assignment.

"It's only for a little Sunday supplement that goes out to some small-town newspapers," Claudia said. "But it might lead to other things. Like getting our novel published."

Claudia didn't look much like a social worker to Rhodes. She was carrying a Dooney and Bourke handbag, for one thing. Rhodes had once considered buying Ivy one as a Christmas gift. Then he'd found out the price.

"You've finished the novel?" Rhodes said.

"Yes. It's a mystery, not a romance novel. We're looking for an agent now."

"As soon as we heard about the murder here, we called the editor at the weekly," Jan said. "We got the assignment because of the Bigfoot connection. We'll call the article 'The Bigfoot Murders!' Can't you just see how that will look in print?"

Jan was shorter than Claudia. She smiled a lot and had plenty of enthusiasm. Since she was a college dean, Rhodes wondered if she knew Tom Vance.

"There's no Bigfoot involved," he said. "But there's a mammoth. Do you know Dr. Thomas Vance?"

"The one who teaches biology at the community college campus here?"

"That's him," Rhodes said.

"I've met him. Both our schools have football teams, and he was on the conference athletic committee. He's one of the best in his field."

"Tell us about the mammoth," Claudia said, and Rhodes told the little he knew.

"That's another great angle for the story," Claudia said when he was finished. If we can't have Bigfoot, we can at least have a mammoth. We can call the article 'The Mammoth Murder' instead."

"Vance doesn't want to reveal the location of the dig," Rhodes said.

He'd called Vance the previous evening to tell him what Bolton had said, and Vance had told him that he'd call Bolton immediately. He wanted to meet Bolton at his lawyer's office and get the waivers as early as he could. He planned to start the dig as soon as he had signed his own copy. He'd get the other people he'd lined up for the dig to sign theirs as quickly as possible, and then he'd get everyone to work.

"We won't tell anybody where it is," Jan said. " 'Digging up Bones.' There's another great title."

"I think Randy Travis has already used that one," Rhodes told her.

"Who?"

"Randy Travis. He's a country singer. It's an old song."

"Oh. Well, you can't copyright a title, so we can use it if we want to. What do you think, Claudia?"

Claudia said she still preferred the Bigfoot angle. "We can work that into the story right at the beginning," she said. "And then put in the mammoth, too."

"You'll be the hero, of course," Jan told Rhodes.

"I thought this was supposed to be nonfiction," he said.

"It is. But even nonfiction needs a strong central character."

"By the way," Claudia said, "did you know that the motel is full of Bigfoot hunters? We were lucky to get a room."

"You're kidding me," Rhodes said. "I hope."

"We wouldn't do that," Jan said. "The place was full by the time we got there last evening."

Rhodes came close to groaning aloud, not because he was still sore from the kicking he'd gotten the day before, although he was, but because the idea of dozens of Bigfoot hunters tramping through Big Woods was enough to make anybody groan.

"We heard some of them talking," Claudia said. "They mentioned that they had friends who'd be camping out. There'll probably be hundreds of them."

Hundreds, not dozens, Rhodes thought. This time he did groan.

"Are you all right?" Claudia said.

"I'm fine," Rhodes told her.

He could hear Hack laughing from across the room.

13

▼

RHODES HAD PLANNED TO GO BACK TO BIG WOODS TO CHECK
on the camp house that Bolton was having remodeled, but he
called Bolton first, to let him know that he'd be on his property.

"I was just about to phone you, Sheriff," Bolton said. "I just
heard from Tom Vance, and he says that people are setting up
tents on my property. I want you to run them off while you're
there."

Rhodes said he'd do what he could.

Jan and Claudia had gone back to the motel to change into
jeans. Rhodes had promised to drive by there and let them follow
him so they could have a look at the woods and the place where
the mammoth bones were, but now he wished he hadn't. Things
were getting too complicated. Still, a promise was a promise.

The Western Inn, just off the highway that led to Obert, was
Clearview's newest motel, which meant that it was around thirty
years old. Blacklin County wasn't exactly the state's most popular

tourist attraction. When Rhodes arrived, Claudia and Jan were waiting in the parking lot, which was full of the biggest pickups on the market, mostly four-door models with big mud tires.

Jan and Claudia stood beside a black Lincoln Aviator. They were wearing jeans and hiking boots. Claudia's Dooney and Bourke bag had been replaced by a backpack. Both women waved when he drove into the parking lot, and he pulled up behind the big SUV.

When they'd visited him at the jail, he'd told them as much as he knew about Larry Colley. He'd also told them about Louetta Kennedy, and he figured that by now they'd have all sorts of theories to share with him. He was wrong. They didn't even want to talk. They wanted to get on the road.

Jan climbed into the driver's seat of the Aviator, and Claudia came over to the county car.

"You lead the way, and we'll follow," she said. "Don't drive too fast. We don't want to get a ticket."

Rhodes looked at her.

"Just kidding. We want to stop at the store where Ms. Kennedy was killed first, if that's all right."

Rhodes said that it would be all right. He pulled out of the parking lot, and the Aviator followed.

When they stopped at Louetta's store, the old Ford was still there. Rhodes wondered what would happen to it. He pointed out to Claudia and Jan that the yellow and black crime-scene tape meant that they couldn't go inside. They didn't like that, because they wanted pictures. Rhodes told them that they'd have to be satisfied with exterior shots. Jan got a digital camera out of the Aviator and started walking around the building, taking the photos.

"I thought you two would have solved the crime for me by

now," Rhodes told Claudia. "Surely you must have some theories about what happened."

"We'd like to think it was a Bigfoot. He killed Larry Colley because Colley was invading his territory. Then he killed Ms. Kennedy."

"Why would he kill her?"

"We're working on that," Claudia said. "It's the only thing that makes sense."

"Let me give you a crime-solving tip," Rhodes said. "You know you're in trouble when your best theory pins the murders on Bigfoot."

"Do you have a better one?"

Rhodes had to admit that he didn't. He was saved from elaborating by Jan, who came back to the Aviator and said that she had enough pictures. So they left the store to go to the site of the mammoth dig.

They went to the site from the correct side of the bridge, so they didn't have to cross Pittman Creek. Tom Vance was the only one there. Rhodes assumed that no one else had signed Bolton's waiver yet. Vance was working on the canopy he was going to put over the dig to protect everyone from the August sun.

He didn't seem to mind talking to Claudia and Jan about what he was planning, so Rhodes decided to leave them there to get some background material while he looked at the camp house.

"Have you had any trouble with feral hogs?" Rhodes asked Vance as he was getting into his car.

"Feral hogs?" Jan said. "What feral hogs? Nobody said anything about feral hogs."

"You can tell them about the hogs," Rhodes said to Vance, and then he drove away, smiling.

Rhodes hadn't wanted Claudia and Jan with him while he evicted the campers on Bolton's land. You never knew when someone might get a little rowdy, and Rhodes didn't want any civilians getting hurt unless they deserved it. He was pretty sure that Jan and Claudia didn't deserve it, but he wasn't so certain about the campers.

Rhodes was glad to see that there were only a couple of tents near the woods. He'd been afraid that there might be more. They were close together, so he figured he could save time and give his little speech only once.

When he stopped the county car, the first thing he saw was Bud Turley's Jeep. Bud was standing not far away.

"I can't believe this," Rhodes said as soon as he got out of the car. "You know better than to have people camping out here, Bud. This is Gerald Bolton's land. And a crime scene."

"I tried to tell them that," Bud said. "They wouldn't listen."

Rhodes looked around, but he didn't see anyone else. "Who's this *they* you're talking about? And how did they find out about all this in the first place?"

"I told them," Bud said. "You can't keep it a secret when there's a Bigfoot sighting."

"There hasn't been any sighting," Rhodes said.

"I talked to Chester Johnson. He says he saw something."

"He didn't see anything. He was just spooked by finding Colley."

"That's your version," Bud said. "Chester's pretty sure he saw and heard something. It could have been Bigfoot."

"So you called every Bigfoot hunter in the state to let them know."

"No, I just put a notice about the sighting on the Internet."

"Even worse," Rhodes said. "Well, we can't do anything about it now. You're just going to have to get your friends out of here, and you need to tell the rest of them holed up at the Western Inn that this is private property. It's also a crime scene, and it's off-limits to Bigfoot hunters."

"You're letting Vance dig up bones."

"That's different. He's not in the woods, and he's not causing a nuisance. And he has permission from the landowner, which you don't. The people who own these tents are trespassing. Now where are they?"

Turley took off his welder's cap and wiped the top of his shiny head. He put the cap back on and said, "They're in the woods."

"You shouldn't have let them go in there," Rhodes said. "It's dangerous, and you know it."

For some reason Turley looked startled. He opened his mouth to say something, then shut it, then opened it again. "How could it be dangerous? You claim there's no Bigfoot in there, so they don't have anything to worry about."

"I said there was no Bigfoot, but I didn't say there weren't any hogs."

Turley laughed. "They're not afraid of hogs. They have their rifles."

"Yes," Rhodes said. "And your friends with rifles are more dangerous than the hogs are. A lot more dangerous than Bigfoot, too."

Turley opened his eyes wide, as if that idea had never occurred to him. "They . . . uh, they'll be careful."

"Sure they will," Rhodes said.

He could see only one vehicle besides the county car and Turley's Jeep. A big Dodge Ram pickup, black and dusty, was parked behind one of the tents.

"How many hunters are here?" Rhodes asked.

Turley still looked a little upset. He said, "Just two. There might be some more later."

"There won't be any more," Rhodes said. "I'm going to have a look at the camp house where Colley was supposed to have been working. I shouldn't be gone more than half an hour. When I come back, I want these tents gone, and I don't want to catch you or any of your Bigfoot-hunting friends here again. If I do, you'll get to spend a while in the friendly confines of the county jail."

Turley's face reddened. "You don't mean that."

Turley was wearing his concealed-carry vest, and Rhodes could see that there was a pistol in one of the inside pockets.

"I do mean it," Rhodes said. He hoped Turley wouldn't do anything stupid, like reach for the pistol. "And you'd better believe it. So go find your friends and get these tents down. Half an hour."

"I . . . I can't go in there."

"You can, and you will," Rhodes said.

He didn't bother to listen to Turley's response. He just got in the car and left.

Glancing at the rearview mirror, he saw Turley standing there, watching the car, clenching and unclenching his hands.

As Rhodes remembered it, Bolton's camp house was a little more elaborate than the words implied. Staying there wouldn't be at all like camping out in one of the tents that Turley's friends had set up. Though the house had only one big room, there was a sleeping loft with real beds, and it was furnished with a couch and comfortable chairs.

Bolton had arranged to have electricity run to the camp house, and Rhodes didn't even want to ask what it had cost him to do that. An air conditioner stuck out of a side window. Rhodes seemed to recall that there was a TV set inside, and even a chemical toilet in a little area that had been walled off from the main room. There was also a small refrigerator.

Bolton had paid to have a well dug in the back of the house, so there was water for washing dishes in the little kitchen area on one side of the room. You could even drink the water in a pinch, but it wasn't recommended.

All the comforts of home, Rhodes thought, but the place had been allowed to run down after the family reunion and the disappearance of Ronnie Bolton.

There was a fence around the house, leaving a yard all around, but it was overgrown with weeds. Rhodes parked near the gate and got out. He could see some cattle grazing about a hundred yards away, but they didn't appear to have any interest in him.

The house was shaded by oaks and elms. Rhodes pushed open the gate and walked to the house through the weeds and the rotten branches that had fallen from the trees.

He stood for a minute on a concrete porch that was level with the ground. A couple of rusted metal lawn chairs sat beside the front door. Rhodes could see some signs that Colley, or someone, had been at work on the house. A couple of boards had been replaced near the front window, and the entire door facing was new and unpainted. Rhodes could smell sawdust and wood. The screen door was also new, shiny and unrusted.

The house wasn't locked, so Rhodes went inside. The air conditioner wasn't on, and the air was stale and hot. A ceiling fan hung down in the middle of the room, with a cord danging from it. Rhodes pulled the cord and the fan came on, stirring the hot air around.

Rhodes didn't know what he expected to find in the house, but whatever it was, it wasn't there. The only jarring note was the power saw that sat in the middle of the floor by a toolbox. Then again, even if they didn't belong in a living room, the saw and toolbox were just part of the equipment Colley had used for his repair work.

There was an unemptied trash can under the sink, but that was no surprise, either. Rhodes already knew about Colley's poor housekeeping. Colley had brought his lunch with him, and Rhodes saw plenty of fast-food wrappings in the trash.

The exposed rafters under the high ceiling were lined with mounted deer antlers. For years there had been deer in Big Woods, and there still were, but not nearly as many as in times past. The hogs were seeing to that. They ate the fawns and chased the grown deer away.

Baseball caps hung from quite a few of the horns, as if someone had thrown them there and left them. The antlers and the caps reminded Rhodes of the skunks in Bolton's house: another meaningless accumulation, unless you were the owner.

Rhodes climbed the ladder that led to the low-ceilinged sleeping loft. It wasn't an easy climb, as the ladder went straight up from the floor, so he didn't go all the way. Even if he had, he wouldn't have been able to stand up. He would have had to search the loft in a crouch.

When his head was high enough to see above the floor of the loft, he noted that there was nothing there except four beds and one old chair. He climbed back down, looked around the big room one more time, then went outside.

It was hot, but the porch was in the shade and there was a light breeze, so Rhodes sat down in one of the rusty lawn chairs to think things over. He had that same feeling that he'd missed something, that something he'd seen inside the house had a connection to the murders. Maybe if he sat there and thought about it, it would come to him.

He'd been in the chair for less than a minute when he heard rifle shots.

14

▼

RHODES BRAKED THE CAR TO A FAST STOP NEAR THE TENTS AND jumped out. The dust cloud that had trailed behind him from the camp house rolled over him and past him as he looked for Bud Turley.

Turley wasn't there, which meant that he was in the woods, which was where the gunshots had come from. Rhodes ran down the path and into the trees.

He hadn't heard any more shots, but that didn't mean there had been none. Closed up in the car and bouncing along two dry ruts with weeds slapping at the car's sides, he might not have been able to hear them.

Before Rhodes had gone twenty yards into the trees, he saw Bud Turley coming toward him at a lope. Rhodes moved off the trail and waited for him.

Turley didn't stop. His eyes were wild, and he hardly even glanced in Rhodes's direction. Rhodes called his name, but Turley ignored him. So Rhodes turned and followed him out of the woods. Since there didn't appear to be anyone, or anything, chasing Turley, Rhodes took his time.

When Turley reached his Jeep, he leaned against it breathing hard. By the time Rhodes got there, Turley's breathing was still ragged, and his eyes were still wild.

"What happened?" Rhodes said.

"I don't know," Turley said. He took off his cap and wiped his head. His hands were shaking. "I didn't want to go in those woods, but you made me. I was looking for the fellas you told me to find, and somebody started shooting at me."

"There's nobody else in there except your friends," Rhodes said.

"If they were my friends when they got here, they're not now, not if they're shooting at me."

"I told you your friends would be dangerous with those rifles. You get people stirred up about Bigfoot, they're likely to shoot anything that moves."

"You're the one that sent me in there." Turley took a deep breath and let it out slowly. "You must have wanted me to get shot."

"If I'd wanted you shot," Rhodes said, "I could have done it myself. Your friends should be more careful."

"Maybe it wasn't them. Why don't you go and have a look for yourself. You're the sheriff. It's your job to investigate when somebody gets shot at."

Rhodes hated to admit it, but Turley actually had a point. It was indeed a part of the county sheriff's job to make sure that idiots didn't kill each other by accident. However, now that Turley was back at the tents, he was out of danger, a fact that Rhodes pointed out to him.

"That doesn't make a damn bit of difference, and you know it," Turley said. "They shot at me!"

His voice shook with anger. He was more disturbed than Rhodes had first thought.

"And it's your fault," Turley said.

"Don't blame me," Rhodes told him. "And don't say it's my fault. It's the fault of your buddies, the idiots with the rifles. Now how are we going to get them out of there?"

Rhodes could see that while Turley didn't object to the word "idiots," he did object to the "we."

"That's your problem," Turley said. "It's not my job."

"You're the one who brought them here," Rhodes said. "You have a responsiblity."

Turley didn't reply. He just stood by his Jeep and looked at Rhodes.

Rhodes looked back.

After a while Turley said, "I can't go back in there. I just can't. I don't want to get shot."

Rhodes couldn't say that he blamed him.

"At least you can see the problem," Rhodes said. "You can see why those two, not to mention all those other Bigfoot hunters who've checked into the Western Inn, need to get out of town and let things settle down here. If they don't, someone's going to get hurt."

"They won't like that idea. They think Bigfoot's in these woods, and that he killed Larry. They want to find him. Some of them have been waiting for years to get a chance like this."

"That's too bad," Rhodes said. "Because you're going to have to convince them that they're wrong about Bigfoot and about this being a chance to find him. I'll get those two out of the woods, but you'll have to do the rest."

Turley shook his head as if he didn't believe Rhodes could do it. "How are you going to get them out?"

"Like this," Rhodes said.

He walked over to the Jeep and started to honk the horn. He kept on honking until he was sure the men in the woods must have heard it.

His only mistake was forgetting what generally happened when cattle heard a horn honking. Often a rancher would honk to call the herd when he wanted to feed them, so when Bolton's cattle heard the Jeep's horn, they responded by starting toward the sound. Before Rhodes had stopped honking, the entire herd that Rhodes had seen near the camp house had come into sight, all of them ambling in the direction of the Jeep. Rhodes didn't mind the cattle, but they might cause some problems if they stepped on the tents.

On second thought, he didn't care what happened to the tents. He honked the horn a few more times.

"Maybe they don't hear it," Turley said. "They're pretty deep in the woods."

"If the cows can hear it, your buddies can hear it," Rhodes said, honking the horn again.

As slow as the cattle were, they arrived at the Jeep before Turley's friends. They surrounded the tents and the vehicles, nosing around, looking for food, mooing when they didn't find it.

"I hope they don't go in the woods," Rhodes said. "Your friends might shoot them."

Turley didn't respond. He stayed close to his Jeep and tried to keep the cows from licking the sides. They weren't going to do any damage to the front of the Jeep or the headlights, thanks to a heavy-duty brush guard that was protecting them.

Finally Rhodes saw two men coming along the path in the woods. They were both carrying rifles, and as they walked along one or the other of them would look over his shoulder back down the path.

When they came out of the trees, they walked over to Turley, who introduced Rhodes as the sheriff.

"This here's Charlie and Jeff," Turley said.

The two men nodded to Rhodes. Both wore faded jeans and T-shirts. Jeff's shirt was emblazoned with a picture of Dale Earnhardt Jr. and the number 8, while Jeff Gordon was smiling from the front of Charlie's shirt. Both Jeff and Charlie wore NASCAR pit caps. Jeff's was a red and white Earnhardt that sported the Budweiser logo. Charlie's was purple and gray. It had the number 24 on it, and it advertised DuPont Motorsports. Neither man said anything to Rhodes, and they didn't offer to shake hands.

"The sheriff says we gotta leave here right now," Turley told them. "He says we're trespassing on private property and you'll have to take down the tents and leave."

The men stared at Rhodes with silent disdain from under the bills of their NASCAR caps. They looked so much alike that he thought they must be brothers, with their pointed, unshaven chins and their lank hair hanging out from under their baseball caps. The bills of the caps were pulled low so that Rhodes could hardly see their eyes. He didn't like that.

"We can't leave," one of the men said. His jaws worked in a rhythmical movement as he chewed what Rhodes supposed was tobacco. "There's a Bigfoot in there, for sure. We spotted him a while ago. Ain't that right, Jeff."

"Sure is," Jeff said. "We took a couple of shots at him. We'd a-got him if he hadn't been able to run so fast. That sucker can really move. No wonder nobody's ever got a picture of him."

Rhodes looked at Turley. Turley looked at the ground.

"Bud," Rhodes said.

Turley's head came up.

"Tell them," Rhodes said.

"Hell, that was me you shot at," he said. He swallowed hard. "If I hadn't run like a jackrabbit, and if you two were any better shots, I'd be dead back in those woods."

Jeff and Charlie shook their heads.

"Sure as hell didn't look like you," Charlie said. "I'd a-swore what we was shootin' at was ten feet tall."

"Me, too," Jeff said. "At least ten feet. You really sure it was you, Bud?"

"Damn right, I'm sure. I know when someone's shooting at me. You think I'm an idiot?"

Jeff and Charlie looked at each other, then shook their heads. Charlie surprised Rhodes by blowing a big pink bubble. First Chester Johnson with his Juicy Fruit and now Charlie with his Dubble Bubble. Or Bazooka. Whatever it was, it wasn't tobacco. Could it be that everyone in the world was on a health kick?

"All right, then," Rhodes said after he got over his surprise. "Now that we've got it settled about who you were shooting at, you two can pull up stakes and get out of here. The owner of this property doesn't want anybody trespassing, and if you come back, I'll have to arrest you."

Charlie's bubble popped.

"What about the rest of the society?" Jeff said.

"What society?" Rhodes asked.

"The Bigfoot Hunters of Texas Society, that's what society. We're all meetin' tonight at some restaurant in town to plan our strategy."

"The Round-Up," Charlie said, having cleaned the gum off his chin. "That's the name of the restaurant."

"You don't need a meeting," Rhodes said. "I'll tell you what your strategy is. It's to stay away from these woods. I meant what I said about arresting you. Ask Bud if you don't believe me."

Charlie and Jeff turned to Turley, who nodded. "He means it."

"Yeah," Jeff said. "But we're the ones with the guns."

"I'm not worried about your guns," Rhodes said.

"You must be crazy, then."

"I'm not crazy," Rhodes told him. "I'm just doing my job. And you need to get started. Bud will help you with the tents. Right, Bud?"

"I guess I will," Bud said.

Jeff and Charlie stood there for a while. Charlie blew another bubble. Rhodes wondered if someone hiding in the woods would play the song from *Deliverance* on a banjo, but it didn't happen. Finally Jeff and Charlie looked at each other and nodded.

"We'll just put these rifles in the truck," Jeff said.

"You do that," Rhodes said.

They put the rifles in the big Dodge and slammed the door.

"I'll trust you to be gone when I check back here," Rhodes said. "You be sure of it, Bud."

He could feel their eyes on him as he walked to the county car. When he got there, he called in the license number of the truck to have Hack run it through the computer and check for any outstanding warrants or traffic violations. There weren't any, which surprised Rhodes a little.

He looked over to see what Jeff and Charlie were doing. They were standing near their truck with Bud, watching him. Rhodes started the car, and by the time he pulled away, they'd begun taking down the tents.

Claudia and Jan were excited.

"This is even bigger than the murder," Jan said when Rhodes walked up to the spot where she, Claudia, and Vance were standing under a tarp that now stretched from a tree on the creek bank to some poles that Vance had set up near the trickle of water in the creek itself. Rhodes didn't know what anchored the poles, but he figured Vance knew what he was doing.

"What she means," Claudia said, "is that we have an assignment to write a separate story about the mammoth."

"Congratulations," Rhodes said. "How did you get it so soon?"

Claudia pulled a cell phone out of her backpack and held it up. "I can send pictures on this thing," she said. "Isn't technology great?"

Rhodes wasn't so sure he agreed, so he made a noncommittal noise.

Claudia didn't seem to notice. She said, "When the editor saw the dig and heard what Dr. Vance had to say, we got the assignment with no trouble at all."

"Won't the publicity cause a problem?" Rhodes asked Vance.

"Not by the time the article's published," he said. "I'll be back in school, and we'll have this site covered up for the winter. I don't think anyone will bother it then."

"Did you find anything today?"

"That's the best part," Jan said. "We did find something." She paused. "Well, Tom did."

"Just another tooth," Vance said, "but I think we can get to the jaw pretty easily, and I'm almost as sure that the tusks will be here somewhere. There could be a pretty complete skeleton. That would make this an excellent find."

"And if there are any arrow points associated with the mammoth, it would make the story even better," Claudia said. "There are lots of mammoths, but only a few have been linked with the human population."

Rhodes thought that Claudia had become an expert on mammoths pretty quickly, but maybe writers were quick studies. Or maybe Vance was just a good teacher. Anyway, Rhodes liked it that Claudia and Jan were excited about the idea of writing a story on the mammoth. That might keep them out of the murder investigation.

"Better a real mammoth than an imaginary Bigfoot," he said to encourage them. "You have some real physical evidence you can talk about and photograph here."

"That's right," Jan said. "Dr. Vance is going to let us help with the dig, so we'll have plenty of authentic details for the story. You can go on back to town without us."

"Can you find the way?"

"If they can't, they can follow me," Vance said.

He seemed glad of the company and the help, and he was welcome to it, Rhodes thought.

"Do you have plenty of water?" Rhodes asked.

"I brought a whole case," Vance told him.

"And we have some in the Aviator if we need it," Jan said.

"All right, then," Rhodes said. "If you need me, just give me a call."

He turned to leave, but Vance stopped him. "Speaking of needing you, we thought we heard gunshots a little while ago. It sounded as if they came from back in the woods somewhere."

"You did hear them," Rhodes said. "It was nothing much, and it's all been taken care of."

"I get a little worried about being out here," Claudia said, looking around. "There's not really anybody around, and I don't think more than one car has passed on the road the whole time we've been here. When I think of two people being killed, it makes me a little nervous."

"They were alone," Rhodes said. "And someone had a reason to kill them. I just haven't figured out what it was yet. There are three of you, and you all have cell phones. Nothing will happen to you."

"I know. But just the same . . ."

"Just the same, my foot," Jan said. "There's nothing to worry about. We'll be fine. Isn't that right, Sheriff?"

"That's right," Rhodes said, thinking of all the Bigfoot hunters back at the motel. If they showed up, armed to the teeth and looking for Bigfoot, all bets were off. They weren't going to show up, though. Bud Turley was taking care of that.

Or he was supposed to. Rhodes thought it might be a good idea to make sure.

15

▼

WHEN HE GOT TO LOUETTA KENNEDY'S STORE, RHODES DROVE into the shade of a tree and stopped the car. He wanted to have another look around, and he wanted a Dr Pepper. He didn't think that taking one from the cooler would contaminate the crime scene. In fact, he was sure that he and Ruth had learned as much from the scene as they were going to.

Before he went into the store, he had a look in the building that held the cattle feed. It was dark inside, and Rhodes could smell cottonseed meal. There were only a few sacks of feed. Louetta's business had dropped off to almost nothing.

Not finding any new clues, Rhodes went to the store itself. He took down the crime-scene tape from across the door, went inside, and got a Dr Pepper. He put a dollar on the cash register and went outside to sit in Louetta's chair and think things over while he drank his DP.

The way he put things together, someone had killed Larry Colley in Big Woods, then returned later and killed Louetta, maybe because she would somehow have been able to implicate him in Colley's death.

Colley's trailer had been searched by someone looking for something small enough to have been stuck in a cereal box, and that something, whatever it was, might or might not have a connection to Colley's death. Rhodes thought it was likely that it did.

So far, Rhodes had come up with no motive for Colley's death. It seemed that nobody liked Colley very much, and no one Rhodes had spoken to, except for Bud Turley, had expressed any grief at his passing. Even Gerald Bolton didn't seem unduly upset, and Colley had been working for him.

Turley wanted to blame the killing on Bigfoot, which was plainly ridiculous, unless you believed in Bigfoot. Turley did, or claimed he did. Rhodes didn't, but it appeared that a surprising number of people were on Turley's side, and most of them were currently registered at the Western Inn, ready to have a big meeting and plan their strategy.

Rhodes knew that no matter what Turley told them, they'd have their meeting. He thought he might as well pay them a visit. Maybe he'd take Ivy for that steak Sam Blevins had mentioned. Ivy would be opposed to that because steak was not one of the items on the low-fat diet she advocated. For that matter, Rhodes couldn't think of a single thing on Sam Blevins's menu that *was* on the diet. Maybe that explained why Rhodes wanted to eat at the Round-Up.

As he thought things over, Rhodes was struck again by the idea that he was somehow missing a bet. There was something that wasn't registering with him. Something he should have noticed but hadn't, or something that he'd noticed but whose significance hadn't registered. No matter how many times he went back over things in his mind, however, nothing would come to him.

He finished the Dr Pepper and took the bottle back inside the store, putting it in a case beside the cooler. He gave the place a last once-over, but he couldn't figure out what he was missing. He told himself, not for the first time, that it would come to him sooner or later.

He went outside and replaced the crime-scene tape at the door and wondered if anyone would ever buy anything at Louetta's store again. He didn't really think so.

When Rhodes got back to the jail, Hack informed him that they were soon going to have a visit from the FBI.

Such a comment clearly required Rhodes to ask why, but the sheriff didn't fall into the trap. He knew better than to do that. If he did, Hack and Lawton would go into a long and complicated explanation that Rhodes didn't feel like hearing.

So Rhodes said, "I always welcome federal assistance," and sat down at his desk to do some of his paperwork.

Hack didn't let it go. He said, "It's about Al Lancaster."

Rhodes looked up from the arrest report he was reading. Lancaster was well known in the county for filing lawsuits. It seemed to be his only hobby, even though all of them were thrown out by the first judge to see them, because they were totally lacking in merit.

"All right," Rhodes said, "what is it?"

"You didn't seem like you wanted to know," Hack said. "Lawton and I, we don't like to bother you if you don't really want to know about something. Ain't that right, Lawton?"

Lawton nodded. "The high sheriff has a lot on his mind. Wouldn't want to add to his burdens."

It was all Rhodes could do not to bang his head on his desk. He said, "You won't be adding to my burdens. I want to know. Who's Al having trouble with now? Is it his neighbor again?"

"Greer's his neighbor's name," Lawton said. "Bob Greer. Al's sued him a time or two already."

"Once for that time his cat got in Al's yard and peed in his flower bed," Hack said with a warning look at Lawton. Rhodes knew Hack didn't like interruptions. "The second time was when he said Greer was getting grass clippings on his lawn."

Rhodes remembered both incidents. Lancaster had complained to the sheriff's office each time, and each time Rhodes had told him that there was no basis for an arrest. Quarrels between neighbors were civil matters. So Lancaster had gone to court.

"Old Bob has one of those ridin' mowers," Lawton said. "He gets that thing going about as fast as it'll run, and it really does sling the grass. If he'd just mow more often than once ever' two or three weeks, it wouldn't be so bad, but he lets it go too long, and after he mows, his yard looks like a hay field."

Hack was getting a little red-faced and frustrated because Lawton had taken over the story. When Lawton had to pause for breath after his last long sentence, Hack jumped in to take over again.

"His clippings were an inch or two deep on Lancaster's yard. Al said it caused his grass to die and damaged his property. The judge didn't let it go to court, though."

As well he shouldn't have, Rhodes thought.

"This ain't about the grass," Lawton said. "It ain't even about Greer."

Hack glared at him.

"What's it about?" Rhodes asked.

"A car," Hack said. "One he bought from Jim Lucas's lot."

Jim Lucas had a place out on the highway. Sometimes Rhodes thought it looked more like a junkyard than a used-car dealership, but Lucas seemed to do all right with it. The car he drove looked a lot better than the ones he sold.

"How could a deal on a used car be a federal case?" Rhodes asked.

"Preowned," Hack said. "Not used. Nobody's said 'used' for years. You need to keep up."

"It ain't really the car that makes it a federal case, anyway," Lawton said.

"But the car started it," Hack said. "Al claims it was a lemon. Stopped runnin' two days after he bought it, right in his driveway. It's been sittin' there ever since, leakin' out oil. Al claims there's a big black stain under the engine."

"So naturally Al wants you to arrest Lucas," Lawton said.

"Lock him up and throw away the key," Hack added. "Or better yet, send him to Huntsville and have 'em give him the needle."

"A lemon is another civil matter," Rhodes said. "Like everything else Al complains about. I can't arrest anybody for that. Al can check out the state's lemon law and see what his rights are."

Hack nodded. "That's what I told him. Not that I was advisin' him in a legal matter or anything. I'm an employee of the county, and I know better'n to do that. I just said that it was a civil case and that you wouldn't be able to help him."

Rhodes still didn't see how the FBI could be involved. So, against his better judgment, he asked.

"Well," Lawton started, but Hack glowered him into silence.

"See," Hack said, turning back to Rhodes, "the thing of it is that Al's got himself a disability. Americans with Disabilities Act applies, Al says."

Rhodes thought over what he knew about Al Lancaster, but no disability occurred to him.

"He's just got one eye," Lawton said.

For just the fraction of a second, Rhodes thought that Hack might jump over his desk and go for Lawton's throat. The thought of the two old men flailing away at each other made Rhodes smile. He didn't think they'd do much damage. Hack controlled himself, so Rhodes didn't get to find out.

"Bet you didn't know about that glass eye," he said to Rhodes.

He was right. Rhodes hadn't known.

"Best glass eye I ever saw," Hack went on. "Not that I've seen that many of 'em. But I do remember the one old Blimp Connor wore. You should, too."

Rhodes nodded. Blimp Connor got his nickname because of his general size and shape, and he'd lost an eye in World War II, or, as he'd always called it, "the Big One." Exactly how he lost the eye depended on which story Blimp was telling at the time. It had been gouged out by a German bayonet in one version, punched out by another GI's thumb in a barroom brawl in another, pecked out by a giant raven while Blimp lay wounded and unable to move in a third.

The eye itself, which Blimp referred to as "a VA special," didn't look real at all. The white wasn't white. It was a curious shade of yellow, and Blimp liked to say that the color was a result of the jaundice, which was about as likely to be true as most of his other stories. If you asked him to, he'd take it out and pass it around so everybody could have a good look at it, or so Rhodes had heard. He'd never been curious enough to ask.

Al Lancaster's eye wasn't like Blimp Connor's. It looked absolutely real. Rhodes would never have known it was glass if Hack hadn't told him.

"You know something?" Lawton said. "Callin' an eye a glass eye don't make it one."

Hack opened his mouth, closed it, and just stared at Lawton, who, Rhodes realized, had a point.

"Knowing Al, his eye's as good as yours or mine," Rhodes said. "I wouldn't put it past him to try to fool the feds, though."

"Couldn't he get in trouble for that?" Lawton said.

"You're danged right," Hack said, recovering from his surprise at Lawton's comment. "We should warn him about that."

"Why?" Lawton said.

"We'd be accessories if he got caught, knowin' what we know. Aidin' and abettin'."

"That right, Sheriff?" Lawton said.

"Could be. You two better be sure nothing happens. I'd hate to see you locked up in one of those federal pens along with Al Lancaster."

"Country clubs is what those places are," Hack said. "They play tennis. Get three squares a day. Probably watch HDTV."

"Don't count on it," Rhodes told him, and turned back to the paperwork.

Ruth Grady came into the jail a little after two, just as Rhodes realized that he'd missed lunch again and started to think about a Blizzard. He forgot about that when he heard Ruth's news.

"Larry Colley's car was a Chevy pickup," Ruth said. "A

twenty-year-old S-10 model. I don't know where it is, but I have the license plate information."

She pulled out her notebook and read off the combination of letters and numbers. Rhodes said he'd put out a bulletin on it.

"Larry Colley had a cell phone, too," Ruth said. "You know how those things save the numbers you call and the numbers of the people who call you?"

"Sure," Rhodes said. "I was hoping he'd have a phone on him and that it would give us a clue. We could use one."

"Well, we might not have the phone, but we have the next best thing. I talked to the people at Clearview Cells, and they said Colley had bought a phone from them. Knowing that, I called the company and got his records."

"And you found a clue."

"I'd call it that."

Rhodes wondered if she'd been taking lessons from Hack and Lawton on how to stall him. He said, "Are you going to tell me what it is?"

"Colley had two calls from the Sandstroms' number," Ruth said.

Rhodes wasn't really surprised. He'd believed Karen Sandstrom when she told him that she'd had no contact with her ex-husband, but he'd been lied to before. He was disappointed, however, both in himself and in Karen Sandstrom.

"And the calls from the Sandstroms' number aren't even the best part," Ruth said.

"What is?"

"There were two calls on there to someone else you've met recently."

She'd definitely been taking lessons from Hack and Lawton, Rhodes thought.

"And that was?"

"Chester Johnson," Ruth said.

16

▼

CHESTER JOHNSON WAS SITTING ON THE DENTED TAILGATE OF his GMC pickup kicking his feet in the air when Rhodes arrived. He was wearing his Clearview Catamounts cap, jeans, and an aloha shirt. The last item seemed a bit incongruous to Rhodes, but more and more people were wearing them lately, even in Blacklin County, which was about as far away from Hawaii as you could get.

The pickup was parked in the shade of a plum tree. Johnson jumped off the tailgate of the truck and walked over to the county car when Rhodes got out. Johnson's jaws were working, and Rhodes smelled the Juicy Fruit.

"What can I do for you, Sheriff?" Johnson said.

Johnson had a little vegetable stand not far from his house on a farm road between Clearview and Obert. He raised tomatoes, beans, potatoes, corn, okra, peas, peaches, and just about anything else that would grow in the Blacklin County soil. People who wanted fresh produce could always find something at Johnson's stand from early spring until late fall, when he closed up shop for the winter.

"I have some nice corn," Johnson said. "I didn't grow it, though. It was shipped in. I got it from a grocery supply place. And I got some okra. Some squash, too. Grew that myself. Go mighty good with cornbread if you'd make you some."

The vegetable stand was just an open-faced shed with a front that swung up and was propped on a couple of poles to create a little shade. The vegetables sat in boxes on long tables, and Johnson had a cashbox on a smaller table. The yellow squash and green okra looked good to Rhodes, who liked both vegetables fried. Frying wasn't on the current agenda at his house, however.

"I didn't come for the vegetables," Rhodes said. "I wanted to talk to you about Larry Colley."

Johnson turned away, walked back to his pickup, and sat on the tailgate again.

"That was a damn shame," he said. "Poor old Larry."

"You and Larry weren't exactly friends, though, were you?"

"Well, I guess we weren't buddies if that's what you mean."

"Funny," Rhodes said. "You never mentioned before that you even knew him, not even when we were looking at his body."

Johnson adjusted his cap and looked off into the distance.

"I didn't see much point in it."

"I called Bud Turley before I came out here," Rhodes said. "He told me that you'd had some trouble paying for the work he and Colley did on your pickup."

Johnson patted the tailgate with his right hand. "This old truck's got a lot of miles on it. I need it to haul things in, and I don't make enough out of this vegetable stand to buy a new one."

He looked as if he might want to say more, but Rhodes thought he knew what was being left unsaid. "You don't make enough to pay your bills, either, I guess."

"I pay my bills." Johnson's voice rose. "But they overcharged me for the work they did. A hundred and fifty dollars for a tune-up! And this old hoopie don't even have all that fancy computer stuff."

"Bud didn't think it was too much to charge. He said that Colley came out here to ask you about making a payment."

"Ask, my ass. He came out here to kick the crap out of me." Johnson gestured toward the little white house where he lived. "My wife was here, too. He wanted to kick the crap out of me and make me look bad in front of my wife."

"But he didn't," Rhodes said. "Not the way I heard it. You stopped him before he could do anything. You want to show me the rifle?"

Johnson jumped off the tailgate and walked over to the table where the cashbox was. Rhodes went right along behind him.

A cardboard box stood beside the table. Johnson pushed aside a flap and brought out his rifle, a .30-30 Winchester.

"That the one you took hunting with you?"

"Yeah. It was my daddy's gun," Johnson said. "He bought it right after World War II, around the time I was born. He always called it 'the Big One.' The war, not the rifle."

Just like Blimp Connor, Rhodes thought. And most likely a lot of others.

"I need to have a gun handy, living out here and running a business the way I do," Johnson said. "Somebody could drive up and rob me and be gone in half a minute. Not being critical, Sheriff, but by the time you or one of your deputies got here, he'd be long gone, and I could be lying dead on the ground."

"Like Larry Colley," Rhodes said.

"I didn't kill him, Sheriff, if that's what you're thinking. When he came out here that day, all I had to do was give him a look at this gun and he changed his mind real quick about whipping my butt. He decided he'd give me another week to come up with the money, if that's how long I needed."

"So you didn't call him up to go hunting for hogs the other day, get him out there in the woods, and bash his head in with your rifle barrel."

"No sir, I did not."

"He called you a couple of times on his cell phone. What about?"

"It wasn't about me taking him out in the woods and killing him. It was about that bill I owed. That's all."

"And you didn't arrange to meet him at Big Woods for a little hog hunting?"

"You don't really think I'd have gone off in the woods with him, do you?" Johnson said. "Or that he'd have gone with me after getting a look at my rifle?"

"I don't know," Rhodes said. "I was just wondering if you could bash somebody's head in with that thing. It looks heavy enough."

"Dang right it is. But why would I do that? I could've just shot him if I'd wanted to kill him. Anyway, if I'd done either one, would I have called you and told you about it?"

"I don't know why you called. Maybe it was just to throw off my suspicions. Is that it?"

"Hell no. I could've just left him there for the hogs to eat up.

There wouldn't have been a sign of him left after they got through with him, or at least not enough for anybody to put a name to. That ought to prove I didn't kill him."

It made sense to Rhodes, but he also knew that people will lie to save their necks. He said, "If you didn't kill him, I guess you won't mind if I take your rifle in and have it checked out." Rhodes put out his hand. "Just to make sure it wasn't used on the back of someone's head."

Johnson hesitated, but he gave up the rifle. Rhodes took it and held it with the barrel pointed down at the ground.

"I guess you know you're leaving me defenseless," Johnson said. "Somebody could come by here and rob me, and there's not a thing I could do about it."

"You could close for the day," Rhodes said. He looked up and down the road. "You're not doing much business anyway."

"You gonna bring my gun back tomorrow?"

"No. It'll take a while to get the tests done."

"What am I supposed to do for protection, then?"

Rhodes nodded toward a tarp-covered lump beside the vegetable stand. "Is that a four-wheeler under the tarp?"

"Sure is. Handy for getting around the farm."

"If someone tries to rob you, jump on and ride away," Rhodes said.

"Take a while to get it uncovered and started. Might be dead by that time."

"Hope for the best," Rhodes told him.

The Round-Up was crowded, but that was nothing unusual. People in Clearview liked the kind of food Sam Blevins served, and he served plenty of it, at what he liked to call "small-town prices."

Blevins met Rhodes and Ivy at the door. He shook Rhodes's hand and said, "Glad you decided to have a steak, Sheriff. And you, too, Ivy."

Ivy said, "You're sure you don't have a chicken breast you could grill for me?"

Blevins gave her a horrified look. "Don't even say that word in here," he told her. "I can fix you a nice lean filet, but nothing that clucks and flies."

"The filet sounds fine," Ivy said. "Where's the Bigfoot convention?"

"In the private dining room. There must be thirty of them."

"I might need to talk to them later," Rhodes said.

"Fine with me," Blevins said. "You want me to let them know you're here?"

"That might not be a good idea. We'll let it be a surprise."

Blevins shrugged and led the way through the crowded restaurant, weaving between the tables with the expertise of long practice. Rhodes and Ivy trailed along behind, with Rhodes stopping now and then to acknowledge the people who spoke to him.

"Here you are," Blevins said, putting the menus down on a clean wooden tabletop. "Mary Jo will be your waitress."

"Isn't that Larry Colley's ex-wife?" Ivy said when Blevins left the table.

"One of them," Rhodes said. "I need to have a talk with the other one later tonight."

"Assuming that the Bigfoot hunters let you leave here alive."

"They're fine folks," Rhodes said, knowing that he was being a little too optimistic. "If Bud Turley doesn't get them too stirred up, they won't be a problem."

"You said that Bud was going to be sure there wasn't any trouble."

"He's supposed to. I'm not so sure I trust him not to do just the opposite."

"I don't blame you for not trusting him." Ivy opened her menu. "Where's that filet Sam was talking about?"

Before Rhodes could point it out to her, Blevins was back at their table. Claudia and Jan were standing right behind him, smiling at Rhodes over his shoulder.

"These two say they know you," Blevins said to Rhodes. "They said they hoped you wouldn't mind if they joined you for dinner."

Rhodes looked at Ivy, who nodded.

"They're welcome to sit with us," Rhodes said, standing up as Blevins put a couple of menus down on the table.

Rhodes introduced the two women to Ivy and explained who they were and what they were doing in town.

"After they finish the articles they're working on," Rhodes said, "they're going to get their novel published. It's about a handsome crime-busting sheriff."

"A fantasy, then?" Ivy said.

Everyone laughed, except Rhodes, and Mary Jo appeared to take their orders. No one had decided on what to eat, but when Ivy mentioned the filet, Claudia and Jan said they'd have that as well. Rhodes went for the rib-eye.

"Full of fat," Ivy said.

"That's what makes it good," Rhodes said, and got a disapproving look even though he'd smiled to show he was kidding.

After Mary Jo repeated their orders to make sure she had them right, she took the menus and went away.

Claudia said to Ivy, "It's noisy in here, isn't it?"

"Eating out is a social event in Clearview," Ivy said, speaking loud enough to be heard over the general buzz of talk, the clatter of silverware, and the piped-in country music. "People have a lot to talk about."

"We'll just have to talk loud enough to be heard, then. We wanted to tell you our latest theory about the murder."

"I was sure you'd have a new one," Rhodes said. "Let's hear it."

"Larry Colley was killed by Bigfoot."

"That's not a new theory. That's the same one you had the last time."

Ivy gave Rhodes a puzzled look.

"They're not crazy," Rhodes said. "Jan's just joking. I think. Right?"

"Not really," Claudia said. "Tell him, Jan."

"It's simple," Jan said. "Have you read today's *Clearview Herald*?"

Rhodes confessed that he hadn't. He'd planned to, but he hadn't had time.

"There's a good story about Larry Colley's murder by someone named Jennifer Loam. Do you know her?"

Rhodes nodded.

"We'd like to meet her," Claudia said. "She can give us some pointers about writing."

Jan agreed. "She surely can. Anyway, she says in the story that she interviewed the man who found the body."

Rhodes hadn't known that, and Johnson hadn't mentioned it. Jan bent down and pulled a little notebook from her purse. She flipped the notebook open and read what was written there.

"Chester Johnson. That's the man's name. And he claims that he saw Bigfoot."

"That's not exactly true," Rhodes said. "He saw a shadow if he saw anything. He was just spooked."

Or he was the killer himself and making things up to make people think he wasn't, but Rhodes didn't add that.

"What if he really did see something?"

Rhodes started to say that was impossible, but Jan held up her hand. Rhodes wondered if that was how she got people to be quiet in faculty meetings.

"Maybe *something* is putting it a little strongly. But what if he just saw a shadow or saw something move?"

"I don't think he did."

"But he might have," Claudia said. "We're not saying it was Bigfoot. But what if someone is in those woods posing as Bigfoot?"

"Why would anybody do that?" Ivy asked. "Those woods are full of feral hogs. Hanging around there would be dangerous."

"There must be something there besides the hogs," Jan said. "Something someone's protecting or hiding or looking for."

"For example?" Rhodes said.

"A meth lab," Claudia said. "We think the woman at the store was killed by someone who was stealing ammonium nitrate fertilizer to use for making methamphetamine in an illegal lab. And he's posing as Bigfoot to keep people away from the lab that's hidden in the woods."

"That's not bad," Rhodes said, "except for the fact that Louetta didn't sell fertilizer. Just cattle feed. And there's no meth lab in those woods."

Rhodes had dealt with meth labs before, and he knew how easy they'd become to set up, hide, and move around. Nobody would set one up in the woods where the feral hogs were a problem. There were too many other places.

"It's a good try," Rhodes said. "But I'm afraid it's not quite right. What's your next theory?"

"We don't have one. You'll have to come up with something better if you want one."

"What if I can't?"

"You will," Claudia said. "That's why they pay you the big bucks."

Rhodes didn't have a response to that, but he didn't need one. Mary Jo arrived at the table bearing food.

Mary Jo was professional and efficient, but Rhodes thought she seemed preoccupied. When he mentioned it to the others, they agreed.

"Maybe she just needs a cigarette," Rhodes said.

"Or maybe she's just realized that Larry's really dead," Ivy said.

"I don't think it really bothers her that Larry's dead," he told them.

"You mean she didn't care about him?" Jan said.

"Not much, or so she says."

Claudia and Jan got very interested in Mary Jo as a possible suspect. They told Rhodes that they were going to ask her for an interview.

Rhodes said that would be fine with him. He was beginning to wonder if Mary Jo might have lied to him, too, the way Karen Sandstrom had. Mary Jo's number hadn't shown up on Colley's cell phone, but they might have met and talked in person.

"She's a big woman," Claudia said. "Big enough to kill somebody, if she hit him hard enough."

"I don't think Mary Jo is the kind of person who'd be hiding out in Big Woods," Ivy said. "Not for any reason whatsoever. And certainly not posing as Bigfoot."

"Well, somebody took her ex-husband there and killed him," Jan said. "Maybe she's the one. It's nearly always the ex-wife or the ex-husband that the police suspect. They never admit it, though. They just say something like 'Naturally we want to ask him some questions.' Or 'her.' But in the end it turns out that the ex is the one who did it."

"Nearly every time," Claudia said. "Isn't that right, Sheriff?"

Rhodes said he never excluded anybody from an investigation.

"A typical nonanswer," Claudia said. "But I think the article in the paper said that there were two ex-wives. Isn't that right?"

Rhodes said that it was.

"Makes it a little harder for the handsome crime-busting sheriff," Ivy said, grinning at Rhodes. "He has to make a choice."

"That's why they pay him the big bucks," Rhodes said.

17

▼

THE STEAKS WERE EXCELLENT, OR AT LEAST RHODES'S WAS. HE carefully trimmed off the excess fat, but the meat was marbled with plenty more.

All the time they were eating, the noise from the private room rose in volume. It had been hardly noticeable at first because of the other noise in the restaurant, but it finally became something of a distraction. Sam Blevins went into the room several times to quiet things down, and the other diners occasionally gave it a curious glance when there was a particularly loud burst of laughter or yelling. The two waitresses who were working the tables for the Bigfoot hunters came out looking harried.

"The handsome crime-busting sheriff is going to have a word with those people shortly," Ivy told Claudia and Jan.

"About the noise?" Jan asked.

"No. He's going to tell them that this town isn't big enough for them and him."

Jan's eyes lit up. "Is there going to be trouble?"

"No," Rhodes said. "And it's not quite as dramatic as Ivy makes it out to be. I'm just going to tell them that they need to leave because there's no Bigfoot in the woods, that they'd be trespassing if they went to look for the Bigfoot that's not there, and that they're going to cause themselves more trouble than they need to if they don't leave town."

"Just like in the movies," Claudia said. "*High Noon.* Or maybe *Shane.*"

"Or *Dirty Harry,*" Jan said. " 'Do you feel lucky, punk?' "

It was possibly the worst Clint Eastwood impression that Rhodes had ever heard, but then Claudia said, "Come on, punk. Make my day," and that was even worse.

"It's not anything like that," Rhodes said. "Mainly because there won't be any shooting and there won't be any fighting."

"Speaking of no shooting," Jan said, "I don't ever see you with a gun or in uniform."

"The sheriff is the only member of the department who doesn't have to wear the uniform when he's on duty," Rhodes said, "and I'm on duty twenty-four hours a day. I do carry a sidearm, though. You just can't see it."

"Is it under your shirt?"

"It's in an ankle holster," Rhodes said.

He'd just started wearing the ankle holster a week or so earlier, and he wasn't fond of it. It did, however, keep his .38 out of sight, and it was secure. He'd read about people in other departments who'd had trouble with various sidearms and holsters, including a couple of cops in Houston, one of whom had accidentally released the safety slide of his automatic when he slid into the seat of his car. The pistol fired a bullet into his foot. Rhodes didn't like automatics in the first place, and he also didn't like having his weapon out for all to see, so he'd decided to give the ankle holster a try. The disadvantages were that it put the gun out of easy reach and it was uncomfortable. Rhodes told himself that he'd get used to it sooner or later.

"If you have to use the pistol, I hope you can grab it before someone shoots you," Ivy said.

"No one's going to shoot me, and I'm not going to have to use the pistol."

Rhodes finished his steak and stood up.

"Now, if you'll excuse me," he said, "I'll go have a talk with those Bigfoot fellas."

"Be careful," Ivy said.

Claudia and Jan didn't say anything. Rhodes thought that they were rather hoping he *wouldn't* be careful. They might be hoping for some untoward action to spice up their article.

Rhodes was determined not to give it to them. He'd go in, make his statement, and leave. Simple as that.

Except that it didn't quite work out the way he'd planned.

Sam Blevins met him as he reached the big double door that went into the private room.

"They're a little bit rowdy in there, Sheriff," Sam said. His voice had a nervous edge. "I just want you to know that I don't serve any beer or liquor here. If they have it, they didn't get it from me."

It was illegal to sell hard liquor in Blacklin County, but restaurants could serve beer if they had a license. Blevins liked to think he ran a family establishment, and he had never applied for a license, as far as Rhodes knew.

"Are you trying to tell me something?" Rhodes said.

"Yeah." Blevins avoided Rhodes's eyes. "I think some of those fellas are drinking liquor, but every time I go in, they hide it. One of the waitresses said she saw a flask or two. Are you gonna make any arrests?"

"I just want to talk to them for a minute. I'm not working for the Alcoholic Beverages Commission tonight."

Blevins relaxed a little. "I just wanted you to know that if they have it, they didn't get it here. If they brought it with them, I can't be responsible."

Rhodes said that he understood and went into the room. The Bigfoot hunters were laughing and talking and shouting to one another up and down the long tables that seated six on a side. Rhodes saw glasses of iced tea, water, and sodas, but he didn't see any flasks, and he didn't see anyone spiking the soft drinks. The nearly empty plates in front of the men were smeared red with ketchup, barbecue sauce, and steak sauce.

Rhodes's entrance didn't disturb anyone for a while. The talking and laughing went right on as it had before he'd come in. Then Bud Turley, who was sitting not too far from the door, noticed him and stopped talking to the man next to him.

The man turned to look at whatever had caught Bud's attention, and Rhodes saw that he was Jeff, and sitting next to him was Charlie, who also turned toward Rhodes when Jeff jabbed him with an elbow.

They were still dressed as they'd been earlier that day, even including the caps. For that matter, practically everyone in the room except Rhodes had on a cap. Rhodes could remember when men removed their head coverings when going into a building, and they certainly would never have worn a cap or hat inside a restaurant. Now, hardly anyone took off his cap, no matter where he was. Rhodes didn't know for sure, but he suspected that some men must wear their caps to church. Maybe they even slept in them.

Charlie nudged the man next to him, and in a short time everyone had been nudged, poked, or kicked under the table. The room became very quiet, and Rhodes could hear the piped-in music clearly for the first time that night. It was some current country song, he supposed, since he didn't recognize either the tune or the singer. He'd stopped being interested in country music when it got taken over by the hat acts, and he hadn't gone back to it.

Bud Turley was the first one to speak. He said, "Hey, Sheriff. Glad you could join us this evening."

He didn't look glad to Rhodes. He looked as if a skunk had just come into the room and filled the air with his spray. Turley stood up, looking a little unsteady on his feet, and waved an arm in Rhodes's direction.

"Boys," he said, "I want you all to meet Dan Rhodes, high sheriff of Blacklin County. I expect he's come to welcome you to Clearview and then to tell you to get your sorry butts out of town."

People started talking in low voices. Rhodes couldn't make out what they were saying. He had a feeling that it was about him and that it wasn't complimentary, but maybe he was being paranoid.

Bud sat down, and most of the men in the room looked at Rhodes as if they wouldn't mind if he disappeared or if his head exploded, with a slight preference for the latter. So he hadn't been paranoid, after all.

"I'd like to welcome you all to Clearview," he said.

Jeff and Charlie looked at each other and laughed. After a slight pause, the others joined in, except for Bud, who didn't seem amused.

"But I'm not here to tell you to get your sorry butts out of town," Rhodes continued.

The laughter died down. Rhodes thought he had them a little off balance.

"What I do have to tell you is that you'll have to stay out of Big Woods. Besides the fact that it's the scene of an ongoing investigation into a murder, it's owned by a man here in town. His name is Gerald Bolton. He's told me that he doesn't welcome trespassers, and he'll be obliged to press charges if I catch any of you out there."

Bud Turley muttered something under his breath.

Rhodes pointed in Bud's direction. "Bud is likely to say that he's been hunting arrowheads on that land since he was a kid, and that's a fact. Mr. Bolton didn't mind that. But he doesn't want a lot of people trampling over his property, and I don't want anybody messing with my crime scene."

Rhodes was exaggerating Gerald Bolton's wishes a little bit, but he didn't think anybody in the room was going to check up on him.

"So the deal is this," Rhodes said. "You're welcome to stay here in Clearview, have your meetings, enjoy the hospitality of our fine business and eating establishments like the Round-Up here, and generally have yourselves a good time. You can even look for Bigfoot in our parks or any public land. But you're not welcome to go messing around in Big Woods."

Bud Turley muttered again, and this time Rhodes didn't let it go. He knew he should have, but something in him just wouldn't allow it.

"You have something to say, Bud?"

Bud got up again, not a bit steadier than he'd been the first time he did it. He stepped over to stand near Rhodes, who got a whiff of liquor.

"Maybe you'd better not say anything, after all," Rhodes told him.

Rhodes left him and went to the table. He picked up the glass that Turley had been drinking from. It was about half full of what looked like a soft drink. Rhodes sniffed it. It might have started out as a soft drink, but something definitely had been added to it.

Rhodes put the glass back on the table as Jeff and Charlie poked each other and snickered like a pair of high school Harrys. They reminded Rhodes of an aging Beavis and Butthead. In fact, if Beavis and Butthead were still around, they'd probably be hunting for Bigfoot on weekends. It was for sure they wouldn't be having dates.

"Bud," Rhodes said, "it might be time for you to go home."

Bud gave him a defiant stare. "Not going anywhere. You let that professor stay out there on Bolton's land. No reason we can't go there."

"Dr. Vance isn't in the woods," Rhodes said. "You can visit him at his dig if you want to, but that's all."

Jeff spoke up. "How about us? Me and Charlie, I mean. All right if we visit that professor?"

"No, it's not all right," Rhodes said. "We can't have too many people trampling around the dig. It would mess everything up."

He wasn't sure just what would be messed up, since people had been trampling up and down that creek for a lot longer than anybody could remember, but Bud Turley seemed to have some ideas on the subject.

Bud got a panicked look on his face at the mention of the dig.

He said, "The Sheriff is right. That dig's important. Don't want anybody out there causing problems."

Rhodes hadn't expected Bud to agree with him, but it made sense that he would. There was no Bigfoot in the woods, and nobody was likely to find a trace of one, but the mammoth was real, and the person who'd found it was Bud Turley. He wouldn't want anybody to mess up his claim to fame.

"Bud," Rhodes said, "I've been visiting with two women who say they're going to write a magazine article about that mammoth. They'll be wanting to interview you and take a picture or two to put in the magazine."

"See?" Bud said to Jeff and Charlie. "You can't go making trouble. This's too important for that."

"Who's more important?" Jeff said, standing up. "You? That mammoth?" He paused and looked around the room. "Or Bigfoot?"

The men at the tables stared at Bud and started muttering to each other. Rhodes couldn't make out all the words, but it was clear that some of them thought Bud was a glory hog who'd gladly sacrifice their chance to find Bigfoot just to get his picture in some magazine.

Bud struggled to say something to refute them, but the words didn't come out, and nobody was listening to him anyway. So instead of saying what he wanted to say, he pushed Rhodes aside and shoved Jeff hard in the chest with both hands.

Jeff fell backward, overturning his chair and kicking the bottom of the table as he flipped over. Plates, glasses, and silverware rose in the air and clattered back down onto the wooden table. One plate missed the table and shattered on the floor. Men pushed out of the way as water, tea, and spiked soft drinks flowed across the tabletops and dripped into their chairs and onto the floor.

Charlie didn't even look at his fallen friend to see if he was hurt. He jumped for Bud, but Bud was too quick for him. He grabbed hold of Charlie's neck with both hands. Charlie's eyes bugged out, and his face reddened. He didn't try to break Bud's grip, however. He clapped his hands around Bud's neck and started to choke him in return.

The two men tumbled to the floor, locked together, their faces contorted as they struggled to breathe.

Rhodes moved a chair out of the way to get to them, but as he bent to separate them, someone yelled, "Let them fight it out!"

Rhodes looked up to see who'd yelled, and a cold, wet napkin slapped him in the face, covering his eyes. As he tried to peel it off, two or three men jumped him, and he went down.

This was just what Claudia and Jan had wanted, Rhodes thought as he fell. He hoped they'd brought their camera.

18

▼

THE NAPKIN SLIPPED AWAY FROM RHODES'S FACE, BUT HE couldn't see much, just feet and chair legs, mainly because the left side of his face was pressed against the bare wooden floor of the restaurant. He didn't need to see much, however, to know that there was someone on his back and that a fight was going on around him.

Rhodes moved his head slightly, rubbing his cheek on the floor as he did, and saw that the lower part of a boot wasn't too far away. His hands were free, and he managed to twist around and get a grip on the boot with one of them and then to give the boot a quick jerk to the side.

Someone cried out and fell, and at the same time Rhodes felt the weight begin to lift off his back. He pushed upward to help his burden along and found himself on his knees.

A chair was in front of him, and behind the chair Bud and Charlie thrashed on the floor, their hands still around each other's necks. They flipped from side to side, their boots kicking against the floor. Amazingly enough, their caps hadn't fallen off.

Jeff was crouched beside the men, his hands on Charlie's shoulders as he tried to pull him away from Bud. He wasn't having much luck.

Rhodes took hold of the chair and shoved himself to his feet. The other Bigfoot hunters had gathered on the other side of the table, and they were leaning over it to shout encouragement to whoever it was they might have been cheering for. Rhodes's judgment was that about three-quarters of them were rooting for Charlie.

A couple of them were banging on the tabletop with the handles of their silverware and making serious dents in the wood. Sam Blevins wasn't going to like that.

The men who had jumped Rhodes had now mingled with the crowd, and he had no idea which ones were the guilty parties. The man he had tripped was sitting up, rubbing the back of his head and staring around with a dazed expression. Rhodes figured he'd hit the back of his head when he fell.

Rhodes put a foot on the chair in front of him and shoved it out of his way. It scooted past Jeff and the two men on the floor and banged into another table. Nobody paid it any attention.

"Move out of the way, Jeff," Rhodes said.

Jeff didn't look up. He shook his head and kept pulling at Charlie, who wasn't twisting around much now. Bud was hardly moving at all. Each man still had his opponent locked in a chokehold. Their eyes were distended, their tongues protruding, their faces turning black.

If they were trying to strangle each other, and it seemed certain that they were, they might very well succeed if someone didn't do something. Jeff was trying, but he wasn't having any success, and nobody else seemed interested in helping. Rhodes thought that it wouldn't be long before people started betting on which man would turn completely purple first.

Rhodes wasn't overcome with good feelings for either Bud or Charlie, but he was the sheriff, so he'd have to be the one to separate them.

He moved over to Jeff and tapped him on the shoulder.

"Move out of the way," he said again, but this time he used what they called the command voice in cop school.

Jeff moved. He let go of Charlie's shoulders and scooted back across the floor. Rhodes took hold of Bud's fingers and tried to prize them away from Charlie's neck. It was like trying to move the bars of one of the cells in the Blacklin County jail.

"Burn him with a cigarette," someone up at the table suggested.

"Kick him in the balls," someone else suggested.

"He can't do that, dumb-ass. Can't get to 'em."

Rhodes didn't pay any attention to the comments. He flipped off Charlie's cap, hoping he wasn't as bald on top as Bud was.

He wasn't. At least not quite. He had his black hair arranged in a combover that the cap had held in place.

Rhodes got hold of a good handful of hair, which is about all there was, and jerked as hard as he could. Even a man being choked to death, even if he was intent on choking someone else to death, could feel his hair being jerked out by the roots. Sometimes he'd even respond.

Rhodes was gratified, after the second hard pull, to discover that Charlie was responsive. He let go of Bud's neck and started kicking harder than he had for a while. He might even have yelled if Bud hadn't been throttling him.

Bud was so surprised by Charlie's releasing him, and so intent on sucking in air, that he relaxed his grip on Charlie's neck, and Rhodes quickly let go of Charlie's hair and pulled Bud's fingers apart. Charlie rolled away, gasping, and Rhodes knelt between the two men before they could get to each other again, not that they seemed to feel like it. They both lay on their backs and sucked in air.

Then Charlie started to choke and cough. His heels drummed on the floor.

"Jesus!" someone said. "Charlie's dying! Bud's killed him!"

"No he's not," Jeff said. "I think he swallowed his gum. Heimlich! Heimlich!"

Wondering what kind of person would chew gum right after eating, or, worse, *while* he was eating, Rhodes grabbed Charlie under the armpits and pulled him to his feet. While Charlie hung in his arms, coughing, Rhodes made the proper fist and pressed Charlie's upper abdomen.

Nothing.

Rhodes pressed again, and a wad of gum flew out of Charlie's mouth and struck the floor near Jeff's foot. Jeff kicked it out of the way.

Rhodes lowered Charlie to the floor, where Charlie resumed gasping.

"Never chew gum when you're gettin' choked," someone said.

"Good advice," another man responded as if he'd just heard the wisdom of the ages.

"I hope you'll throw their butts in the jail," Sam Blevins said.

Rhodes looked at the restaurant owner, who had materialized at his shoulder as soon as the fighting was over.

Rhodes stood up and let his gaze roam around the room. The Bigfoot hunters were all back in their chairs except for the two men lying on their backs and Jeff, who had moved over against the wall after picking up Charlie's purple and gray cap, which was now clutched in his hands.

All the Bigfoot hunters were pretending nothing had happened. That was fine with Rhodes. He turned to Blevins and said, "Are you going to press charges?"

Blevins thought about it. "Well, I don't know. They didn't break anything." He looked down at Bud and Charlie, who were still lying on their backs struggling to breathe. "Maybe they've had enough punishment."

Rhodes agreed. He didn't want to have to take them to jail and then have their pals bond them out fifteen minutes later. He didn't want to try to discover which of the other ones had jumped him and which ones had been drinking, either. It wasn't worth it.

"Have the servers bring in the bill," Rhodes told Blevins. "Who's going to pay?"

"Their treasurer's supposed to," Sam said. "That's him over there."

He pointed to Jeff, who was twisting Charlie's cap in his hands and looking as if he wished he were elsewhere. Out hunting for Bigfoot, maybe.

"All right," Rhodes said, looking back to the tables. "The rest of you can leave. Quietly. And go straight back to the motel. If you've been drinking, you'd better have someone else drive. I'll have a deputy right outside in the parking lot to make sure you follow instructions. You call it in, Sam."

Sam nodded and left the room. As he went out the door, Rhodes saw Ivy, Claudia, and Jan standing there. He didn't see a camera, for which he was grateful.

"You can forget what I said about enjoying our Clearview hospitality," Rhodes told the Bigfoot hunters. "I've decided that I *am* going to throw your sorry butts out of town, but I don't want you on the highways tonight. You can check out of the motel first thing in the morning."

One or two of the men seemed about to protest, but after they took a good look at Rhodes, they changed their minds. They muttered a little among themselves about not having had their cobbler, but Rhodes didn't blame them for that. Sam's cherry cobbler topped with ice cream was even better than his steaks. Rhodes felt as if he were punishing a bunch of kids, sending them to their rooms without dessert.

"Clear out," Rhodes told them, and they did, still muttering.

As soon as they cleared the door, brushing by the women who still stood there watching, one of the servers came in holding the bill.

Rhodes pointed to Jeff. "Give it to him."

The woman stooped down and held out the bill. Jeff had to let go of the cap with one hand to take it. When he did, the server retreated.

"Get up, Jeff," Rhodes said. "You're not hurt."

Jeff got up. "What about Charlie?"

"Give me a hand," Rhodes said.

Jeff came over, and they tried to get Charlie to his feet. It wasn't easy.

He tried to say something, but he still couldn't get any words out. Jeff seemed to understand him, however. He pushed the combover into place as best he could and stuck Charlie's cap on his head to cover it.

Rhodes draped one of Charlie's arms over Jeff's shoulder, and Charlie hung there like a wet sock.

"Can you get him to the motel?" Rhodes said.

"Yeah. We came together in my truck," Jeff said. "Come on, Charlie."

After paying the bill, Jeff went out with Charlie wobbling along beside him. Rhodes thought that Charlie would fall over at every step, but somehow he didn't.

Jeff got Charlie out of the room, and Rhodes looked down at Bud, who was gradually returning to something resembling his normal color.

"I hope you're ashamed of yourself," Rhodes said.

Bud wheezed out something that sounded like "Not really," but Rhodes couldn't have sworn that's what it was. He got behind Bud and took hold of him under the armpits. With a little effort he heaved Bud into a chair.

"You'd better sit there for a while," Rhodes said. "Then you can go home. You be careful, you hear?"

Bud wheezed out a reply that might have been "Yeah."

"Have a nice night," Rhodes said, and left him there.

"We were wrong," Claudia said when Rhodes joined them at the door.

"We certainly were," Jan said. "Clint Eastwood is all wrong. John Wayne would be much better."

"Or Rambo," Ivy said. "Who played Rambo?"

"Sylvester Stallone," Rhodes said. "Let's stick with John Wayne, pilgrim."

* * *

Rhodes didn't feel like talking to Karen Sandstrom that night. He wished Claudia and Jan a pleasant evening, and he and Ivy went home.

"I think the handsome crime-busting sheriff had better practice his John Wayne impression," Ivy said after Rhodes came in from playing with the dogs.

Yancey yipped as if in agreement.

"I thought I was pretty good," Rhodes said.

Yancey disagreed, and Ivy shook her head.

"How about this one," Rhodes said. "It's from *The Train Robbers*. Big John says it to Ann-Margret. 'Lady, I got a saddle at home older than you are.' "

Ivy laughed, and Yancey ran in a circle around Rhodes's feet.

"That's even worse," Ivy said.

"Then I give up."

"That's the best idea you've had all day," Ivy said.

"I have another one."

"What?"

"It's even better than the last one. Trust me."

"We'll see," Ivy said with a smile.

19

▼

THE NEXT MORNING RHODES WENT TO THE JAIL, EXPECTING Hack and Lawton to start in on him immediately about the ruckus at the Round-Up.

They didn't disappoint.

"I heard you had to fight off five different men in a big free-for-all at the Round-Up last night," Lawton said. "I heard they were all bigger'n you, too."

"It was only four men," Hack said. "Not countin' the two on the floor chokin' each other. Ain't that right, Sheriff?"

"I didn't fight off anybody," Rhodes said. "It was just a little scuffle, and it was over before it even started."

"That ain't the way I heard it," Lawton said. "And that reporter for the *Herald*'s already called. She'll be here in a few minutes to talk to you about it."

Rhodes sighed. He'd read the article about the murder in the paper before breakfast, and he knew there'd be another one today about the mammoth dig. He wasn't looking forward to one about the tussle at the Round-Up.

He didn't have time to worry about it long. Jennifer Loam arrived and got right down to business. She turned on her little recorder, and Rhodes told her the story pretty much as it had happened.

"That's all?" she said.

"That's all," Rhodes said. "Nothing much in it. You'll do better with your mammoth story. And I have a couple of people who'd like to talk to you about that, and about your story on Larry Colley." He told her about Claudia and Jan. "They admired your work and want some writing tips."

"I might be able to help them," Jennifer said. "Where are they staying?"

Rhodes told her, and she said she'd pay them a visit.

"You sure worked that out slick," Hack said after the reporter left. "Just eased her right on out of here without even tellin' her about fightin' off the four men at the Round-Up."

"Five," Lawton said. "The way I heard it, it was five men. Big ones, too."

"I didn't fight anybody," Rhodes said, and he was saved from defending himself any further when Ruth Grady came in.

She asked if he'd heard anything about Colley's truck, and Rhodes said that he hadn't. Then she asked if he'd visited Karen Sandstrom.

"He was too busy," Hack said. "Takin' on four men in a big fight out at the Round-Up."

"Five," Lawton said. "It was five men, the way I heard it."

Rhodes gave Ruth a helpless look. Ruth grinned.

"I heard it was seven," she said.

Rhodes stood up. He said, "I'm going to have that talk with Karen Sandstrom," and started for the door.

But he stopped before he got there. Something had been gnawing at him for a couple of days now, and it was time to do something about it.

"I need the file on the Ronnie Bolton case," he said, turning back.

"That happened before we got all computerized," Hack said. "What do you want with it?"

Rhodes didn't know for sure himself. He said, "I want to look it over. I keep thinking there might be some connection between what happened to him and what happened to Larry Colley."

"Don't see how there could be. That was a long time ago."

"I still think I'll have a look at the file."

"Hope you can find it," Hack said.

"You don't have to worry about that," Rhodes said.

As Rhodes read through the file, things about Ronnie Bolton's disappearance started to come back to him.

The family reunion had been put together by Gerald Bolton, and it had been a big deal. People from both sides of the country had come for a visit. Most of the guests had come from Texas, of course, but Bolton had cousins in California and Virginia, and they'd attended, looking forward, no doubt, to seeing their Texas cousins for the first time in years. No one could have guessed how the reunion would end.

Ronnie Bolton had played with his young cousins and then had wandered off sometime in the afternoon with one of them. According to what Gerald Bolton had told Rhodes, Ronnie and the other children had been warned repeatedly not to go beyond the fence that surrounded the camp house, and Bolton had put special emphasis on the dangers of the woods.

One of the California cousins had a son named Elliott, who was about Ronnie's age. Elliott dared Ronnie to go into the woods with him. Gerald said that Ronnie was something of a daredevil and probably hadn't needed much encouragement. So he and his cousin slipped away from the adults, all of whom were occupied with their own visiting and weren't really paying much attention to the kids.

Ronnie and Elliott went to the edge of the woods, where Elliott had second thoughts and decided to go back to the camp house, being a lot more of a city boy than someone used to the outdoors. He'd told Rhodes that he didn't like the way it got dark back in the trees.

Ronnie hadn't wanted to go back to the camp house, though. He'd called his cousin a baby and gone right on into the woods without him.

Nobody ever saw him again. Everyone assumed that he'd become disoriented and lost in the woods and been unable to find his way out. As soon as Elliott returned to the camp house, the adults had begun to search, but they found no sign of Ronnie. They called Rhodes's office, and a larger search had been organized. The searchers kept looking for a week, and Rhodes had looked on his own after that. Nobody had found a trace of Ronnie Bolton.

Rumors about Bigfoot, feral hogs, and serial killers naturally made the rounds as people struggled to find some kind of explanation for what seemed to be unexplainable. The resident Bigfoot experts, Bud Turley and Larry Colley, had joined in the search. No one found a trace of Bigfoot, either.

None of that was news to Rhodes. What he'd really been interested in seeing was the list of people who'd been at the family reunion, and, sure enough, there was a name on the list that tied directly to the things that were happening now.

One of Bolton's Texas cousins was Buck Sandstrom, Karen Sandstrom's husband.

Gerald Bolton was surprised to see Rhodes, who hadn't called ahead this time.

"You're always welcome here, Sheriff," Bolton said, being the good host. "What can I do for you?"

Rhodes thought the direct approach would work best. He said, "I want to ask you a few questions about your family reunion."

Bolton looked over his shoulder to see if his wife was anywhere around. She wasn't. Rhodes heard music from the other room.

"Come on in," Bolton said, closing the door behind Rhodes. They went into the den, and Bolton asked Rhodes to have a seat. Rhodes took his place in the platform rocker, and Bolton sat in the La-Z-Boy.

"I wouldn't want Edith to hear us," Bolton said. "We talk about Ronnie, but not with strangers. No offense, Sheriff."

"None taken," Rhodes said.

"What kind of questions did you want to ask?" Bolton said. "Do you have some new information?"

Rhodes shook his head. "Not a bit. But I'm curious about a couple of things."

"You know I'll help you if I can."

"Thanks. You have a cousin named Buck Sandstrom. He was at that reunion."

"Sure. Buck and I grew up together. We were friends for a long time. I was older, sort of the leader, I guess you could say. I haven't seen Buck for a good while, though."

"Why not?" Rhodes asked.

"Edith and I don't see people much, not since that reunion. Edith, well . . . she just doesn't feel like it."

The muted music from the other room played on. Rhodes couldn't quite make out the tune.

"I don't know exactly how to explain it," Bolton went on. "It just seems that people get uncomfortable around us. It's not so much that we've changed, which we have, of course, or that they've changed. It's like the whole situation between us has changed. They've moved on. We haven't. Not really."

"Buck moved on to marry Larry Colley's ex-wife," Rhodes said.

Bolton managed to smile a little. "One of them," he said. "You don't think he killed Larry, do you?"

Rhodes said that he didn't know what to think. "I was just wondering if he was around all the time at the reunion or if he was out of sight part of the time."

Bolton frowned and sat forward in the chair, which wasn't an easy trick in a La-Z-Boy. "Which part of the time?"

"The part where Ronnie went to the woods," Rhodes said.

Bolton leaned back in the chair and didn't say anything for a while. Rhodes didn't prod him. Finally Bolton said, "I can't remember. It's just been too long, and there were a lot of people there."

"Twenty-eight," Rhodes said. He'd counted the names on the list.

"And they were all talking, moving around, swapping stories. We were getting ready to grill some hamburgers and hot dogs. People were going to their cars and getting drinks and food. It was all pretty confusing."

"Do you remember swapping any stories with Buck?"

"I must have. We had plenty of tales to tell in those days. But I just can't remember."

"What about your wife," Rhodes said. "Do you think she would have noticed anything?"

There was a pause, and Rhodes heard the music again. He still couldn't make out the tune.

"I hate to ask her," Bolton said. "Like I said, we don't talk about Ronnie with other people. Edith gets upset pretty easily."

"I'll try not to upset her, and she might be able to help me out," Rhodes said. He wished he knew what he was hoping to find out.

Bolton rocked forward in the La-Z-Boy and pushed himself to his feet. "I'll ask her," he said, and left the room.

While he waited for Bolton to come back, Rhodes looked at the collection of glass skunks. There was one that looked familiar, and Rhodes finally realized that it was Flower, from *Bambi*. He looked around to see if the amorous Pepé Le Pew was there—after all, if there was one movie skunk present, there might be another—but if he was, Rhodes didn't see him. He was thinking about getting up and walking over to the shelf for a closer look when Bolton came back into the room. Edith was with him. Rhodes stood up.

"Hello, Sheriff," Edith said in her wispy voice. "Please, keep your seat."

She walked over to the couch and sat down. Bolton went to his La-Z-Boy. Rhodes remained standing.

"Gerald says you want to ask something about That Day," Edith said. Rhodes could hear the capital letters on the last two words.

"It's about Buck Sandstrom," Rhodes said. "Do you know him?"

"Oh, yes. We used to see Buck often. Not so much anymore, though. I can't remember the last time."

"I was wondering about that day," Rhodes said, hoping he hadn't put the capitals into his own voice. "At the reunion. Did Buck ever wander off away from the rest of the group?"

Edith sat and thought it over for even longer than her husband had. Her eyes took on a faraway look, and Rhodes was beginning to wonder if she'd forgotten that he was even in the room.

Evidently she hadn't. She said, "I wish I could help you, Sheriff. I really do. But I just can't remember. We were all having such a good time . . ."

Her voice trailed off, and she looked down at her hands. Rhodes saw that she had a tissue crumpled up in one of them. She smoothed it out on her lap and then dabbed at her eyes.

Rhodes was sorry he'd bothered her. This visit had been a mistake from the beginning. He should have gone straight to Buck Sandstrom, but he'd thought maybe he could find out something that would give him an edge. Instead he'd just upset Edith Bolton, and probably Gerald, too.

"I'd better be going," he said.

Bolton got up to show him to the door. As they were leaving the room, Edith said, "There was one thing."

Rhodes barely heard her. He turned around and said, "What?"

"Ronnie liked Buck. He looked up to him because Buck was older. Like Buck looked up to Gerald."

She almost managed to smile at her husband, but it didn't quite come off.

"So I'm sure Buck and Ronnie did spend some time together That Day. I don't know if that means anything."

Rhodes didn't know, either, but he thanked her for the information.

When Bolton and Rhodes got to the front door, Bolton said, "Tell me the truth, Sheriff. Is Larry Colley's murder connected to Ronnie's disappearance? Is Buck?"

Rhodes told him the truth. He said, "I don't know."

20

▼

BUCK SANDSTROM HAD HIS OWN BUSINESS, A QUICKIE LUBE THAT specialized in oil changes and state inspections. It had three bays, and it was busy most of the time.

Rhodes parked the county car away from the tiny office and away from the bays. When he got out of the car, he saw heat waves rising off the concrete.

He started toward the bays, but he hadn't gotten more than a couple of steps before he was accosted by a young man in a khaki-colored jumpsuit with QUICKIE LUBE stitched on the left front side over the name LANNY. His khaki cap had the bright yellow and black Quickie logo on it.

"Ready to switch the county business over to us, Sheriff?" Lanny said.

He was smiling, and Rhodes knew he was kidding. Still, he gave him an answer.

"We're still getting our oil changed at the county barn," he said. "Is Buck here today?"

Lanny laughed. "He's always here. Not that he doesn't trust us, but he likes to be here in case there's a problem. Not that we ever have a problem."

Lanny laughed again, but this time there was a hint of nervousness in it. Rhodes figured that was because one of the things every employee at the Quickie Lube did was try to sell every customer an additional product or service: an air filter, a radiator flush, a transmission fluid change, something that the customer hadn't come in for and had no thought of buying. It wasn't illegal, but it sometimes caused a problem when a customer thought he was being hassled or cheated. Rhodes had heard from more than one of them.

"You want to talk to Buck?" Lanny said. "I can get him for you."

"Fine. I'll wait here."

"Cooler in the office."

The office held a counter, a soft drink machine, and several chairs for the customers. Through the full-length windows, Rhodes could see people sitting in the chairs.

"I'd rather talk to him in private."

"Sure, sure," Lanny said, laughing even more nervously. "I'll get Buck right now."

He went into the first bay and disappeared down a red metal stairway into the pit that ran along under all three bays. In a couple of minutes, Buck Sandstrom came climbing up the stairs and walked over to Rhodes, wiping his hands on a red rag. He stuck the rag in his side pocket and put out his hand.

"Don't worry," he said. "My hand's clean."

Rhodes wasn't worried. He'd shaken plenty of greasy hands in his time.

"Is this about Larry?" Buck said, releasing Rhodes's hand.

Buck was wearing the company jumpsuit, too, but his didn't fit him very well. He was too big for it, and the shoulders looked tight and uncomfortable. Rhodes remembered that Buck had played linebacker for the Clearview Catamounts during his high school days and then went on to play at the junior college where Tom Vance taught. Buck had been good enough to get a lot of offers from big universities, but he'd torn up a knee during his sophomore year and had given up on education and football. He'd come back to Clearview and worked at a couple of different jobs before getting the Quickie franchise.

"What makes you think it's about Larry?" Rhodes said.

"Karen told me you'd talked to her. I figured it would be my turn next." Buck turned and gestured with his thumb. "It'd be cooler in the shade."

There was a pecan tree sticking up through a big square hole in the center of the concrete near the side of the office. Buck started toward it without waiting for Rhodes to say anything. Rhodes followed him.

Buck was right. It was cooler in the shade. A locust whined somewhere up in the tree.

"What I was wondering," Rhodes said, "is why Karen lied to me about Larry."

"She didn't lie to you," Buck said.

Rhodes was willing to concede the point. After all, he wasn't a hundred percent certain.

"Maybe not. But she told me she hadn't seen Larry or talked to him in years. I'm not sure that's strictly true."

Buck put out a hand and leaned against the pecan tree. "She didn't say she hadn't seen him. She said she hadn't talked to him."

So Karen and Buck had discussed her conversation with Rhodes. For some reason, Rhodes had thought that Karen might not mention it to her husband.

"So she's seen him?" Rhodes said.

"You could say that, but it's stretching. He's been kind of hanging around."

Rhodes thought back over what Karen had said to him. She'd told him that she hadn't had any contact with Colley—no cards, no calls—but she hadn't said anything about hanging around. Rhodes asked Buck to explain what he meant.

"Now and then he'd be outside the library when she left to come home. He never spoke to her, and she wouldn't even look in his direction. She didn't like him much."

"Why would he be doing that?" Rhodes asked.

"I don't know. I can tell you what I think, but that's about it."

"That's fine." Rhodes was willing to listen to anything that might help him. "Tell me what you think."

Buck pushed away from the tree and folded his arms across the front of his jumpsuit. "Larry was always a jerk."

That isn't exactly news, Rhodes thought, but he didn't say so. He waited for Buck to continue.

"So I think he was sorry about what had happened between him and Karen, the divorce and all. He never paid her much attention, just went right on living the way he had before they were married." Buck grinned. "I never made that mistake."

"You're smarter than Larry, then."

"That's right, I am. But Larry's getting older. *Was* getting older. I guess he won't be getting any older now."

Not unless he knew a secret the rest of us don't, Rhodes thought.

"Anyway," Buck said, "I figure he was wondering what his life would've been like if he'd had any sense. If he'd acted like a husband and stayed with Karen. Maybe he even missed her, missed being married to her and having a real life. So he sort of started hanging around her, wondering if there was any way they could ever get back together."

It was an interesting theory, but nobody was ever going to be able to test it. So Rhodes didn't see any need to keep discussing it. He said, "Someone made a couple of calls to Larry's cell phone from your number. Was that you or Karen?"

"She told you she hadn't talked to him, and she hadn't. I'm the one who called him. She doesn't even know I did it."

"How did you get his number?"

"It's in the ads for that repair business he and Bud Turley have. Had. Whatever."

Rhodes hadn't seen any ads and said so.

"You should look at the *Clearview Herald.* There's one in there every week. 'Call Bud or Larry, day or night' and then the numbers. So I called."

"And what did you tell him?"

"What do you think I told him? I told him to stay the hell away from my wife or we'd both have to go to the hospital."

Rhodes looked out across the concrete parking area and saw the heat waves shimmering up from the surface. He didn't ask why they'd both have to go to the hospital, but Buck told him anyway.

"Because I'd kick his ass so hard, it'd take major surgery to get my foot out."

"And what happened then?" Rhodes asked.

"Nothing." Buck pushed his cap up on his head. "Nothing except that he didn't turn up outside the library again. If you're thinking I killed him, you're barking up the wrong tree."

"What kind of car do you drive?" Rhodes asked.

"What does that have to do with anything?"

"Humor me."

"Sure," Buck said. "Come around to the back."

They left the shade of the pecan tree and walked behind the office.

"There she is," Buck said, pointing to a Chevrolet pickup that Rhodes guessed must have been nearly forty years old. It was a bright cherry red, and the Quickie Lube logo was painted on the doors.

"You must have seen me around town," Buck said. "It's hard to miss me. Good advertising for the business, and it still drives like a new one."

"I have an Edsel," Rhodes said. "It doesn't drive like a new one, though."

"Maybe it does," Buck said. "From what I've heard about those things, they didn't drive all that good when they were new."

Rhodes grinned. "You could be right. Let's get back to that shade."

They went to stand under the pecan tree again, and Rhodes said, "Here's another question for you."

"What's that?"

"You only talked to Larry on the phone, right? You never confronted him in person?"

"Nope. He didn't even have his oil changed here. Probably did it himself out there at Bud's place."

"Probably," Rhodes said. "You were at Gerald Bolton's the day his son disappeared, weren't you?"

Buck moved closer to the tree and leaned his shoulder against it. The locust was still whining somewhere up above, and another one joined in. Rhodes looked into the tree but couldn't see either of them.

"I was there," Buck said. "What's that have to do with anything?"

"Maybe nothing. But sometimes things that don't get closed out in the past can have an effect on what's happening now."

"Ronnie was a good kid. He and I got along. I've always wondered what happened to him. He was just gone, like he'd never been there."

"Were you with him that day?"

"Some. We played horseshoes for a while that morning, but he was more interested in visiting with his cousin from California than with me. He could see me any old time."

Buck stopped and seemed to think about that last sentence.

"He didn't see you again after that day," Rhodes pointed out.

"I've thought about that a lot. Whose fault it was, I mean."

"It wasn't anybody's fault, the way I heard it."

"Maybe not. I've wondered about a few things, though."

Rhodes asked him what things he'd wondered about.

Buck pushed away from the tree, seeming to use only his shoulder. Rhodes tried to remember if he'd ever been quite that spry.

"I shouldn't have said anything. It's nothing."

"Tell me anyway."

"Well, you know how Gerald tells everybody that he warned Ronnie and his cousin not to go in the woods?"

Rhodes said that he knew.

"I'm not so sure that's true. I'm the one who told Ronnie a lot of stories about the wild hogs, but they were more funny than scary, the way I did it. Gerald was drinking some beer that day. Hell, everybody was drinking some beer, I guess. Anyway, I don't remember him telling Ronnie anything, or even paying much attention to him. I don't think he even knew the kid had wandered away. I'm the one who noticed. When I told Gerald, he waved me off. He didn't even get worried for another half hour or more."

Rhodes thought back over the file he'd looked at that morning. "I don't remember seeing an interview with you in my files," he said. "I thought I talked to just about everybody who was there."

"You didn't talk to me, and if you had, I wouldn't have mentioned anything like what I just said. It's just something I've wondered about over the years."

Rhodes thought it over. If Bolton felt guilty about what had happened to his son and had lied to cover it up, that was one thing. It would explain a little about the Boltons themselves, too.

On the other hand, Buck might be lying. People lied to Rhodes all the time. It was part of his job to separate the true from the false in what he was told.

"All right," Rhodes said. "Thanks for telling me and for taking the time to talk to me."

"Don't mention it," Buck said. "I try to stay on the right side of the law all the time."

Rhodes went back to his car. As he was driving away, he looked in his mirror and saw Buck talking to Lanny. Lanny was probably getting a price on a new timing belt that he wanted to sell to somebody, Rhodes thought. Just a couple of semihonest businessmen hard at work.

Rhodes was headed to the Dairy Queen to get himself a Blizzard when Hack came on the radio to tell him that there was a disturbance at the public library. He wasn't clear on what kind of disturbance it was.

"Lots of yellin' goin' on in the background," Hack said. "I couldn't make out just exactly what the caller was sayin'." The caller, he told Rhodes, was Dora Foley, the head librarian. "She was kinda excited. They don't get a lot of disturbances at the library. They like it quiet."

Rhodes said he'd get right over there.

The Clearview Public Library was big and square and white, a slab-sided building that sat right in the middle of an entire block surrounded by a wide lawn on all sides.

There was plenty of parking, but Rhodes had to walk what seemed like quite a distance to get to the door. When he got there, he had to push through a group of five or six people who were gathered to watch the fun inside. They were cheering someone or something, and they didn't much want to give up their positions when Rhodes asked them to move aside.

He was able to clear a path through them, however, and he was glad to get into the cool air-conditioned library. He saw Dora Foley, who wore glasses and put her graying hair up in a bun on top of her head, as if she'd studied pictures of librarians in books from the 1940s and decided that she wanted to look as much like them as possible.

Dora stood behind the circulation desk, and Karen Sandstrom was beside her. As Rhodes watched, a book came wobbling through the air from the children's section, pages flopping like useless wings. The two women at the desk leaned to the left and right. The book passed between them and hit the wall behind them.

Dora picked it up and put it in a stack of books on the desk. Then she saw Rhodes and said in a loud voice, "The sheriff is here. You're in big trouble now."

"I'm not afraid of the sheriff," said a woman from somewhere in the children's section.

Rhodes couldn't see the speaker, but he recognized her voice.

"What's going on here, Mary Jo?" he said.

"She's crazy, that's what," Dora said. "She came in here and started yelling and throwing books. She's going to have to pay for the ones she's mutilated, too. I won't put up with that kind of thing."

"I'm not crazy," Mary Jo said. She walked out where Rhodes could see her. "I'm just pissed off."

She was wearing her tight jeans and western shirt, as if she'd dressed for her job at the Round-Up, but she didn't have on her cowboy hat. Her hair was loose and fell around her face.

"We don't allow that kind of language in here, either," Dora said. "It's against library rules."

Dora hadn't been in Clearview long. She'd moved there about six months earlier from a branch library in Houston. Jennifer

Loam had interviewed her for the paper, and Dora had said that she'd left the city because she wanted to get away from the crude habits and manners of the people who lived there.

Little did she know what she was getting into, Rhodes thought. Small towns were not necessarily places of gentility and elegance.

As if to prove what Rhodes was thinking, Mary Jo said she didn't give a damn about library rules.

"Arrest her, Sheriff," Dora said, pointing in Mary Jo's direction. "Arrest her right now."

"I'll take care of this, Dora," Rhodes said. "Mary Jo, you and I need to have a talk."

Mary Jo told him what he could do with his talk.

"See what I mean?" Dora said. "She's crazy as a bedbug. We can't have language like that in the library!"

Mary Jo grabbed a book off a shelf and heaved it in Dora's direction. It was a heavy book, and it didn't make it to the desk. It hit on the floor and slid a foot or two. Rhodes could see the title. Something about Harry Potter.

"Arrest her, Sheriff!" Dora yelled.

"Not right now," Rhodes said. "She and Karen and I will just borrow your meeting room for a little while and talk things over."

Rhodes went into the library and walked around the far end of the desk.

"The room's right back here, Mary Jo. Come on. You, too, Karen."

He went on to the room and sat down to see if anyone would show up. After a few seconds Karen came in.

"Hey, Sheriff," she said.

"Have a seat," Rhodes said, and she did.

They waited without talking for another minute or two. Mary Jo stuck her head in the door. She looked to Rhodes like a woman who badly needed a cigarette. Rhodes knew that if she lit one in the library, Dora would have a stroke, so he didn't suggest it. Mary Jo might very well have taken him up on it.

"I'm not going to jail," Mary Jo said, still showing no more than her head. "All I did was throw a few books."

"We'll see," Rhodes said. "Come on in and sit down. You'd better close the door, too."

Mary Jo came in. She closed the door behind her and went to a chair at the end of the table, as far from Karen as she could get.

"So," Rhodes said. "What was all that about?"

"You'll have to ask Mary Jo," Karen said. "I was just doing my job when she came in and went nuts."

"I'm not nuts, and you and old lady Foley better quit saying I am. I could sue you for something or other if you don't."

"Just calm down," Rhodes said.

He waited while the two women glared at each other for a little while. Then he said to Mary Jo, "Now tell me why you came in here and started throwing books."

"Ask her," Mary Jo said, nodding in Karen's direction. "She knows."

Rhodes looked at Karen, who shrugged.

"I'm asking you, Mary Jo," he said.

Mary Jo gave a theatrical sigh.

"I guess I was a little upset."

That was better than "pissed off." Rhodes figured that Mary Jo was calming down.

"Why were you upset?" he asked.

Mary Jo looked at Karen and pushed her hair away from her face. Rhodes thought she might say "Ask her" again. Mary Jo fooled him, though.

She said, "Because she killed Larry, that's why."

21

▼

NOBODY SAID ANYTHING AT FIRST, AND THEN KAREN STARTED TO laugh.

"What're you laughing at?" Mary Jo said.

"You," Karen said when she got her laughter under control. She got a tissue out of her purse and wiped her eyes. "I thought you said you weren't crazy."

"I'm not crazy, and you know it."

"Then why are you saying I killed Larry?"

"You think I don't know he was sniffing around you? I knew, all right."

Karen sneaked a look at Rhodes and said, "I don't know what you're talking about."

"I do," Rhodes said. "I've already talked to Buck today. You didn't quite get around to telling me everything you know during our first conversation."

Karen slumped back against her chair. "I should've known you'd find out. I don't know why I didn't tell you."

"Because you killed Larry," Mary Jo said, slapping the tabletop with the flat of her hand. "That's why."

Karen opened her mouth to argue, but Rhodes stopped her. He was afraid things were about to degenerate into a *Did not, did so* shouting match.

"What difference would it make to you if she did kill him?" Rhodes asked Mary Jo. "As I remember, you told me that you weren't sorry Larry was dead. You called him a lowlife, not to mention a couple of other things. And you said he never spent any time with you."

Mary Jo's mouth twisted, and a tear trickled out of the corner of her eye.

"Maybe I exaggerated," she said. "Me and Larry had some good times. Not many, but a few. It wasn't right that he was sniffing around Karen again."

Karen's eyes widened. "You were jealous?"

Mary Jo sniffled. "Maybe," she said.

Karen handed her a tissue.

"Thanks," Mary Jo said.

She took it and wiped her eyes, then blew her nose. She got up and threw the tissue in a trash can that sat in the corner of the room. When she sat back down, she was more composed.

"I drove by here one afternoon and saw him watching the door," she said. "I knew what he was waiting for. I think he missed you even when he was married to me. After all, you were a librarian, and I was just a waitress, which is all I'll ever be."

That wasn't much different from what Buck Sandstrom had

said about Larry earlier, and for all Rhodes knew it was equally accurate.

"I don't know what he was thinking," Karen said. She got up and moved over to sit beside Mary Jo, whose hands were clasped on top of the table. Karen put her hand on top of Mary Jo's. "But whatever it was, it didn't matter to me. I didn't want him back. He wasn't worth even thinking about, and you shouldn't worry about what he thought of you. You have a good job, you take home a salary, you're responsible for yourself. Larry wasn't any of those things. You're a lot better than he ever was."

"Maybe he was trying to be responsible," Mary Jo said. "Maybe he'd thought about how empty his life was and wanted to do better."

It sounded to Rhodes like something Mary Jo might have heard on a soap opera, but again it echoed Buck's assessment. Somehow it seemed to Rhodes that what they said should have meant more to him, that it tied into something that he'd overlooked, something that had been trying to get his attention but that he kept missing.

Karen and Mary Jo continued to talk, and it was as if Rhodes weren't even in the room. He decided that he might as well leave. Mary Jo wouldn't be throwing any more books, and the library could go back to its normal routine.

Rhodes closed the door quietly as he left, and he stopped at the front desk to speak to Dora Foley. As far as he could tell, the disturbance seemed to be forgotten. People were using the computers and flipping through the magazines. One young woman was helping her little boy pick out a book in the children's section.

Dora Foley was behind the desk. She had a harried look. "I hope you're going to arrest that woman," she said, pushing at her bun to straighten it. "It will take us quite a while to reshelve the books she threw, and some of them might need repair. We don't get a lot of money from the city for things like that."

"I don't think it will break the city to pay for a few book repairs," Rhodes said.

"And that's not all," Dora said, as if Rhodes hadn't spoken. "You heard the language she used. I'm sure that's against the law."

"I'm afraid not," Rhodes said. "That is, unless you want to file a specific complaint. Disturbing the peace, maybe, or causing a public nuisance."

Dora folded her arms across her chest. "I don't want to cause trouble. But still . . ."

"Mary Jo was upset," Rhodes said. "You have to make allowances for that sort of thing."

After a pause, Dora said, "I suppose that's true. If you say so. But I feel it was highly inappropriate."

"It was. But it won't happen again."

"I don't see how you can be sure of that."

"Because I'm an experienced lawman," Rhodes said.

Dora Foley grinned. "Well," she said, "I guess that settles that."

At times when Rhodes needed to get away from everyone, he liked to visit his "official" office in the courthouse. He could have worked out of it all the time if he'd wanted to, but that would have involved some changes in his routine that he wasn't ready to make. So he went there only when he wanted to get away for a while. Even at that, he had to call the jail to let Hack know where he'd be. He got on the radio.

"Just as well you called in," Hack said.

Of course, he didn't say why. He wanted Rhodes to ask, and rather than prolong the agony, Rhodes gave in and said, "Why?"

"Because we've had a couple of calls," Hack said.

"What kind of calls?"

"The kind of calls the sheriff needs to know about."

Rhodes didn't sigh into the mike, as he figured it would give Hack too much satisfaction. He said, "Are you going to let me know what they were?"

"You don't have to get snippy about it," Hack said.

"I'm not getting snippy."

"Yes, you are. I know snippy when I hear it."

"Never mind about snippy. Tell me about the calls."

"One of 'em was from that Dr. Vance. He just wanted you to know that he'd talked to Bob Anderson, the biology teacher out at the high school, and some of Bob's students are going out to the mammoth dig this afternoon to help out. They're prob'ly there by now. He mentioned those two women friends of yours, too."

Rhodes waited. Hack said nothing. Rhodes didn't try to outwait him. He said, "What did he say about them?"

"That they'd been a big help to him. They don't mind gettin' dirty, he says. He meant that as a compliment. He thinks they've located where a tusk might be. You might want to let Bud Turley know."

Rhodes hadn't thought about Turley and his friends all day. "I will if I see him. Why don't you call the motel and see if those Bigfoot hunters checked out. I meant to do that, but I didn't."

"You must be gettin' old and forgetful. Anyway, you don't have to worry about it. Ruth went by there around noon, which is checkout time in case you didn't know. She said the parkin' lot was clear."

Rhodes was glad to hear that someone was taking care of business. He said, "Good. Is there anything else I need to know about in those calls?"

"Just the usual. Some stray horses on the road out by Obert, windshield wipers stolen off a car parked downtown. Some trucker got lost on the way to the power plant and called for help."

"I'm guessing that all that's been taken care of."

"Yeah. But you're the sheriff. You need to be informed of what's goin' on."

"And I appreciate it," Rhodes said. "If there's an emergency, give me a call at the courthouse."

"What's an emergency?"

"Stray horses don't count," Rhodes told him.

No trials were going on that afternoon, and the high-ceilinged halls in the courthouse were quiet. There were the usual lines in the county clerk's office, but even there it wasn't as hectic as it sometimes was. Rhodes's rubber-soled shoes squeaked along the marble floors.

Rhodes went first to the new Dr Pepper machine, which he didn't like at all. For as long as he could remember, he'd been able to get Dr Pepper in glass bottles from an old machine that, he was forced to admit, had seen better days. But when it had broken down a month or so ago, it had been replaced by a garish new eight-foot-tall monstrosity that looked more like some kind of futuristic jukebox than a soft drink machine.

Not that Rhodes cared much about its appearance. What mattered to him was that it dispensed Dr Pepper in large plastic bottles.

The plastic bottles were better than cans, of course, and there was quite a bit more Dr Pepper in them than in a can or the old glass bottles, but the fact was that Dr Pepper just tasted better in glass.

Taste, Rhodes supposed, was relative. He had never quite recovered from the big changeover to the use of corn syrup instead of sugar as the sweetener in his favorite drink. A lot of years had gone by, and by now he should have adjusted. Others may have been able to, but he hadn't.

He was sure that a spokesperson for Dr Pepper would maintain that the taste was unaffected by the change, but Rhodes knew better. At least one bottler, in Dublin, Texas, still made Dr Pepper the old-fashioned way, and Rhodes had once ordered a case of the "real" ones and had it sent to him. He'd parceled the drinks out over a month or so, enjoying every sip.

Now, however, Rhodes had to settle for what he could get, and that was a big clear plastic bottle, dispensed with such a clunking frenzy that it was well shaken by the time it arrived in the slot. He had to wait a couple of minutes before opening it to be sure it didn't fizz all over his hand and the courthouse floor.

While he was waiting, he bought a package of orange crackers with peanut butter filling from another new machine. When the crackers fell into the bin, Rhodes got them out and went to his office.

He brushed away a spiderweb that dangled from a light fixture. He was going to have to come in more often.

Rhodes sat in his chair and put the crackers on his desk while he opened the Dr Pepper. It fizzed, but only a little. He took a swallow and opened the crackers, thinking that he really needed to do something about his eating habits.

He usually managed to eat some shredded wheat in the mornings. He figured that had to be good for him. Ivy said it was like eating hay, but he told her that fiber was important for a healthy diet.

Then Ivy saw to it that he had something in the evenings, something that was considerably better than the beanie-weenie, bologna sandwich, or occasional bowl of canned chili that had been his staples before he'd married her. She insisted that he eat a low-fat meal, but the menu was at least a little bit varied.

It was lunch that was doing him in. A Blizzard wasn't a balanced meal, no matter how you looked at it, and you couldn't say much more for a Dr Pepper and a package of peanut butter and crackers, either.

I'll do better, Rhodes thought as he picked up the crackers and opened the cellophane wrapper. *Starting tomorrow. Or the next day.*

The cellophane crackled open, and Rhodes got out the first orange square.

Protein, he thought as he took a bite of the cracker. *Peanut butter has protein. Protein's good for you.*

He finished the cracker and washed it down with Dr Pepper. He leaned back and got comfortable in his chair. All he had to do was decide how all the pieces fit together, and he'd know who'd killed Larry Colley and Louetta Kennedy.

The only problem was that he didn't know for sure if he had all the pieces, much less how to fit them together.

He started by thinking about cars and trucks.

22

▼

WHAT CONCERNED RHODES WAS LOUETTA'S MURDER. HE WAS convinced that she'd been killed because she'd seen the car or truck that Colley's murderer had driven.

She'd liked to sit out on the front porch of her store in her lawn chair, and she'd kept an eye on the road to see who passed by. She hadn't had a lot of other entertainment, what with no TV set or even a radio in the store.

So Rhodes started with the assumption that she'd seen her killer drive by with Larry Colley. He must have had a distinctive vehicle because otherwise he wouldn't have been worried. Louetta's eyesight couldn't have been good enough to allow her to see who was in a particular car, but what if the killer had been driving a Jeep, say, or an old red Chevrolet truck with an advertising sign painted on the side? Louetta wouldn't have needed twenty-twenty vision to make either of those out easily.

Then again, certain cars and trucks, even if not distinctive, would have been familiar to her. Colley's S-10, for example, would have passed by often, what with Colley working on Bolton's camp house, and Colley would have stopped at the store to buy a snack now and then.

Chester Johnson went by there all the time to hunt hogs on Bolton's land. Louetta would have known his truck by sight, too, not that it mattered. Chester had gone to her store to call Rhodes about finding Colley's body, and he'd insisted that he wouldn't have called if he'd been the killer.

Rhodes didn't necessarily believe him. Johnson actually had a motive for killing Colley. It wasn't much of a motive, but it was more than enough to cause a murder. Rhodes had known of people being killed for sillier things. Johnson might have called just to fool the sheriff, which was why he had sent Johnson's rifle off for testing just in case.

Buck Sandstrom might also have had a motive, and Karen might have as well. She could have driven the truck as easily as Buck. But why would either of them take Colley to Big Woods to kill him? It didn't make sense.

Johnson, on the other hand, was going there to hunt, or so he claimed, and Colley was working on Bolton's house. The two might easily have run into each other and gotten into an argument that resulted in Colley's death. Johnson might even have arranged to meet him, for that matter.

Bud Turley didn't have a motive that Rhodes could think of, but he'd been in the vicinity on the day Colley had died. However, since he'd been there and admitted it, having found the mammoth, he wouldn't have had to kill Louetta just because she saw his Jeep.

All of which left Rhodes pretty much right back where he'd started, with a lot of questions but no answers.

He finished the crackers, drank the rest of the Dr Pepper, and left the courthouse.

Rhodes called Hack on the radio to say that he was going to have a look at the mammoth dig. He didn't ask if there had been any important calls about stray horses. He knew Hack would have told him.

The mammoth dig had undergone a transformation in the short time since Rhodes had last seen it.

The canopy was stretched out, but it wasn't making a lot of shade over the dig because the sun was too low in the sky. There were little red triangular flags stuck into the ground, and Rhodes tried to determine if there was a pattern. If there was, he couldn't see it.

Bob Anderson, the biology teacher from Clearview High, was supervising a group of students who were crouched over a shallow trench someone had dug. High school had already been in session for a couple of weeks. It seemed to Rhodes that it was starting earlier every year. If the trend continued, it wouldn't be long until the break between the spring and fall semesters was hardly longer than the Christmas vacation.

Anderson was decked out in a floppy cotton safari hat and a pair of old boots. The students had on their school clothes, jeans mostly.

Tom Vance was brushing off something he held in his right hand. Claudia and Jan were leaning in to have a look at it. They had both managed to find Clearview Catamount caps, and they had them pulled down over most of their hair.

Everybody was dirty enough to be in need of a long shower, but nobody seemed to mind. In fact, it seemed to Rhodes that they were all having a good time.

"What do you have there?" he asked Vance.

The professor looked up to where Rhodes was standing at the top of the bank and said, "A little piece of a jawbone, I think. Bob's got his students looking for the tusk."

"Finding the tusk is a good thing, right?"

"If it's intact. We'll have to wait until tomorrow to find out. We're about ready to quit for the day. It's getting a little late for digging, and we don't want to harm anything."

Rhodes looked over toward the woods. It wouldn't be long before the sun sank behind the trees.

"This is just great," Jan said. "I never thought we'd get involved in something like this when we came here to do a story about a murder. We're going to make this mammoth famous."

"More important," Claudia said, "now that we've got two stories to write, *we* might become famous."

Rhodes thought that their plans for articles might have made them forget about selling their book with a handsome crimebusting sheriff as the hero. In a way it was too bad. The world needed more books like that.

"Has Bud Turley been here today?" he said.

"We haven't seen him," Claudia said. "Maybe after what happened last night, he's ashamed to come out in public. I certainly wouldn't blame him."

Rhodes had to grin at that. He couldn't think of anything that would keep Bud away from something that might bring him a little publicity.

"I take it that you haven't had any trouble from that bunch you met at the restaurant," Rhodes said.

"Not a bit," Claudia said. "But we told Tom about it, and he's a little worried."

"Vandalism," Vance said. "Those fellas might want to get a little revenge for what happened to them, and since they can't do anything to you, they might decide to do it to us."

"I don't think you're in any danger," Rhodes told him.

"I didn't mean *us*, exactly. I meant to the site. They could do plenty of damage here if they wanted to."

Rhodes wasn't too worried about it. He said, "They've cleared out of the motel. I'm pretty sure they're all back home by now, thinking about Bigfoot again. Only a couple of them really even know this dig is here, and Bud won't tell them. He doesn't want this place messed up any more than you do."

"Well, I hope they don't decide to come around here and cause problems," Bob Anderson said, coming over to join Vance and the two women. "My students will never get another chance like this. It's something they can put on their college applications that nobody else is going to have."

"Bud Turley providing educational opportunities for future college students," Rhodes said. "That's something I never thought I'd say."

"He's done a lot of people a good turn by making this find," Vance said. "Whether he intended to or not. And I have to give him credit for bringing that tooth to your office instead of digging this whole place up by himself. He'd have made a mess of it."

It wasn't that Bud was such a good guy, Rhodes thought. If he'd known he'd found nothing more than a mammoth's tooth, he probably wouldn't even have bothered with it. It was the thought that the tooth came from Bigfoot that motivated Bud, at least at first. Now he might be interested in the mammoth because it was going to get his name in the papers.

"We'd better get back to work and finish up while we have the light," Vance said. "I wish we could keep on with this during the school year."

"Maybe you could work something out," Jan said. "I'm sure I could get down here on weekends, if nothing else."

"I know I could," Claudia said.

"Maybe I could, too," Vance said. "Bob, what do you think?"

"We'd love to do it," Anderson said. "Or I would. And I'm sure most of the students would, too."

Even if they wouldn't, Rhodes thought, they'd want it on their college applications. He said, "I have to go back to town now. It looks like you have things under control here, but be sure to call if you need anything from my office."

Vance said that he would.

On his way back to town, Rhodes stopped by Bud Turley's place. He could hear the loud country music playing from the shop in back, so he went that way and found Bud working on a four-wheel ATV.

When Bud saw Rhodes, he wiped his hands and turned down the radio. His neck was purple with bruises, and Rhodes figured it hurt, but he didn't mention it. Instead he asked him about the ATV.

"That yours?" he said.

"Belongs to a friend," Bud said. His voice was husky. "I'm

working on it for next to nothing. It's kind of like working on a big lawn mower."

"How long have you had it here?"

"It's been a few days, why?"

"I was just wondering. Will it run?"

"It'll run," Bud said, "but it runs rough. Just needs tuning up is all. Won't take me long, now that I've got started."

Rhodes changed the subject to ask about Larry Colley's truck.

"I hadn't thought about that truck," Bud said. He was wearing his welder's cap tonight, and he took it off to wipe the top of his head with the rag he'd used on his hands. "I didn't know it was gone, and I don't know where it could be. He took good care of that sucker. It was old, but it still ran good. You think the killer stole it?"

Rhodes said he didn't know. "How about your Bigfoot friends? Did they all get out of town all right?"

"Friends, my foot." Bud touched his neck with the tips of his fingers. "You saw what that damn Charlie did to me last night."

As Rhodes remembered the incident, Bud had been the aggressor, but if Bud wanted to remember it differently, Rhodes didn't mind.

"I just want to be sure he and the others got out of town," Rhodes said. "I don't want them causing any trouble out there at the mammoth dig."

"You think they might?" Bud seemed genuinely concerned. "That woman reporter talked to me about it today. She even took my picture. There's gonna be a big story about it in the paper in a day or so."

"Those women I told you about last night want to interview you, too. You'll be a celebrity, Bud. That is, you will if nothing happens to the dig."

"Nothing will happen. I'll make sure of that. I'll call Jeff and Charlie and give them the word. You can count on me, Sheriff."

Rhodes said that he hoped so. As he drove away, he was thinking about ATVs. Whoever had clobbered Rhodes at Colley's trailer had been riding on one, and both Johnson and Bud had access to one. Rhodes wondered if Buck Sandstrom did. It was likely, since nearly everyone who lived outside the city limits owned one, and a lot of the people in town did, too.

Rhodes wondered if all the trails to the killer had grown cold already, but he didn't think so. If he kept worrying at the things he'd heard and the things he'd seen, something would point him in the right direction.

Something always did.

The next day Rhodes was up early and out in the yard with Speedo and Yancey when Ivy called him to the door. She'd been dressing for work and had her robe and house shoes on.

"It's Hack," she said, handing Rhodes the phone. "He sounds happy."

Ivy knew as well as Rhodes that nothing made Hack happier than an emergency call.

Rhodes took the phone just as Yancey sank his sharp little teeth into the bottom of his pants leg and started to shake his head from side to side. Rhodes bent over and took hold of Yancey's jaws. Yancey didn't want to let go. He growled, but a growl from Yancey wasn't exactly intimidating. Rhodes persuaded him to let go. Then he told Hack to go ahead.

"You need to get out to the mammoth dig soon as you can," Hack said.

Typically, he didn't say why.

"Why?" Rhodes said after a short pause.

"Looks like they got big trouble out there," Hack said. Ivy had been right. Hack sounded delighted. "The whole dang place has been torn up. Somebody's vandalized it."

23

▼

RHODES DROVE TO THE SITE OF THE DIG. VANCE AND BOB ANDER-son were there, but the students hadn't arrived yet. Rhodes figured they were in class and wouldn't come out until that afternoon. Claudia and Jan weren't there, either. Maybe they weren't early risers.

Hack hadn't been exaggerating much when he'd said that the place had been torn up. Chunks of earth were rooted up every-where. Some of the little red flags were still in place, but others had been trampled into the ground. One of the canopy ropes was broken.

"I guess those Bigfoot hunters that Claudia and Jan told us about didn't get the message," Anderson said. "They must've de-cided to come out here and see how much damage they could do, just to get back at you."

Rhodes had considered calling in a bulletin on Jeff and Charlie as soon as he'd gotten the call from Hack, but he'd thought it might be a good idea to wait and have a look at things first. Now he was glad he'd made that decision.

"I don't think those Bigfoot hunters did this," Rhodes said. He pointed toward the trees. "Look all along the creek bank back that way."

Anderson and Vance turned to look in the direction Rhodes had pointed.

"See how the bank's torn up?" Rhodes said. "It looks to me like the feral hogs have been out here during the night, having themselves a little fun. They're the ones to blame, not the Bigfoot boys."

"I think you're right," Vance said. "I should have known. They skipped a stretch before they got here to the dig, though. That's what threw me off."

"How messed up are things?" Rhodes asked.

"It could be worse. They didn't really dig up anything. Mostly they just messed up our markers. Some of them we can get back in about the right place. Maybe most of them."

"Not all, though," Anderson said.

"No," Vance agreed. "Not all. But enough. I took a few pictures of the layout before we left yesterday, and that'll be a big help. If we'd been farther along, it might have been worse, but this can be fixed. I was afraid when we first got here that somebody had dug up the tusk and stolen it. That would've been a real setback. But it didn't happen." He looked back toward the trees again. "I'm sorry we called you out here, Sheriff. It was just a wild goose chase."

"That's all right," Rhodes said. "I've been on a lot of those."

* * *

Back at the jail Rhodes had to deal with the usual routine things. No matter how important a single case might seem, there were always other calls coming in.

A fisherman at the lake had been backing his boat into the water and had kept on going. He was all right, but his truck was underwater. Rhodes had the man call a wrecker for that one.

There was a complaint that during the night some young women had been driving around town mooning other drivers.

"Nobody ever moons me," Hack said when he mentioned the complaint to Rhodes.

"You're too old," Lawton said. "Nobody's gonna moon an old geezer like you."

"You're not any spring chicken yourself," Hack told him. "I'd say you were just as much of a geezer as I am."

"Maybe so, but I'm not the one whinin' because young women don't ever moon him."

"I wasn't whinin'. I was just sayin' that it never happened to me."

"Sounded like whinin' to me."

"Well, it wasn't."

Rhodes stopped the argument by asking about another report he had. Someone was dumping trash illegally on one of the county roads.

"Same place they've been dumpin' it for weeks," Hack said. "You want me to tell Buddy to stake the place out?"

Rhodes told him that he didn't think so. "Buddy will catch them sooner or later. He doesn't like people who dump trash on the roads."

"Nobody does," Hack said. "But that ain't ever stopped 'em from doin' it."

The rest of the day went pretty much like that—lots of petty complaints, all of which could be handled by the deputies or left alone, and all accompanied by expert commentary from Hack and Lawton, who had opinions on everything. The problem was that all the complaints had to be dealt with, and many of them required a decision by Rhodes. They kept him busy, and they kept him from being able to devote all his attention to the murders.

It was the middle of the afternoon before things slowed down enough for Rhodes to get out the reports on the disappearance of Ronnie Bolton and start reading through them again. He couldn't help thinking that if he just read over the reports enough times, whatever he'd overlooked would jump out at him.

It didn't. He was flipping through the pages for the third or fourth time that day when the phone rang yet again and Hack answered. Rhodes could tell from his tone that he was getting excited only a few seconds into the call.

"I'll get the sheriff right out there," Hack said. "Don't touch anything."

Those last words were the ones that bothered Rhodes. They never meant anything good.

Hack hung up the phone and turned to Rhodes. There was a smile on his face, another sure sign of trouble. "You need to get back out to the mammoth dig. They've found something."

Rhodes hoped Hack was going to tell him it was a tusk. Or maybe some Clovis points that would prove that the mammoth had died at the hands of ancient hunters. The news, however, wasn't that good, not that Rhodes had expected it to be.

"What have they found?" Rhodes said.

"More bones."

There was nothing surprising in that, so Rhodes just waited. He knew there was more to come, and eventually Hack would get it told.

"Human bones," Hack said.

"From mammoth hunters?"

"No," Hack said. "They're not that old. Tom Vance says they're not very old at all."

Rhodes stood up.

"I'm on the way," he said.

When Rhodes arrived at the mammoth dig, the canopy was stretched out, and the little flags were all back in place, at least as far as Rhodes could tell, but nobody was there. Vance, Anderson, the students, Claudia, and Jan were all fifty or sixty yards away in the direction of the trees. They stood in front of three tall native pecan trees and looked down at something on the ground as they talked together.

Rhodes walked along the bank to where everyone was. Jan saw him first.

"You need to have a look at this, Sheriff," she said. "Toby's the one who found it."

A girl from Anderson's class gave Rhodes a shaky smile. "I didn't mean to," she said. "I was just walking along down here to, well . . ."

Her voice trailed off, and Rhodes looked along the bank at a thick stand of what his father had always called privy cane. Rhodes thought it might be some kind of bamboo. At one time, people had grown it around their outhouses to hide them. These days, when there weren't a lot of outhouses, a stand of it could provide a place to have a little privacy for bodily functions if you were caught short out in the country.

"I think the hogs rooted it up," Vance said. "It must have been buried in the bank at one time."

Rhodes didn't have to ask what *it* was. He could see the bones sticking out of the earth. He was surprised the hogs hadn't made more of a mess of them, but the hogs hadn't really been feeding. They'd been more interested in just rooting up the earth and moving along than in more serious matters.

The bones looked small. Remnants of cloth clung to some of them.

"We haven't touched anything," Vance said.

"Good," Rhodes said. "This is a crime scene now. You can all go back to your own excavation, but I might want some expert help later."

"Who is it?" Claudia said. "Do you know?"

"Maybe," Rhodes said, thinking of Ronnie Bolton.

After Rhodes had looked over the site, he called on Vance for the expert help. Vance carefully unearthed the rest of the bones, and it didn't take an expert to see that they had once belonged to a boy of about Ronnie Bolton's size. Rhodes could see the rib cage, and one of the bones had a large chunk missing. It might have been broken off by a bullet.

Ronnie's dental records would be easy to get, but Rhodes was already convinced from what he'd seen that the bones were Ronnie's remains and that he'd been shot. Soon after that, he'd been buried at the foot of the three pecan trees, which had been a little smaller then.

Rhodes looked up toward the road. A row of bushes and high weeds grew all along it. From the road it would be hard to see anyone down where Rhodes stood, and it had probably been much the same when Ronnie had been buried.

Not that many years ago, Ronnie Bolton had been having a good time at his family reunion. He'd wandered off with his cousin, the way boys will, and someone had killed him. Rhodes had never really expected that Ronnie would be found alive, but now that he was seeing what he believed to be solid evidence of the boy's death, he felt a little hollow inside. It was bad enough when someone as old as Louetta Kennedy was deprived of the remaining days of her life, but it seemed even sadder and more unfair when the victim was someone as young as Ronnie Bolton had been.

Rhodes tried to shake off the feeling. It wouldn't do him any good. He looked around at the burial site. He didn't expect to find any clues, not after the years that had passed, and he didn't. He went back to the county car and radioed Hack.

"You got an ID yet?" Hack asked when Rhodes told him the situation.

"No," Rhodes said. "Just a guess."

Hack had the same guess. "Ronnie Bolton."

"Maybe." Rhodes wanted to be sure he hadn't missed anything. "Get hold of Ruth and send her out here to work the crime scene."

"Ten-four," Hack said.

* * *

"I think we have three stories to write now," Jan said when Rhodes went back down to the dig.

"Maybe they're all connected," Rhodes said. He didn't mention Ronnie Bolton or his disappearance. "Sometimes things we think are over with aren't finished after all."

Jan said, "Larry Colley was killed in the woods over there, and the body of somebody else was found right here. So we have a kind of connection already. Propinquity."

It was a college-professor word, but Rhodes thought he knew what she meant.

"You could start with that," he said. "And see where it leads you."

"The question," Claudia said, "is where does it lead *you?*"

Rhodes said he wished he knew.

"See," Hack said. "This is when you need *CSI: Blacklin County.* Those CSI fellas could tell you plenty just from examinin' those bones."

"I already know plenty," Rhodes said. He was looking through the reports on Ronnie Bolton's disappearance one more time. "I know he was shot, and I know he was buried. What more do I need?"

"You need to know who it is," Lawton pointed out.

"The dental records will tell us," Rhodes said, but he was already convinced he didn't need them. He thought that Hack and Lawton were, too. "Anyway, I've sent the remains to the state crime lab. They'll be careful and thorough."

"Well, they better be." He confirmed Rhodes's suspicions by adding, "Have you called the Boltons yet?"

"I had to call them to get access to the dental records. Dr. Lowery will send them to the state lab."

Rhodes thought about how Bolton had sounded when they'd talked. He hadn't been excited about the news. If anything, he'd been subdued, but maybe he was keeping his voice down because he didn't want his wife to hear.

"Do you think it's Ronnie?" he'd said.

"I can't be sure," Rhodes had told him. "We'll have to wait for the lab to give us a positive ID. My guess is that it's him, but I don't think you should mention it to your wife yet."

"I won't. I hope . . . I don't know what I hope."

Rhodes didn't know what to say because he couldn't imagine what Bolton was feeling. For years there had been at least a chance, no matter how slim, that Ronnie was alive—and an even slimmer chance that one day he might somehow return. If the story the bones told turned out the way Rhodes thought it would, then even that slim hope was gone.

On the other hand, while it would be the end of hope, it would also be the end of uncertainty, and that might be a good thing. Rhodes wasn't sure, though, whether the two things balanced out. Only Gerald and Edith Bolton would ever know that.

"I'll let you know as soon as we're sure," Rhodes had said, and Bolton had thanked him before hanging up.

"You think you're gonna find some kind of answer in those old reports?" Hack said, breaking into Rhodes's thoughts.

"We'll have to wait and see," Rhodes told him, forgetting about his phone call to Bolton and concentrating on the papers scattered around on his desk. "I might."

His eyes wandered to one page in particular, the one that contained a description of the clothing Ronnie Bolton had been wearing on the day he disappeared: a Dallas Cowboys cap, jeans, a blue and silver Cowboys jersey.

Rhodes read the description again, thinking about the scraps of clothing that remained with the bones that the hogs had turned up. He looked back at the report. Cap, jeans, a blue and silver jersey.

Then Rhodes knew what he'd been overlooking all along.

24

▼

IT WAS THE CAPS.

Everybody wore caps. Even Claudia and Jan had gotten them for the dig.

There had been no cap on or near Larry Colley's body in Big Woods, but Rhodes couldn't remember ever having seen him without one.

Louetta had been wearing some kind of cap when Rhodes had last seen her alive. He tried to remember what the words on it had been, and after a second they came to him. CORNELL HURD BAND. The band was a group of ten or eleven musicians from Austin. Rhodes had heard one of their CDs and enjoyed it, which was why he'd remembered the name.

But there hadn't been a cap near Louetta's body when Rhodes had found her, either. There hadn't even been one in the store. The cap had disappeared.

And there was nothing that looked like a cap among the scraps of clothing with the bones that had been unearthed on the creek bank.

Three people, all dead.

Three caps, all missing.

It was possible that Rhodes just hadn't seen the pieces of the cap with Ronnie's bones—he couldn't stop thinking of them as Ronnie's—but the other two were clearly missing.

Rhodes reminded himself that Larry Colley might not have been wearing a cap when he was killed. The wound in the back of his head wasn't a clue. Colley had been hit on a spot a bit lower than where a cap would have been, so no trace of the cap would have been embedded in the wound.

Colley always wore a cap, though, Rhodes told himself. He was sure of it. Colley and Bud both wore the same kind, the long-billed welder's model.

So where were the caps?

Rhodes wondered if he could be dealing with a serial killer, the kind who took souvenirs from his victims. It hardly seemed likely that a serial-killer could be roaming loose in Blacklin County, es-pecially one who killed only three people, one long ago and two hardly a day apart. Serial killers weren't supposed to work like that. Then again, serial killers weren't exactly operating along the lines of anything resembling so-called normal behavior.

"You're lookin' mighty serious," Hack said, interrupting Rhodes's train of thought for the second time. "You must be onto somethin'."

"Maybe I am," Rhodes said, "but if that's so, I'm not sure what it is."

"You could ask me and Lawton about it. We might not be hotshot professional lawmen like you, but we're both pretty smart fellas."

"Did you ever see Larry Colley without a cap on?" Rhodes said.

"Now what kind of a question is that? It's not much of a challenge."

"It might be for somebody with a memory like yours," Lawton said. "Why don't you tell him the answer, if you think you know what it is."

"I know what it is, all right, which is more than I can say for you. You're about as likely to know as a one-eyed alley cat."

"Why don't you both tell me at once," Rhodes said. "On three. One. Two . . ."

"Yes," both men said almost together.

"Dang cheater," Lawton said to Hack. "You're supposed to wait till he says *three*."

"Yeah? What about you, I didn't hear *you* waitin'. Who's the cheater?"

"I don't know who the cheater is," Rhodes said, "but I do know who the sheriff is. And he's going to arrest both of you for disturbing the peace if you don't behave yourselves."

"I'm behavin'," Hack said. "He's the cheater."

"Never mind," Rhodes said before they could get started again. "Here's another question for you. And no cheating. What kind of car does Mary Jo Colley drive?"

That quieted them down because, as it turned out, neither one of them knew the answer.

"Who cares, anyway?" Lawton wanted to know.

"I do."

206

"Why?" Hack said.

"I have a curious nature," Rhodes said.

The truth was that while Rhodes hadn't considered Mary Jo a suspect, he was now having his doubts. The incident at the library could have been her attempt to throw suspicion on Karen Sandstrom in order to avoid being suspected herself.

Would Mary Jo collect the caps of her victims? She didn't wear a cap. She wore a western hat, or she did at work. Rhodes couldn't imagine why she'd take caps from murder victims. Of course, he couldn't imagine why anyone else would, either.

Rhodes picked up his phone and called Sam Blevins. When Sam came on the line, Rhodes asked about Mary Jo's car.

"An old Ford, I think. Don't know what year. Gray. They all look alike to me these days. Far as I know it could be a Chevrolet or even a Buick. Why?"

"I was just wondering," Rhodes said.

He thanked Sam for his help, such as it was, and hung up. It seemed safe enough to disregard Mary Jo as a suspect. Louetta wouldn't have paid much attention to her car, and if she had, it wouldn't have mattered with a vehicle so nondescript.

The Sandstroms were still in the mix, though. It was time to start checking up on where they were the day Larry Colley was killed.

Lanny, the Quickie Lube employee Rhodes had talked to, turned out to be Lanny Langstrom, and he wasn't too happy to see Rhodes show up at his door late that afternoon. He was still wearing his jumpsuit, but he didn't have on his cap. His dark hair was plastered down on his head. Rhodes could hear a TV set playing somewhere inside the house.

"My wife's fixing supper," Lanny said, coming out onto the porch and closing the door behind him. "I'd just as soon talk out here if it's all right with you."

It was fine with Rhodes. He told Lanny that he wanted to ask a question about his employer.

"I don't know if you're supposed to tell stuff about someone you work for," Lanny said, looking doubtful. "I think you're supposed to keep it confidential."

"That's lawyers and doctors," Rhodes said, wondering where Lanny had picked up that nugget of misinformation. "They have confidential relationships with their patients and clients. Everybody else is allowed to talk."

"Well, you're the sheriff," Lanny said, rubbing the side of his head just above his right ear. "I guess you'd know about stuff like that. Unless you were trying to trick me."

"I'm not trying to trick you. It's just a simple, straightforward question."

"OK. Go ahead and ask me."

"When I was at the Quickie Lube the other day, you said Buck Sandstrom was there all the time. Is that strictly true?"

"What do you mean by 'strictly'?"

"I mean is he there all the time."

"Well, everybody has to have lunch," Lanny said.

Not everybody, Rhodes thought, remembering that he hadn't, but he nodded his agreement.

"So he's not there *all* the time," Lanny said. "He takes a break from about noon till one, or that's what he always says. 'I'll be back at one.' He gets back early, though. Sometimes I wonder if he thinks we'd screw things up if he left us for very long."

"He never takes a long lunch hour?"

"Shoot, no. He's all over us, down there in the pit, checking up on the office worker, making sure we do the whole checklist instead of just part of it, and telling us what we can do to . . ."

Lanny's voice trailed off before he admitted that Buck was engaged in helping sell the customers an air filter or set of wiper blades, but Rhodes wasn't interested in that. If Lanny was telling the truth, and Rhodes didn't doubt him, then Buck wouldn't have had the time to kill Larry Colley or Louetta Kennedy.

Just to be sure, Rhodes said, "What about this week in particular? Any late lunches, any time off?"

Lanny rubbed his head again, as if doing so helped him to think. "Like I said, he's always there, checking on us. This week, every week. Not that he stays late or comes early. He's always right on time. Opens up on the dot, closes on the dot. He says a man should be at home with his family as soon as the whistle blows."

Lanny looked over his shoulder at the door, a sure sign that he was hoping Rhodes would go away and let him be with *his* family.

"Not that we have a whistle," Lanny said. "But you know what I mean."

Rhodes said that he knew and thanked him for the information.

"You're not gonna mention to Buck that I talked to you, are you?" Lanny said. "I mean, you're like a lawyer and a doctor, right? You have to keep stuff confidential."

"I won't tell anybody," Rhodes said. "You can trust me on that."

Lanny stood on the porch watching as Rhodes went to the

county car. It was a shame, Rhodes thought, that some people didn't trust their local sheriff.

Rhodes didn't bother to check up on Karen Sandstrom. She was too frail to have killed Colley and Louetta. She could have done it with a pistol, but not by brute force.

As Rhodes drove home, he thought that he was narrowing down his list of suspects pretty well.

In fact, there was now only one name left on it.

Bud Turley.

25

▼

"YOU DON'T REALLY THINK BUD WOULD KILL HIS BEST FRIEND, do you?" Ivy said.

She and Rhodes were sitting in the kitchen, eating their low-fat meal, veggie enchiladas, which Rhodes had to admit weren't bad. They were spicy, and the mushrooms inside the rolled corn tortillas were almost as good as meat. The other vegetables—zucchini, spinach, black beans—were also tasty and filling.

Of course, a platter of cheese enchiladas at the Jolly Tamale, Rhodes's favorite Mexican restaurant—which was, for that matter, the *only* Mexican restaurant in Clearview—would have been a little more satisfying, but Rhodes didn't think it would be a good idea to mention that.

"Bud's the one it comes down to," Rhodes said. "I'm still trying to figure out the motive and everything else, but Bud is definitely the number-one suspect."

Rhodes wondered what Lanny would think if he knew that the sheriff was discussing suspects with his wife. Lanny would probably think Rhodes was betraying confidential information and should be kicked out of office.

Ivy wasn't buying Rhodes's idea. She said, "I just don't think a man would kill his best friend. There's an article in the paper today about how Bud found the mammoth, and it mentions all the years that he and Larry Colley palled around together. Bud sounds awfully upset that his friend's dead."

Rhodes hadn't seen the paper, but he was sure that Jennifer Loam had done her usual excellent job of reporting. He wondered if Claudia and Jan had gotten any pointers from her. He also wondered if Claudia and Jan were doing any writing of their own, or if they were just working at the mammoth dig. Maybe he should have asked them if they had any new theories about Larry's death. He could use the help.

"Besides," Ivy said, "how does all this fit in with Ronnie Bolton?"

Rhodes had told her about the discovery at the mammoth dig, and she'd hit on another point he hadn't quite worked out.

"I don't know," he said. "Yet. But I will."

"You think there's a connection?"

"Sure. Don't you?"

Ivy got up from the table and started clearing away the dishes. Rhodes finished up his enchiladas, along with what was left of his pinto beans and Mexican rice, two more low-fat foods that he liked just fine, especially with salsa on them.

"I wouldn't be so sure of any connection," Ivy said.

She set two slices of red-meated seedless watermelon on the table in big plates. Rhodes liked watermelon, but he had an odd habit, one that he'd picked up as a kid. He liked to put salt on it, something that Ivy couldn't understand.

"It's the combination of sweet and sour," he said as he sprinkled on the salt. "It makes the watermelon even better."

Ivy shook her head. "If you say so."

Rhodes hadn't told her about the missing caps, but he thought he'd wait until he finished eating.

When he'd scraped the watermelon right down to the rind, Rhodes pushed back his chair and told her his theory about the caps.

"That's pretty shaky if you ask me," Ivy said when he'd laid it out for her. "Anything could have happened to Louetta's cap. What if somebody came by the store and just took it?"

"Why would anybody do that?"

"I don't know, but it could have happened. And you don't even know for sure that Larry was wearing a cap. Besides which, you don't know for sure that Ronnie's cap isn't buried there near where his bones were found."

"You might as well go ahead and say they aren't his bones," Rhodes told her.

"I wouldn't say that. I believe they are."

"And I believe the rest of it."

Ivy got up and put the watermelon rinds in the trash and the plates in the sink.

"Then you must be right," she said. "After all, you're the sheriff."

"You better believe it," Rhodes said.

The next morning Rhodes thought he had the answers that had been eluding him.

Sometimes it worked like that. He'd go to sleep with a problem on his mind, and during the night his unconscious mind would work it all out.

Not that he trusted his unconscious mind to be a hundred percent reliable. He preferred logic to the mysterious workings of the brain during sleep. After all, if his dreams were anything to judge by, his unconscious mind was a real piece of work.

While he ate his shredded wheat—with low-fat milk, naturally— Rhodes read the article about the mammoth dig in the *Clearview Herald,* but he couldn't really concentrate on it. He was too busy thinking about the connections he'd made while he was asleep.

Ivy came in with Yancey trailing along behind her. He never yipped at her, not the way he did at Rhodes, something that Rhodes had never quite figured out.

As soon as he saw Rhodes, Yancey pranced over to the table and started to bounce around Rhodes's chair. He was quiet for a while, but soon the yapping began.

"He wants to go out," Ivy said.

"I know," Rhodes said. He spooned in a rectangle of shredded wheat. "I'll take him in a little while."

"Don't forget to change the water in Speedo's bowl."

"I won't.

"And feed him."

"I'll do that."

"And be careful today."

"I'll do that, too."

Ivy went away to get dressed, and Rhodes finished the shredded wheat, washed out his bowl, and put the bowl in the dishwasher. Yancey was at his heels the whole time, but he'd stopped barking.

He started up the instant Rhodes opened the door, however, and he bounded out to find Speedo, who was waiting for him. The two of them charged around the yard for a while, with Yancey displaying complete unconcern for the fact that Speedo, a border collie, was several times his own size. Rhodes was certain that Yancey didn't even know that Speedo was bigger, or, if he knew it, he didn't believe it.

While the dogs romped, Rhodes sat down on the step of his little back porch and went through the events that he now believed would lead him to the answer to the question of who had killed Larry Colley.

If it went back to Ronnie Bolton, as Rhodes believed it did, then Bud had also killed Ronnie. Just why was something Rhodes's unconscious mind had neglected to tell him. It would have helped to have a motive. Maybe that would come later.

What Rhodes had been overlooking for a while was something that people had told him about Colley. Maybe he really had been trying to get his life back together, to change the way he was living and become different. Buck Sandstrom had mentioned that idea, and so had Mary Jo.

If Larry had known something about Bud Turley that he'd kept secret for years, and if the secret was something like murder, maybe he'd decided to come clean as the first step on his turnaround.

That by itself might not have been enough to cause Bud to kill him. It would be just Larry's word against Bud's. But what if Larry had some hard evidence, something like Ronnie's baseball cap, for example? That would be enough to cause Bud considerable worry, the kind of worry that might lead him to kill his friend to protect himself from a murder charge.

Friendship was all well and good, but when it came to choosing between friendship and life in prison, Rhodes was cynical enough to believe that most people would say to heck with friendship and do whatever it took to save themselves.

Well, he thought, *maybe not. Not if whatever it took was murder.* He wasn't quite cynical enough to think that most people would commit murder, but he thought a good percentage of them might very well consider it, and some of them would even go through with it.

Rhodes wasn't absolutely certain that Colley had taken the baseball cap, but it made a kind of sense. Someone had searched Colley's trailer, and a boy's baseball cap would fit into a cereal box if you stuffed it inside.

One thing still bothered Rhodes. His idea was that Colley had taken the cap from Ronnie's body, probably to keep it as evidence in case he ever needed to prove that Bud had killed Ronnie.

If that was true, why had Bud taken the caps from Colley and Louetta?

Well, Rhodes had never expected his unconscious mind to provide all the answers.

And, to tell the truth, he wished it had provided him an answer without so many *maybes* in it. That would have made things much easier all around.

One thing he considered was the fact that Bud had been so insistent that none of his Bigfoot buddies disturb the area where the mammoth had been found. As it was, the mammoth bones were a good distance from where Ronnie—if it was Ronnie—had been buried, but if a bunch of people started probing around the entire area, they might well have run across the other bones. Bud wouldn't have wanted that.

Before Rhodes could come up with any more theories, Speedo got tired of running around the yard with Yancey and located his ball. He brought it over and dropped it at Rhodes's feet, and the game began. Speedo never seemed to get tired of it, and neither did Yancey, whose contribution consisted more of yipping and yapping than anything else.

Rhodes enjoyed the game, too, but he couldn't play all morning, as pleasant as that might be. He liked it out in the backyard before the day got started. It was cooler than it would be until the next evening, and playing ball with a couple of dogs was a lot more fun than dealing with whatever problems had occurred in the county overnight.

Someone had to deal with them, though, and he was the one who was drawing a salary. He got up and stretched. After putting out food and water for Speedo, he called Yancey, and they went inside.

"Those women were moonin' people again," Hack said when Rhodes entered the jail. "They've been doin' it for two nights in a row now, and people are gettin' tired of it."

"Did anybody get a license number?" Rhodes asked.

Lawton and Hack laughed at that.

"Nobody was lookin' at a license plate," Lawton said. "Hack here's still jealous that they ain't mooned him yet."

"Don't start that," Rhodes said. "I don't have time for it. I'm going to be out and about this morning, and I might need Ruth to help out. Tell her to stay handy."

"What's goin' on?" Hack said.

"I'll tell you later," Rhodes said, and left, knowing it would drive Hack and Lawton crazy.

He was smiling at that thought when he drove away and headed for Bud Turley's place.

26

▼

TURLEY'S HOUSE WAS QUIET, AND SO WAS THE SHOP BACK IN
the barn. Rhodes got out of the county car and shut the door. He
stood for a minute, listening, but he didn't hear any country music.

He walked around to the barn. The big doors on the front were
closed. Rhodes looked at the cars and trucks parked outside. He'd
seen them in the dark, but he hadn't really examined them.

The best place to hide something was in plain sight, Rhodes
had heard, or at least that had been the theory expressed by one of
his English teachers long ago when the class had discussed some
story by Edgar Allan Poe. So if you followed Poe's logic and you
wanted to hide an old Chevy S-10 pickup, why not park it with a
bunch of other vehicles and hope no one would notice?

It was a good theory, but there was no S-10 anywhere around.
There was, however, a 1957 Oldsmobile, red over white, with
rusted-out fenders. It would look good, Rhodes thought, if someone restored it properly, but he didn't think Bud Turley was the

man for the job. Besides, Rhodes already owned a creampuff Edsel, if there was such a thing, so he didn't need an Oldsmobile. For that matter, he didn't need the Edsel.

He walked along the side of the barn to the open area in back, which hadn't been visited by a lawn mower since the Carter administration. Junked bodies of old cars hulked all around, some of them nearly hidden by grass and tall weeds.

A wrecked black Ford older than Rhodes, maybe as old as Hack and Lawton, sat with its hood up and nothing in its engine compartment except a hackberry tree with a trunk a couple of inches thick growing up through the middle.

This might be an even better place to hide a truck you wanted to get rid of, Rhodes thought, but he didn't find the S-10 there, either.

Rhodes left the cars and checked the barn's back doors. He found them closed and held together with a chain that ran through two holes in the sheet metal. Rhodes rattled the chain and gave it a good hard pull. It clanged against the inside of the doors, and Rhodes decided that the ends were hooked together by a padlock.

The barn had a couple of big windows on each side, but Rhodes couldn't see through them. They were too high. He could peer through the crack between the doors, but he couldn't really see much except the shape of the ATV that Turley had been working on.

Rhodes decided that he didn't need to see much more than that. It was clear enough that Turley wasn't there. His Jeep was gone, so he was, too. Rhodes would just have to look for him somewhere else.

Larry Colley had frequented the Pool Hall and the Dairy Queen. Rhodes thought that Bud would be likely to hang around the same places.

He went to the Pool Hall first. It was a big square building made of concrete blocks painted white. At that time of day, only a couple of cars were parked in the lot, and Turley's Jeep wasn't one of them. Rhodes drove on by.

Turley's Jeep wasn't at the Dairy Queen, either, but Rhodes figured he'd better stop and perform a more thorough investigation just to be sure that Turley wasn't hiding inside. When Rhodes went through the glass door in front, the woman behind the counter looked up and said, "Good morning, Sheriff. The usual?"

Rhodes knew then that he'd been buying too many Blizzards.

"Sure thing, Julia," he said. He'd reform tomorrow.

While he waited for the Heath Bar Blizzard, Rhodes performed a conscientious check of the booths, but he didn't see Bud Turley in any of them.

The mixing machine hummed, swirling together the soft ice cream and the bits of Heath Bar. Rhodes got out his billfold.

Julia set the Blizzard on the counter, and Rhodes paid her. She got his change and said, "Don't see you in here on Bean Day much lately."

The Dairy Queen had a big pot of pinto beans one day a week, and you could have all the beans and cornbread you could eat. Rhodes liked beans and cornbread, but not as much as he liked Blizzards.

"I'll stop by one of these days," he said. He picked up a napkin and a spoon for his Blizzard and went outside.

Rhodes sat in the car in the parking lot and ate the Blizzard while he thought about where Turley might be.

It was possible that Bud had figured out that Rhodes was on to him and left the county, but Rhodes didn't see how that could have happened. He hadn't told anyone his suspicions except Ivy, who certainly hadn't told Bud, and he was unlikely to figure it out for himself.

Only one other place to look came to mind, and that was the mammoth dig. Rhodes finished his Blizzard and got out of the car to throw the cup in the trash.

Getting back in the car, he thought of something else. Jennifer Loam might have asked Turley to come by the newspaper office for an interview. Rhodes started the car and headed over to the building that housed the *Clearview Herald*.

Turley wasn't there, however, and neither was Jennifer Loam. Sharon Moncrief, who sold classified advertising and had a desk in a little cubicle near the front door of the *Herald* building, told Rhodes that Jennifer had called Turley earlier and told him to meet her at the mammoth dig. She wanted to get some photos of him there.

Rhodes thanked Sharon and left to drive to the site. He should have mentioned to Vance and the others that it wouldn't be a good idea to talk about finding the human bones, but it was too late to worry about that now. They would almost certainly say something about them to Turley, who would be very much on his guard.

Rhodes hoped that Turley wouldn't do anything stupid, and then he had to smile at himself for thinking such a thing. If there was any chance at all to do something stupid, Turley would be the one to do it. That was the story of his life.

When he reached the dig, Rhodes saw Turley's Jeep parked off to the side of the road in a line of other vehicles. Jan's black Aviator was there, along with Vance's pickup and Jennifer Loam's little car. Anderson and the high school students hadn't arrived yet, which Rhodes thought was just as well.

He pushed through the weeds in the ditch and walked down to the dig, where he saw Bud Turley crouched under the canopy near one of the little red flags. Bud was holding a little brush in his hand and appeared to Rhodes to be pretending to dust off a rock.

Jennifer Loam took a picture of him, checked it in the viewer, and told Bud that it looked fine. He stood up and handed the brush to Vance.

Rhodes looked Turley over. He was wearing his many-pocketed vest and another T-shirt with the arms ripped away. His tattoos showed up to good advantage on his muscular arms. Rhodes wondered how they'd look in the picture, but what he was really interested in was the way the vest sagged on the left side. Turley was carrying one pistol in the vest, and he might have another one or two concealed somewhere.

Rhodes remembered that he'd told Ivy that he'd be careful. He hoped Turley would let him.

Just then Claudia looked up and saw Rhodes standing there. She nudged Jan, and they waved to him. Rhodes walked down the bank to the dig.

Turley watched him come. He didn't look worried. Maybe no one had mentioned what the hogs had turned up.

"Hey, Sheriff," Bud said. "I'm gonna be a media star."

"I think I can get a whole page in the weekend edition for this story," Jennifer said. "But there's something I need to talk to you about, Sheriff."

Rhodes had a sinking feeling he knew what she had in mind. Bud might not have found out about the bones on his own, but nothing got by Jennifer.

"Can it wait?" he said.

"I don't think so. Claudia tells me there's been another find out here."

"I hope that was all right," Claudia said. "You didn't tell us it was a secret."

Rhodes shrugged. Jennifer would have found out as soon as she read the police reports, which she did nearly every day, but that might have been a little later, and Bud wouldn't have been around.

"It's no secret," Rhodes said.

"Do you know who it was yet?" Turley said.

He hadn't been wearing his cap for the picture, but he had it back on now. Rhodes didn't know where it had been.

"We might never know," Rhodes said, which was no doubt stretching the truth a bit, but he didn't really care. "Even if we find out, it'll take a long time. It's not easy to get a positive ID on remains that have been in the ground for a long time."

Turley seemed to relax a little at that comment, and Rhodes didn't mention that he was having the dental records checked. That shouldn't take long at all.

"It would be easy on TV," Jan said. "For that crew on *CSI,* I mean. They'd do a DNA analysis and have it back before the show was over."

"It always looks easy on TV," Rhodes said. "A real DNA analysis is more likely to take weeks, or even months."

Vance, who had been standing off to the side, walked over to join them. "Besides, there aren't very many crime labs as well equipped as the ones you see in those shows. There's a shortage of money to equip them, and voters don't like tax increases."

"I take it you don't mind paying taxes," Rhodes said.

"Not when they're for a good cause. But the money's probably already available. It's just being spent for other things."

"Not in this county," Rhodes said.

"No. I'm talking about the big cities."

"I hate to change the subject," Jennifer said, "but I think you're trying to avoid my question, Sheriff."

She was right, but Rhodes just gave her a smile and said, "Sorry. I got sidetracked."

"That's all right. I wanted to ask you if you've considered that the remains that were found here might be what's left of Ronnie Bolton."

Turley stiffened and looked at her sharply.

Rhodes said, as if it were the first time he'd thought of it, "Ronnie Bolton? He disappeared a long time ago. You weren't even here then. How did you happen to hear about him?"

Jennifer waved away a bug that had flown in front of her face. "I read a lot of things about this county before I moved here. Well, that's not strictly true. There's not a whole lot available to read. But the disappearance of Ronnie Bolton was big news at one time, and it turns up quite a bit on Internet searches for Blacklin County."

Technology, Rhodes thought. He knew there was a good reason he didn't trust it. The Internet was as bad as gossip.

"You didn't mention Ronnie Bolton to us," Claudia said, giving Rhodes an accusatory look. "What's the story?"

"You can look it up on the Internet later," he said.

"We'd like to know now," Jan said, and Vance nodded in agreement.

Rhodes sneaked a look at Turley out of the corner of his eye. The big man was nervous, but he didn't appear anywhere near panic. Rhodes had planned to talk to him, but he'd intended to ease into the subject of Ronnie Bolton in a roundabout way. He hadn't wanted it brought up so abruptly, and he hadn't wanted anyone else to be around.

He moved a little closer to Bud, who moved over by Jan and said, "That's an old story around here. Nobody's interested in it anymore."

"I am," Jennifer said. "It would make a great article. Can't you just see it? Two sets of bones uncovered along Pittman Creek in the same week. One set is from a mammoth dead thousands of years, and the other is from a young boy who disappeared not that long ago. How long has it been, Sheriff? I can't remember."

"A little over ten years," Rhodes said.

"A great article," Jennifer repeated. She shook her head and looked sheepish. "I'm sorry. I get carried away sometimes when it comes to stories that I might write. I realize that Ronnie Bolton was someone's son, and there must have been a lot of grief over the years, but I can't help being excited about writing about what happened."

"I don't blame you one bit," Claudia said. "We writers have to take our material from life, and we need to find out the truth about things that happened, no matter what."

"We don't know what happened," Rhodes said, more for Bud's benefit than for Claudia's. "And we don't know that we've found Ronnie Bolton. Like I said, it will take a long time to be sure about that."

"What if it is him?" Vance said. "What will you do then?"

Turley had gotten to within only a step or two of Jan, and he'd managed to get her between himself and Rhodes.

Rhodes put out a hand to point down toward the spot where

Ronnie's remains had been found and took a few steps in that direction. Bud had a reputation for violence, and having seen an example of how excitable and quick to react he'd been during the little argument in the Round-Up on the previous night, Rhodes didn't want him to get upset and start something, not with all the civilians around.

"If there's been a crime, we'll investigate," Rhodes said. "That's what we always do. But we don't know that it's him, or even that there's been a crime committed."

"Dental records," Jennifer said.

Great, Rhodes thought. *I should have known someone would come up with it.*

"That's right," Vance said. "A good lab can compare the Bolton boy's dental records with the teeth in the skull we found here. That wouldn't take long at all."

Rhodes could have said that Ronnie Bolton had never been to a dentist in his life, but he knew nobody would believe him, least of all Turley, who was swiveling his head to look from his Jeep to Rhodes as if trying to determine his chances of getting away.

"You said that you'd been looking for Bigfoot out here for years, Mr. Turley," Jennifer said, seemingly unaware that he was becoming more and more jittery. "Were you here when Ronnie Bolton disappeared?"

That was it for Bud. He said, "I'm leaving. I gotta get to work."

"You don't have to be in such a rush," Jan said. "You know this area as well as anybody, and we'd like to talk to you about what might have happened here."

"You can go with me, then," Bud said.

He took hold of Jan's arm and started up the creek bank, dragging her along with him.

"What are you doing?" Jan said, slapping at Bud's arm. She might as well have been slapping a log for all the good it did. "Let go of me."

Bud didn't let go. "You wanted to ask me questions, you can ask. Come on."

"Hold on, Bud," Rhodes said.

Bud stopped. He held Jan's arm with his left hand. With his right, he reached into his vest and brought out a 9mm Glock pistol.

"We're leaving now. She'll be fine. She can ask me her questions while I'm driving. I'll see you all later."

Rhodes knew that Bud didn't have any intention of seeing them later. He might let Jan go, or he might not, but he wouldn't be hanging around Blacklin County. Not that he'd be able to get very far.

"This isn't Bonnie and Clyde days, Bud," Rhodes said. "You'll be stopped before you get fifty miles. Why don't you let Jan go, and you and I will talk things over."

"All right," Bud said. He stopped moving up the bank. "Come on up here, and we'll talk."

Rhodes didn't believe for a second that Bud was giving up that easily, but he didn't see that he had any choice other than to humor him. He walked a couple of steps, watching Bud warily.

But he wasn't wary enough. As soon as Rhodes got a little closer, Bud shoved Jan at him as hard as he could.

Rhodes didn't have time to brace himself. Jan stumbled into him, and he fell backward with her in his arms. They hit the ground and rolled down the bank.

They would have rolled all the way to the creek bed if Claudia hadn't gotten in the way. She jumped in front of them and dropped to her knees. She tumbled over when they collided with her, but she managed to stop their progress.

Rhodes untangled himself from Jan and stood up just in time to see Bud's Jeep pull into the county road, its wheels throwing gravel that banged against the Jeep's undercarriage.

Rhodes could hear everyone yelling behind him as he ran for the county car.

Bud had taken off in the direction his Jeep was pointed, so he was headed away from any populated area.

Rhodes got on the radio and told Hack what had happened. He told him to send Ruth Grady and to alert the Department of Public Safety and the sheriff of the next county. The car rocked from side to side on the rough gravel road.

Rhodes racked the radio just in time to see the Jeep's left front wheel hit a deep chuckhole in the road. It wouldn't have been so dangerous if Bud had been driving at the usual speed for an unpaved county road, around twenty or twenty-five, but Bud was doing at least seventy.

The Jeep bounced up and tilted dangerously to the right, but it didn't flip over. Instead it righted itself, then slewed off the road, plowed through the ditch, and went over the edge of the creek bank.

Rhodes stopped the county car, got his .38 from the ankle holster, and went to see what had happened to Bud.

By the time that Rhodes got to the creek, the Jeep was down at the bottom of the bank, nosed into the shallow water. Bud had already climbed the opposite bank, and Rhodes saw only his broad back as he disappeared into Big Woods.

27

▼

RHODES HAD FOLLOWED ANOTHER MAN INTO THOSE TREES A FEW years ago. It hadn't turned out very well for either of them. Rhodes had wound up in the hospital, and he was the one who'd come out the better of the two. So he wasn't looking forward to going in there after somebody else.

On the other hand, he didn't see that he had much choice. He could have waited for Ruth Grady to show up, but she might not be there for another half hour, depending on where she'd been when Hack called her. Half an hour was too long. Rhodes couldn't afford to wait. Turley could get himself good and lost in that length of time.

If he didn't get lost, he'd have to leave the woods sooner or later, but there were so many places that he could get out that there would be no way to cover them all.

Or he might never get out. It would depend on his sense of direction. He might wander for days. Or if the feral hogs found him and if they were in a bad mood, his wandering would end abruptly, and it would be too bad for Turley. Some of those hogs weighed three hundred pounds. Some of them had tusks as sharp as ice picks.

For just a little while Rhodes considered letting Turley get away. Maybe it would be for the best just to let him disappear, the way Ronnie Bolton had disappeared. He'd fade into the woods, never to be seen again, until someone hunting for Bigfoot, maybe Jeff and Charlie, stumbled across his bones.

Rhodes knew he couldn't let it go like that. His job was to do what he could to bring Bud back.

He trotted down the creek bank and up the other side. He ran a little faster as he crossed the weedy pasture to the trees, but he slowed down when he got to the woods. He was panting a little and sweating a lot. It was definitely time to cut back on the Blizzards.

Rhodes looked into the woods. A real woodsman would be able to track Turley without much trouble, Rhodes thought. Bud would be in a hurry, and he'd be careless. He'd break limbs, step on sticks, and generally leave an easily discernible trail for the trained eye.

Rhodes didn't have a trained eye, so he'd just have to do the best he could. He stuck his pistol in his belt at the small of his back, wishing he hadn't decided to try the ankle holster. It was just too inconvenient when you needed to get at your sidearm quickly.

As Rhodes moved into the trees, he hoped he'd hear Bud blundering along ahead of him. He didn't. He didn't hear much of anything. A locust started up, and then another. That was all.

He walked along, pushing branches out of his way. Some kind of green vine with sharp stickers grew low to the ground and twined into the bushes. Occasionally it would hang on Rhodes's pant leg and pull at it.

The path that Bud had made was easy enough to follow even for someone who didn't have a trained eye, so Rhodes kept going. He hoped that Bud wouldn't try to ambush him. Rhodes didn't think he'd be able to prepare for an ambush.

He didn't think he'd be able to prepare for any feral hogs, either. He didn't see any signs of them, however, and he hoped they were all far away, lying in the shade and napping peacefully, waiting for late afternoon or night to start stirring around.

Rhodes didn't plan to be there when they started getting frisky.

It was a little cooler in the woods than it had been outside them because of the shade, even though there wasn't much of a breeze. The sunlight made crazy patterns on the ground and in the trees.

Rhodes ducked under a low limb and thought about snakes. He didn't like snakes. It might even be fair to say that he'd prefer never to see another snake as long as he lived. He decided not to think of snakes anymore.

Naturally he couldn't think of anything else.

Copperheads.

Rattlers.

Cottonmouths.

They were all pit vipers, they all had homes in Big Woods, and they were all dangerous.

Cottonmouths were aggressive. They wouldn't try to get away if they saw you. They'd attack. They stayed around water, though, and there wouldn't likely be many of them in the woods. They preferred swampy areas. There were a couple of those in Big Woods, but they were well away from where Rhodes was at the moment.

Rattlers, as far as Rhodes knew, weren't fond of water, and they weren't really aggressive. However, they were the most dangerous of the three because their bite was more likely to be fatal.

Copperheads weren't especially aggressive, either, but they weren't what anybody would call friendly. Rhodes knew they were the cause of more reported snakebites than any other species in Blacklin County. Still, while their bite was painful, it was seldom fatal.

So at least there's that much good news, Rhodes thought.

On the other hand, both copperheads and rattlers would attack if they felt threatened and if their escape routes were cut off. Rhodes promised himself that he'd never cut off a snake's escape route.

As he made his way through the trees and undergrowth, trying not to think about snakes, Rhodes was careful to glance up now and then. He didn't think that there were snakes dangling from every limb, but he'd once made the mistake of not thinking someone might climb a tree.

If Bud was agile enough, he could get up high among the leaves and hope that Rhodes would walk right past him. If he was even more agile, he could wait until Rhodes got under him and jump down on top of him. But Rhodes didn't see anything to indicate that Bud had shinned up a tree. He'd just kept right on going, deeper into the woods.

Rhodes came to a place where the trees didn't grow as thickly together as they had. He looked ahead as far as he could see, but there were just more trees, which wasn't exactly a big surprise. There were miles of trees yet to go.

A stick cracked off to the right, and Rhodes dropped to one

knee, pulling his pistol out of his belt as he did. He waited, but no more sound came. Then a mockingbird fussed above him, and Rhodes stood back up.

He walked in the direction from which the noise had come and found that Bud had gone that way. About thirty yards away were three very large black walnut trees. Someone handy at woodworking would probably like to have those trees, Rhodes thought. They'd make some nice furniture. Right now, they might be providing a hiding place for Bud Turley.

"Hey, Bud," Rhodes said. "I'm ready to call this whole thing off if you are. We can go on back to my car and drive to town. I'll send a wrecker for your Jeep. We'll get us a drink of water."

Bud, if he was hiding behind the trees, didn't answer. Maybe he wasn't thirsty, but Rhodes was.

Rhodes started to circle around, keeping his eyes on the three big trees. It wasn't easy because the other trees grew so close together and because he was trying to be quiet. He wasn't succeeding very well.

After he'd taken a few steps, he thought he saw something move behind one of the trees. It had to be Bud. There was nothing else that big, except for the hogs, and the hogs weren't as tall as Bud. At least Rhodes hoped they weren't.

Rhodes stopped trying to be quiet. He said, "I see you back there, Bud. Why don't you come on out? You don't want to get bitten by a snake or gored by some wild hog. We can talk things over, and maybe it will all turn out all right."

Rhodes didn't see how it could possibly turn out all right, not for Bud or anybody else, but Bud might not know that. It was Rhodes's opinion that a man who was guilty of murder or any other crime always wanted to believe that there was a way out, that some way, somehow, things weren't all his fault. Sometimes that was the only way to stay sane.

Assuming that Bud was sane might be a mistake. People had always thought he was strange. Maybe "strange" hadn't been the right word.

Bud, if indeed it was Bud behind the trees, didn't reply to Rhodes's comments, and while at least he hadn't started shooting, he hadn't indicated any willingness to surrender. Rhodes thought that it might be time to try a different tactic.

Unfortunately, he didn't have a different tactic in mind. He stuck the pistol in his belt again and sat down with his back to an elm tree that didn't quite hide him. He had to sit in an uncomfortable position because of the pistol, but he didn't want to put it back in the holster.

From where he sat, Rhodes could see the walnut trees, or at least parts of them. He'd just wait for Bud to make his move.

Bud didn't make his move, not even after Rhodes had waited for a full ten minutes. To Rhodes, it seemed more like an hour or two. He was getting bored, and he was getting worried about Ruth Grady. She'd find his car, and she'd see Turley's Jeep in the creek. Then she might come into the woods. Rhodes didn't know what kind of tracker she was, so he was afraid she might get lost. Worse, she might come upon Turley and scare him. Someone might get shot.

Scaring Turley, though—that wasn't a bad tactic. Rhodes wished he'd thought of it before. Now he just had to figure out a way to do it.

He scanned the area again. There was a thick growth of bushes of some kind not far from where Bud was hiding behind the trees.

If it was Bud, and if he was hiding. Rhodes was no longer sure. Bud might have crept away, though Rhodes thought he'd have noticed a movement had that happened. He wondered if Bud had gone to sleep, though that didn't seem likely. Bud had hardly been relaxed enough for that.

A dead branch lay on the ground not far from where Rhodes sat. It was about two feet long and as thick as Rhodes's arm. He crawled over to it and picked it up.

It wasn't very heavy, but it would do. He continued crawling, keeping an eye on the walnut trees and trying to get close to the bushes that he'd noticed, but not so close that Bud would see him.

When he'd gotten as near the bushes as he thought was wise under the circumstances, he glanced toward the walnut trees to see if he could spot Bud. He saw something, or someone, but he couldn't be sure if it was Bud because of the intervening trees.

Now that he was ready to try it, Rhodes's idea didn't seem likely to work. Since it was the only idea he had, however, he thought he might as well go through with it.

Holding the dead limb in his left hand, he drew his pistol. Then he jumped up and threw the limb into the bushes. At the same time, he started kicking his feet at the leaves and small branches on the ground, snuffling and grunting as much like a feral hog as he could.

Rhodes felt ridiculous, but he had to carry it through. He stopped snuffling and yelled, "Look out, Bud! It's the hogs! They're headed in your direction!"

Bud had been behind the walnut trees, all right. He jumped up from behind the one where he'd been crouched and looked wildly about, but he couldn't see any hogs, mainly because there weren't any.

Rhodes fired a shot into the air. "Run, Bud!" he shouted. "They're right behind you."

Bud started to run, but for some reason, maybe because Rhodes didn't sound anything at all like a real hog, or maybe because he had an inborn distrust of lawmen, he stopped. He turned around and started firing his pistol in Rhodes's general direction.

Rhodes dropped to the ground and fired back. He aimed high, over Turley's head. He didn't want to kill Bud, even by accident.

Turley, however, didn't seem to care in the least if he killed Rhodes, and he was doing his best to accomplish it. He ran toward him, firing off shots from the Glock. Bullets buzzed through the leaves and knocked off small limbs. One bullet tore a chunk out of the ground near Rhodes's left leg and spattered his pants with dirt.

Rhodes aimed lower, toward the ground in front of Turley, hoping to trip him up. He hit the toe of Turley's left hiking boot, and Bud fell forward. He hit the ground and slid on his face. His pistol left his hand and slid in front of him, right into the bushes.

Rhodes got up as Bud scooted forward, trying to reach the pistol. He stuck his hand into the bushes and felt around. Then he screamed.

When he pulled his hand back, Rhodes saw that there was a thick snake hanging from it. The snake—it had to be a copperhead, Rhodes thought, judging from the distinctive brown banding—was nearly a yard long.

Turley jumped to his feet and whirled around, trying to throw the snake off his hand, but it had sunk its fangs into the web between his thumb and index finger, and it wasn't letting go.

Bud was yelling, but Rhodes couldn't understand what he was saying, if indeed he was saying anything.

"Hold still," Rhodes said. "Don't move around so much."

He was sure Turley didn't even hear him. Blood came from the hiking boot, but Bud probably wasn't aware of that, either.

"Bud!" Rhodes yelled.

Bud stopped spinning. He looked at Rhodes.

"You," he said, but that was all he got out before he fainted.

28

▼

RHODES WASN'T AN EXPERT AT DEALING WITH SNAKEBITES, BUT he knew that the first thing he had to do was remove the snake from Bud's hand.

The prospect didn't appeal to Rhodes in the least, though he felt sure that the snake would like to get away from Bud almost as much as Rhodes would like for it to. Or it would if snakes could think. Rhodes didn't have a high opinion of the snake's intelligence level.

Although Bud lay quite still, the snake was thrashing around. Rhodes walked over and looked down at it. He had a knife, and he might be able to sever the head from the body, but he didn't know how the snake would react to that. Probably not favorably. Anyway, Rhodes didn't really want to kill it unless he had to.

If it had been possible, he'd simply have picked up Bud and carried him out of there, with the snake dangling from his hand, but Bud was far too big for that. The snake might not have liked that idea, either, any more than it would like having its head removed.

The snake seemed to be trying to let go of Bud on its own, but its fangs were embedded in his hand and must have been trapped. It flopped haplessly from left to right.

Rhodes sighed and said, "All right, snake. It's you and me. One on one."

He looked around until he saw a stout limb with a fork in it. He broke it off the tree and sharpened the forked ends with his knife. It didn't take long. When he was satisfied, he folded the knife and put it back in his pocket.

He jammed the forked end of the stick into the ground about six or eight inches in back of the snake's triangular copper-colored head and pushed it into the dirt as far as he could. Then he knelt down on the writhing snake and held it in place while he used both hands to open its jaws.

The snake was strong, and it didn't particularly want to cooperate. Rhodes had time to examine the pits behind its nostrils in more detail than he cared to. He really wished he'd brought his latex gloves with him.

The fangs came out of Bud's hand slowly. They didn't squirt any venom, for which Rhodes was grateful. There was a little blood, but not as much as Rhodes had expected.

Bud's hand twitched away reflexively, out of reach of the snake.

Rhodes released the head and stood up, holding on to the stick.

The snake stopped squirming, as if it were just waiting for its chance to bite someone else, preferably Rhodes.

"I'm going to send you on your way," Rhodes said. "Tell all your pals what a friend I am to all the little creatures of the forest."

The snake pretended not to hear.

Rhodes eased the stick out of the ground, and just as it came free, he used it to flip the snake away from him and Bud. It landed near the bushes with a flop, stayed motionless for a moment, then slithered away.

Rhodes sighed again, this time with relief. His clothes were soaked with sweat, and not entirely from exertion. He thought that he liked snakes even less now than he had before, if that was possible.

Now all he had to worry about was Bud Turley. The most important thing was to get him to the ER as soon as he could. None of those old first-aid tricks, like putting on a tourniquet or sucking out the venom, worked with copperhead bites. Not that Rhodes would have sucked out the venom even if it had been recommended.

He looked down at Bud, who hadn't lost any weight in the last few minutes. He was still far too heavy for Rhodes to carry or even drag out of the woods. Rhodes didn't think there was a chance Bud would die, but he might go into shock. For that matter, he might be in shock already. His hand was beginning to swell.

As he was trying to think of some way to deal with Bud, Rhodes heard something in the woods behind him.

Great, he thought. *Now the wild hogs will get me.*

He turned around. He didn't see any wild hogs. He saw Ruth Grady.

"Who's been doing all the screaming?" she said. "I could hear you a mile away."

"That was Bud," Rhodes said, pointing to him.

"Oh. I thought it might have been you. I've heard that you had a run-in with some feral hogs here once."

"This time it was a snake. And I didn't have a run-in with it. Bud did. Besides that, I think he's been shot in the foot. I need to check that."

Rhodes knelt down and took off Bud's hiking boot and peeled down the sock.

"That's one nasty sock," Ruth said, "and I don't mean the blood."

"I expect his feet sweat," Rhodes said.

"Yeah. I'd say they've been sweating for about a week. Or two."

Rhodes got the sock off. It appeared that he'd shot off the end of Turley's big toe.

"You'd better tie that off," Ruth said. "We don't want him to bleed out while we're dragging him through the woods."

"You think we can do it?"

"Sure. The two of us can manage. It's not that far."

"We'll see."

"It won't be a problem. Let's see. You shot his toe off, and what else?"

"He was bitten by a copperhead."

"Then I don't blame him for screaming. I hope he's guilty of something, considering all he's gone through in punishment."

"He's guilty of plenty," Rhodes said.

Of course, the next day Turley denied nearly everything.

Rhodes wondered why hospital rooms were always so cold. Was there some theory that germs didn't like low temperatures?

He was standing by Bud Turley's bed in room 132 of the Clearview Hospital. It wasn't the most cheerful room that Rhodes had ever been in, but it was clean—and cold.

Bud's foot was wrapped up and no doubt cleaner than it had been for about a week. Or two. His arm was swollen, but the doctor had told Rhodes that Bud probably wouldn't lose any tissue.

242

Bud was, in fact, almost completely recovered from his wound and the bite, though the doctor had also confided to Rhodes that Bud would never walk as easily or as well as he had before losing most of his big toe.

"Sure, I ran," Bud was telling Rhodes. "I was scared you'd blame me for killing Ronnie Bolton. I could tell by the way you were looking that you thought I did it. Who wouldn't run?"

Rhodes said, "You jumped me in Larry's trailer the other day. I know what you were looking for."

Turley somehow didn't seem as big, lying in a hospital bed, and nobody looked very frightening in a hospital gown. His tattoos were more ludicrous than intimidating. He looked away from Rhodes and said, "I don't know what you're talking about."

"Oh, come on, Bud," Rhodes said. "I can match the ATV tracks outside the trailer to the tires of the one that's in your shop."

He was lying, since the ground had been too hard to take any tracks from the ATV, but maybe Turley didn't know that.

Bud kept mum for a while. Finally he said, "I didn't really jump you. I thought you were a burglar, and you scared me. I was going to catch you and turn you in, but I decided I'd just get out of there instead."

"You don't really expect me to believe that, do you?"

"I'm having some pain," Bud said, reaching for the call button. "I think I'd better call for the nurse."

"Don't even think about it," Rhodes said, and Bud dropped his hand. "It would be a lot easier on both of us if you'd just tell the truth."

"You wouldn't believe me even if I did."

There were two chairs in the hospital room. One of them could be made into a bed of sorts and wasn't comfortable for sitting. The other was a straight-backed metal chair with a cushioned seat. It wasn't very comfortable, either, but Rhodes sat in it anyway.

"You could always give the truth a try," he said, crossing his legs. "It would be a nice change."

"You think I killed Ronnie Bolton. I can tell."

"You could always change my mind."

"You don't mean that. I know how you sheriffs are. You get your mind made up, and you don't care about the truth. You just want to make an arrest and send somebody to the pen whether they did anything or not."

"You've been watching too many cable TV movies," Rhodes said. "I don't want to send anybody to prison unless he's guilty. If you're not guilty, you don't have a thing to worry about."

"Yeah, right. Tell that to all those guys who've been in the pen for twenty years, and now they finally get a DNA test done and it proves they were innocent all along."

Turley hadn't been watching TV. He'd been reading the newspapers, which surprised Rhodes a little.

"You can't tell me you haven't read about some of those cases," Turley said. "You can't tell me those guys weren't railroaded."

"I'm not trying to tell you anything, but none of those cases were from this county."

"Maybe they just haven't gotten around to those yet."

Rhodes uncrossed his legs and started to get up. "If that's the way you feel about it, I'm not going to waste my time with you."

"You're gonna get those bones tested, aren't you," Turley said. "And check the dental records."

"Yes," Rhodes said. He settled back down on the chair. "But I think we've found Ronnie Bolton. You probably know for sure. If you'd tell me what you know, I might be able to help you with the prosecutor."

Turley leaned back into his pillows and looked up at the ceiling. Rhodes looked up, too. It was just a ceiling. Acoustic tile. Fluorescent light. Nothing new there.

"I didn't kill Ronnie Bolton," Turley said. He was still looking at the ceiling. "I've thought about it a lot, and even if I'd killed him, I don't think you could prove it." He turned his eyes to Rhodes.

Rhodes shrugged. Turley was right. Rhodes didn't have any proof of anything, just a bunch of suppositions, and suppositions didn't cut any ice in a courtroom. With what he had right now, Rhodes didn't think a judge would even issue a warrant for Turley's arrest. He'd hoped to talk to Turley and eventually get a confession, but not under these circumstances. Turley was too much aware and on his guard now.

"I'm right," Turley said. "You think I did it, but you can't prove it. The thing is, though, that I didn't do it."

"If you didn't kill him, who did?" Rhodes said.

"Hell, you should be able to figure that out for yourself."

"I'm a little slow today. Why don't you just tell me."

"Sure," Turley said. "I'll tell you. It was Larry. He's the one that killed him."

29

▼

"It was an accident," Turley said. "Plain and simple. If we'd been thinking straight at the time, we'd have reported it, and that would have been that. Oh, sure, we'd have got a hard time from a lot of folks, but sooner or later they'd have seen it couldn't be helped."

"You were there when it happened, then," Rhodes said. "The accident."

"Yeah, I was there. It was a weekend, and we were out in Big Woods, looking around for signs of Bigfoot. He's out there, you know. I don't care what anybody says. He's out there, and one of these days I'll find him."

Rhodes thought the likelihood of that was small and getting smaller all the time. He said, "We're talking about Ronnie Bolton, Bud. Not Bigfoot."

"It's all tied together, though. See, we were out there, and you know how it can be in those woods. All quiet and scary, especially when you get to thinking about wild hogs and snakes and all." He held up his bandaged hand and looked at it for a second. "Anyway, we were a little skittish, I guess. The kid came sneaking up on us, and Larry turned around and shot him. Just like that."

Turley closed his eyes as if that would keep him from seeing it all happen again. When he opened them, he said, "I thought I'd die, too, just keel over right there. You can't imagine what it's like, to see a kid lying there, blood coming out of a hole in his chest, and you can see just by looking at him that he's dead and that there's not a damn thing you can do about it."

"Why did Larry take the boy's baseball cap?"

Turley's eyes came into focus. "He didn't take the cap. I did. Larry didn't even know I took it. Not then."

Rhodes was beginning to think that maybe Bud was telling the truth. He said, "Why did you take it, then?"

"Evidence. I wanted to be able to prove that even if I was there, I didn't kill anybody."

Rhodes said that he didn't see how the cap would prove that.

"I don't guess it would. But it was something to give me a little hold on Larry if he ever tried to turn me in for doing it. Which I didn't. Do it, I mean. Hell, you could prove the bullet came from his gun if you could find it."

"The gun or the bullet? We'd need both of them, and we'd have to prove he owned the gun. If he was smart, he got rid of it."

"Nobody ever said Larry was smart. He kept the gun in his old truck. I was talking about the bullet."

The bullet hadn't been in the grave. Even the careful excavations by Tom Vance hadn't located it.

"We panicked after we knew the boy was dead," Turley went on. "We thought we'd go to the pen if we told what happened.

People think we're crazy anyway. They'd be just as happy if we were in the pen for life or if we got the needle. That way they'd never have to see us around here again. We started just to leave the boy there for the hogs to find, but we were afraid someone might come looking for him before that happened, and anyway, it just didn't seem right. So we took him to the creek and buried him. The ground was pretty soft, and we buried him deep enough. Or that's what we thought. A lot of that creek bank's washed away lately."

"And you just left him there and went on like nothing had happened. All these years. You were even part of the search party."

"Well, it would've looked pretty funny if we hadn't been. We know that place about as well as anybody. People expected us to help out. And since we were helping with the search we could keep people from looking where we buried the boy."

Rhodes thought it over. It made sense. Except for one thing. The cap.

"Larry had the cap at his place. You were looking for it there. But you told me you were the one who took it."

"I did. Larry got religion a while back, I guess you could say. He started talking about how his life had taken a turn for the worse ever since that day and how he wanted to get it back on track."

Rhodes felt a little better on hearing that. He'd been right about that part of it, at least.

"So he came to my place one day when I was gone and took the cap," Bud said. "It was in the shop, in a box under that table where I keep the radio. I don't know how Larry figured that out, but he did. Maybe he'd looked around for the cap before, different times when I wasn't around. He told me he had it and that he was gonna set things right. I don't know how he thought he was gonna do that. The boy was dead. You can't set that right. You just have to go on with your life."

"After Larry was killed, you wanted the cap back."

"Hell, yes. Wouldn't you? I was gonna burn it. If somebody found it at his place, they might tie me in with the boy's killing, and Larry wouldn't be around to tell them he was the one that did it. You know that. You were there looking for the cap yourself, to use it against me."

Rhodes hadn't been looking for the cap, not specifically, but there was no need for Turley to know that.

"All right," Rhodes said. "Let's say you're telling the truth. I guess you must've killed Larry to stop him from letting people know what happened that day in the woods. You were afraid that if he told the story, you'd be implicated. You couldn't let that happen."

"Kill Larry?" Turley said. "What the hell makes you think I killed Larry?"

No matter how Rhodes pressed him, Bud wouldn't admit that he'd killed Larry. Larry was his best friend, he said, and even if Larry was getting all holier-than-thou, Bud wouldn't have killed him.

"Not even if he was going to ring you in on a murder charge?" Rhodes said.

"It was an accident. I told you that. And he didn't want to ring me in on anything. He just wanted to get it off his chest. He said he'd messed up his whole life, starting on that day, and he wanted to set it right if he could."

"Did he say how he was planning to do that?"

"Nope. Larry was a good old boy, but when it came to making

a plan, he was a little helter-skelter if you know what I mean. He probably didn't even have a plan."

Through everything, Bud was matter-of-fact and convincing, and his story never varied. Rhodes left the hospital thinking that he'd been wrong about nearly everything.

So he went to the courthouse for a while. He drank a Dr Pepper and ate a package of the peanut butter crackers and thought everything through one more time.

Chester Johnson was at his vegetable stand, sitting on the tailgate of his truck, just as he'd been the last time Rhodes had paid him a visit. It was almost as if no time at all had passed.

Rhodes stopped the county car. Johnson slid off the tailgate and walked over to him, just like before. This time, however, Johnson didn't try to sell Rhodes anything.

"You're sure paying me a lot of visits lately, Sheriff," he said. "I didn't know you and I were such good friends."

"This isn't exactly a visit," Rhodes said. "It's more like county business."

"You mean you're gonna give me back my gun?"

"That's not it. It's still at the lab, being tested."

"Waste of time and taxpayer money. Won't find a danged thing on it."

"Speaking of finding things," Rhodes said, and stopped.

Johnson waited a while and then said, "Yeah?"

"I remember that you drove all the way to Louetta Kennedy's store to use the phone that day you found Larry Colley dead in the woods. You must not have a cell phone."

"Don't need one. Don't have anybody to call."

"Oh, I wouldn't say that. You called Larry Colley a few times."

Johnson looked confused. "What's that got to do with anything?"

"His incoming calls were recorded on his cell phone. He had one, even if you don't."

Johnson kicked at the dirt. "I still don't see what that has to do with anything."

"Well," Rhodes said, "there's a little problem. I didn't find Larry's cell phone anywhere in those woods. It just flat disappeared."

"And you think I took it? What would I do with a cell phone? I told you I didn't have anybody to call."

"I know that. But you might have taken it because you knew it had that record of your calls on it. Some of those phones hold a lot of numbers from incoming calls. You might have figured that somebody, like the sheriff, might check those numbers and see that you'd been calling Larry. He'd wonder why. And he might find out about how you'd been having some trouble with Larry over those car repairs that you forgot to mention to me until I'd already found out about them. All that might not look so good for you, so why not just take the phone and not have to worry about it?"

"Lotta 'mights' in there," Johnson said. "And you managed to find out about those calls anyway. So you're just fishin' for an answer."

Rhodes grinned. "People say that to me all the time. But if you don't go fishing now and then, you'll never catch anything."

"You won't catch me, and that's for sure. If I took that phone, you don't think I'd keep it, do you? How dumb do you think I look?"

"Not all that dumb," Rhodes said. "I think the phone was in

one of those side pockets of his overalls, and you saw it sticking out. You figured, 'Why not?' and just grabbed it. No ties to you left behind."

"I'd never do a thing like that," Johnson said with such a pious look that Rhodes knew he had to be lying.

"I'm sure you got rid of it right off the bat," Rhodes said, and Johnson couldn't help but allow himself a brief sly smile of pride in his own cleverness. "So it wouldn't do me any good to accuse you of theft," Rhodes went on.

"Nope."

"Well, I just wanted to know for sure."

"And now you do, don't you?" Johnson said.

Rhodes nodded. "And now I do."

Rhodes drove away from the vegetable stand convinced that Chester Johnson had taken the cell phone. He'd no doubt disposed of it, but Rhodes didn't really care about that. The phone was mainly just a loose end that Rhodes had wanted to take care of. Now there were a couple of other things that he wanted to find. Like those missing baseball caps. And Larry Colley's truck.

And, of course, the killer.

30
▼

EDITH BOLTON ANSWERED THE DOOR AT THE BOLTON HOUSE. She didn't look any better than the last time Rhodes had seen her, but then he hadn't expected her to.

"Is Gerald home?" he said, though he knew the answer already. Bolton's school-bus-yellow Hummer wasn't in the driveway.

"No, Sheriff," Edith said. It seemed to Rhodes that there was less of her voice left now than there had been before, if that was possible. It was as if she were gradually fading away. First the voice would go, then the rest of her. "He drove down to the camp house a little while ago. Do you want me to tell him you dropped by?"

"Thanks," Rhodes said, although he knew he'd be seeing Gerald before she did. "I'd appreciate that."

He went back to the county car and got Hack on the radio. "Tell Ruth Grady to meet me at Gerald Bolton's camp house. You know where that is, don't you?"

"Sure I do. I been livin' in this county a lot longer than you have."

"I know that. The question is, can you tell Ruth how to get there?"

"Are you sayin' I don't know how to give directions? If you are, maybe you ought to get the county commissioners to buy one of those GPS things for all the cars. Or a computer with maps on it. Ever'body else has computers in the cars."

"We're getting those in a couple of months," Rhodes said. "Can you tell her how to get there or not?"

"She was just at those woods close to Bolton's place yesterday. All she has to do is turn off the county road a little sooner."

"Hack."

"Yeah, yeah. I can tell her," Hack said.

"Good. Tell her not to waste any time."

Bolton's Hummer was parked near the gate in the fence that enclosed the camp house. Its vivid color looked right at home in the green weeds, even if the Hummer itself didn't. Rhodes parked the county car beside it and went through the gate into the shade of the trees.

Bolton was sitting on the porch. A hunting rifle leaned against the wall beside him, within easy reach.

"I've been about halfway expecting you to show up, Sheriff," Bolton said.

Rhodes nodded toward the rifle. "More than halfway, I'd say."

Bolton ignored the comment. He took hold of the arm of the metal chair that was beside him and shoved the chair well down the porch. It made a scraping noise that set Rhodes's teeth on edge as it slid along the concrete.

"Have a seat over there, Sheriff," Bolton said.

Rhodes went over to the chair and started to have a seat.

"Better pull it on down to the end of the porch," Bolton said. "Just to be on the safe side."

Rhodes pulled the chair farther away from Bolton. It made the irritating scraping sound again.

"That's fine," Bolton said, and Rhodes sat down in the chair. Bolton reached for the rifle and laid it across his knees. "It was the caps, wasn't it."

"The caps and some other things," Rhodes said. "I should have thought about that Hummer sooner. Probably the only one in the county. Louetta would have been curious about it."

"Curious? She knew who was driving it. I'd stopped at her store a couple of times lately when I came down to check on the work here." Bolton smiled. "I was lying when I told you I only came down here to feed the cattle. I've been here two or three times lately, and I stopped at Louetta's store at least twice."

"You didn't have to kill her."

"What do you know about it? She called me at home, said you'd been to the store after Chester Johnson found Colley's body. She said she hadn't told you that she saw me pass by earlier that day."

Bolton shifted in the chair. It grated against the concrete.

"That store wasn't making any money, she said. Hadn't made any for years. She was just about broke. She said maybe I'd like to help her out. You wouldn't think an old woman like that would turn extortionist, would you? But that's the kind of world we live in."

"Well, you put a stop to that," Rhodes said.

"You don't have to be sarcastic." Bolton leaned back in the chair with a metallic squeak. "I didn't mean to kill her. I went to talk to her. You know. Talk things over logically. She started yelling at me, calling me a killer, saying she was going to turn me in. She started coming at me, and I hit her."

Bolton looked down at his hands and flexed his fingers. Then he looked back at Rhodes. His gaze was steady and hard.

"I didn't even hit her that hard. She was just old and fragile."

"You had to hit Larry Colley a lot harder," Rhodes said.

"Sure. But he deserved it. He killed Ronnie."

"Did he tell you that?"

"Yeah. Can you believe it? Wanted to get his life straightened out, he said. After all, killing Ronnie was just an accident, so he thought I'd be happy to know about it and forgive him. Closure, he said. Now there's a word you wouldn't think you'd hear from Larry. Maybe he'd been watching Dr. Phil on TV. Anyway, that's what he said. *Closure.*"

"You didn't forgive him, though."

Bolton made a sound somewhere between a snort and a laugh. "You've seen Edith. You know what Ronnie's disappearance did to her. It's almost like Larry killed her when he killed Ronnie. He might as well have."

"What about you?"

Bolton looked down at his hands again.

"Me, too, goddammit." His voice broke. "Me, too."

His head jerked up.

"Just sit where you are, Sheriff."

"I'm not going anywhere," Rhodes said. "The caps are inside, aren't they? Hanging from the antlers."

"Ronnie liked caps. He collected most of those in there. Of

course, I helped him. Then Colley showed up with the one Ronnie had been wearing that day. He had it here at the house, and he told me the whole story."

"So you took him down to the woods and killed him."

A dirt dauber buzzed around in the rafters above Rhodes's head. Rhodes didn't look up at it.

"That's pretty much it," Bolton said. "Larry was going to show me where it happened. He said he had to do that, to explain it all. When we got there, he started talking, and I . . . I don't know. I hit him in the back of the head with my rifle butt. He never saw it coming. He was too full of his story, telling me how Ronnie came up on them and how he . . . Anyway, I hit him. Pretty damn hard. I knew he was dead as soon as he fell, so I just left him for the hogs. They'd have gotten him, too, if Chester hadn't come along when he did."

"You took his cap," Rhodes said.

"That's right, I did. Larry still had Ronnie's cap in his hand when he fell, and I took it, and then I took his. Added them both to Ronnie's collection. I thought he'd like that."

"Louetta's, too."

"Yeah." Bolton frowned. "I'm not sure why I took hers. It's in there, though. With the others."

Rhodes thought he should have looked more closely at the caps on his earlier visit, but then, he hadn't been thinking about them as a clue at the time. He shifted in his chair, making sure his pant leg was loose and trying to hike it up a little, though not far enough for Bolton to see the ankle holster. He wondered what was keeping Ruth Grady.

"I haven't quite decided what to do," Bolton said. "I came down here to think it over." He gestured toward the rifle. "I thought I might use that on myself, but when it came down to it, I just couldn't go through with it. I wasn't scared. Far from it. But then I thought about Edith. I'm not sure what she'd do without me, you know? It's hard enough for her when I'm around, but it would be a lot worse if she didn't have me. I thought that when Larry was killed, she might get better, knowing that the man who'd killed Ronnie got what he deserved."

"Does she know you're the one who killed Larry?" Rhodes said.

"I didn't tell her, if that's what you mean."

Bolton ran one big hand down the barrel of the rifle while he caressed the stock with the other. The rifle was a Ruger .44 carbine, around twenty years old, Rhodes figured. He didn't think that particular model was being made any more. It fired .44 Magnum cartridges, and it would make a big hole in a deer, or a man.

"But she knew I did it," Bolton said. "I don't know how."

"And she didn't get any better," Rhodes said.

"That's right. She got worse, if anything. Well, you know. You've seen her. I don't understand it."

Rhodes thought he might, but this wasn't the time to explain it to Bolton.

"One thing I've been wondering about," Rhodes said.

"Just one?"

"Colley's truck," Rhodes said. "What happened to it?"

"I drove it down in the creek bottom and left it. I didn't think anybody would find it there."

"What about Chester Johnson?"

"Yeah, he might have run across it. But like I said, I didn't give Chester any thought. If I had, I wouldn't be in this mess, would I?"

"You probably would. Killing a couple of people isn't something that you can just walk away from."

"I didn't mean for any of that to happen. It was . . . an accident."

Rhodes just looked at him.

"I see what you mean," Bolton said, though Rhodes hadn't said a word. "I'm no better than Larry was, am I? Or maybe I'm worse. I have to pay for it some way. Like Larry did."

"It doesn't have to be like Larry did," Rhodes said.

"I wish I could believe that," Bolton said. His hands tightened around the rifle. "But I don't."

Rhodes heard the distant sound of a car. Bolton must have heard it, too, but he didn't look in the direction it came from.

"You must have some backup coming," he said. "Too late for that, though. Too late for both of us."

He swung the rifle up, and Rhodes dived sideways out of the chair. The rifle blast echoed off the wall of the camp house. The bullet whanged through the metal back of the chair where Rhodes had been sitting and tore big chips out of one of the cedar stanchions holding up the end of the porch.

Rhodes rolled to a half-sitting position and grabbed at the pistol in his ankle holster, but Bolton swung the rifle toward him again, and Rhodes rolled to the right just as Bolton fired. The bullet plowed up a furrow where Rhodes had been. Rhodes stopped himself and rolled right back over the furrow as Bolton got off another shot. Rhodes kept right on rolling this time, and Bolton missed with a fourth shot.

One more, Rhodes thought, still rolling and hoping that Bolton would guess wrong again.

He didn't. Rhodes felt something kick him like a mule in his upper left arm. Oddly enough, instead of increasing the speed of his roll, it stopped him completely.

He squirmed around to a seated position. He wasn't feeling much of anything in his arm now, and he pulled up his pant leg.

On the porch, Bolton pulled back the operating handle of the rifle, and when it locked in place, he inserted a cartridge into the firing chamber. He didn't seem in any hurry. He pressed the bolt release, then turned the carbine over and started pushing cartridges through the loading gate on the bottom of the receiver.

Rhodes had his pistol out. He was feeling dizzy, and his thumb was almost too weak to pull back the hammer of the .38, but he managed it.

"I'm really sorry about this, Sheriff," Bolton said, taking aim.

Rhodes didn't say anything. He pulled the trigger.

The stock of Bolton's rifle splintered in his hand. Bolton yelled as the barrel whipped aside and broke the finger that was trapped in the trigger guard.

Rhodes stood up. He was shaky, but he wasn't going to fall. Bolton was huddled in the chair, holding his hands between his legs. Blood dripped onto the concrete, and Rhodes thought that the bullet that hit the rifle stock might also have hit Bolton's hand.

Ruth Grady walked up to Rhodes, her own pistol in a two-handed grip. It was rock steady and pointed at Bolton.

"What kept you?" Rhodes said.

"Bad directions," Ruth said. "I got lost."

If Rhodes had been feeling better, he'd have laughed.

31

▼

"I DISTINCTLY REMEMBER TELLING YOU TO BE CAREFUL," IVY said.

"It's not as bad as it looks," Rhodes said. "Just a scratch."

It was more than a scratch, but not much. Bolton's bullet had taken out about an eighth of an inch of flesh from Rhodes's arm, and Rhodes considered himself lucky. The Magnum bullet could have shattered all the bones in his upper arm if it had been a solid hit. It might have removed the whole arm, in fact, but Rhodes didn't see any need to go into all that with Ivy.

"Even if it's just a scratch, I still hate for you to get shot," Ivy said.

Rhodes didn't like it, either, but it came with the job. He said, "I think some cheese enchiladas at the Jolly Tamale might make me feel better."

Ivy grinned. "I suppose you'd want some of those greasy high-fat chips to go with them, too."

"Not to mention some guacamole," Rhodes said.

"It's nice that you're wearing short sleeves. That way people can see your bandage. It looks very heroic. Maybe it will get you some votes."

"See?" Rhodes said. "There's always a bright side if you just look for it."

Claudia and Jan were sitting in a booth near the front of the Jolly Tamale when Rhodes and Ivy walked in. Rhodes had called them at the motel and asked them to be there. He was glad they were close to the door. He didn't want to have to explain to anybody about the bandage. Claudia waved, and Rhodes and Ivy joined them.

Mariachi music came from hidden speakers, and the chatter of the diners echoed off the tile floors and walls.

"We want to hear all about it," Jan said when Rhodes and Ivy were seated in the booth. Jan pointed to the bandage on Rhodes's arm. "The big shoot-out, I mean."

"How did you know about that?" Ivy said.

"We heard all about it on KCLR," Claudia said. "The announcer was very excited."

Rhodes wondered if the radio station had finally found someone to replace Red Rogers, who had been at the station for a good while before he was murdered. He'd been a little like Jennifer Loam, always questioning Rhodes about the cases he was working. That was all Rhodes needed: a hotshot youngster at the radio station teaming up with Jennifer Loam.

"It wasn't much of a gunfight," Rhodes said.

"How do you like his John Wayne impression?" Ivy asked.

"Was that John Wayne?" Claudia said. "I wasn't sure."

"I thought maybe he was doing Clint Eastwood," Jan said.

Ivy looked at Rhodes. "I told you it needed work."

Rhodes shrugged, which didn't do his arm any good, but before he got a chance to say anything, the server brought a bowl of warm chips and two bowls of salsa.

After he'd ordered his enchiladas and had a few chips, Rhodes told Claudia and Jan a little about Edith Bolton and what the situation was.

"I thought that since you were a social worker, you might be able to get her some help," Rhodes told Claudia.

"How soon?"

"Tonight would be good."

"I'll take care of everything as soon as we finish eating. In fact, I'll get started right now." Claudia pulled a cell phone out of her purse and slid out of the booth. "What's the address?"

Rhodes told her.

"Does she have friends with her now?"

Rhodes had made sure of that. "Yes," he said. "But she's going to need more than just friends."

"Sure. I'll see to it."

Claudia went outside to talk, and the food arrived in sizzling hot plates just as she returned.

"It's all fixed," she said. "I'm not sure that Edith Bolton can be fixed, though, no matter what we do."

"I appreciate it that you're trying," Rhodes said.

"We still want to hear about the big shoot-out," Jan said. "You're not going to get away with changing the subject."

"It wasn't really a shoot-out," Rhodes said. "We should eat before the food gets cold."

"Don't let him kid you," Ivy said. "It was a shoot-out, all right. And it's not the first trouble he's had down in those woods."

"Really?" Jan said. She took a notebook and pen out of her purse. "That might make another good scene in our book about the handsome crime-busting sheriff. What happened the first time?"

"He was nearly killed by wild hogs," Ivy said.

Jan and Claudia looked at Rhodes, who shifted uncomfortably on the booth's bench seat.

"Really?" Claudia said.

"Really," Ivy told her.

"But you survived," Jan said.

"Here I am," Rhodes said.

"There's always a bright side," Ivy said, smiling at Rhodes. "If you just look for it."